LOST

FINDER

A NOVEL BY
E. GALE BUCK

Spearach Press
*all things magical and
not yet understood*

ISBN: 978-1-7360230-6-8 (paperback)

This is a work of fiction.
   Mystery; Intrigue; Action & Adventure; Romance;
   Amnesia; Organized Crime; Detective

Suitable for Young Adult - Adult

Published July, 2024 by
Speurach Press
all things magical but not yet understood
an imprint of
The Silver Wreath
www.woodsmanstories.com

Printed in United States of America by
Ingram Lightning Source

Other Titles by E. Gale Buck

From Speurach Press
Vrenessbith - two parts
  - Awakening
  - Catharachd
Treasured Adversaries
The Thirstday Cognizance Brigade

From The Silver Wreath
Christmas / Woodsman
Woodsman Stories
Finding Nicholas
Secret Stories of Santa
A Quiet Service - four volumes
        a scandinavian legacy
        exploring a new world
        passion beyond misfortune
        reaching beyond tomorrow

Faith / Inspirational
Secret of the Turquins
Excuse me, My Name is God, do you have a minute or two to
        talk

For Children - Tales from the North Pole
(Illustrated by Christiana J. Buck)
        How Santa's Reindeer Got Their Bells
        The Bethlehem Tree
        First to Fly
        Joy Ride

All titles available through Amazon and other fine bookstores.

For information on new projects follow The Silver Wreath on
Facebook.

There is an old stereotypical image of writers, authors of great stories, tucked away in an attic or some dark room pounding away on a keyboard, their world lit only by a dim light and the magic of the story they were creating. Not so long ago, the keyboard would have been the clicking of a typewriter and there would be a stack of pages beside it; pages with handwritten notes and changes or corrections. Today, there might be a pad with notes of ideas but the keyboard would be almost silent as the author's face is illuminated by the glow of their computer monitor. Corrections and changes invisible as they are accomplished through whatever program / app the author might be using.

That world still exists. Birthing a story idea and creating the tale are still solitary events. The author works within their mind and struggles to get that story into words others can read, experience, and enjoy. Then, when the saga is completed, comes the formatting for the agent or publisher; again working alone as the bits and bytes of story are manipulated into an acceptable presentation. However, in between the beginning and the end most good writers have a team of friends who read and follow the story through its development. Real, live people who read, comment, and challenge the writer's motivations and plot lines.

I would like to thank those who challenged me and kept me thinking beyond my own concepts as *Lost Finder* was developed. This is the fourth journey Drew and Lauren Bridges have taken with me and the first for Bill Finger. Thank you, each of you, for your comments, insights, questions, and yes, even the challenges.

I also need to thank one very special lady who has not only journeyed through every adventure I have developed, but is also my number one critic, editor, and fan. My wife, Christy. Thank you for the inspiration, devotion, challenge, and ideas that continue to emerge from the mist of our existence.

LOST FINDER

Chapter 1

Feeling something like a wild animal tugging at his leg, he woke with a start. Seeing an old man attempting to steal his boot from his foot, he kicked. The boot was worn leather, calf-height with heavy heel and sole. A single strap crossed from the instep over the bridge. Great for kicking, which he delivered with forceful effect. This kick was not wild but direct and powerful. The old man, who had been tugging on the boot, flew backwards toward an open door. Looking around, the now fully awake victim of an attempted assault saw other men on the far side of what appeared to be an otherwise empty freight car. Then he noticed the rhythmic clacking of a train rolling down tracks and subtle deep vibrations of the boxcar filling his legs.

Pulling his boot snug, he felt something inside, below his foot. Curious, but wary, he rose to his feet wondering, *Where am I, and more importantly, how did I get here?* Hoping to find answers, he drew a deep breath of cool air pouring in the open door before walking over and helping the would-be-thief back to his feet.

"That was close. You almost became part of the landscape. What's your name old man?"

"Jacob. You're dressed too good to be ridin' these rails. Who're you? We all thought you was dead."

He started to answer then paused. He had no idea who he was nor how he got onboard this train going to who knew where. Realizing he had to reply, he grabbed a name from the air. "Stan. My name's Stan and my head feels like I should be dead. Where's this fine 'coach' headin?"

"Terra Haute, then on to Indianapolis or Chicago . . . not sure," another old man, this one dressed in army fatigues replied. His voice was coarse, like he hadn't had anything to drink in days. Appearing to weigh about 165 pounds, his skin was bronzed and leathery with a scraggly salt-and-pepper beard hanging from his cheeks and down his neck. Dark blue eyes were lifeless, without compassion, yet still friendly enough to answer. "Don't matter no how. You won't get through Terra Haute. Bulls'll pull ya off when the train stops. Most of us'll jump at Farmersburg; a few'll wait till Youngstown."

"Why doesn't everybody jump off at Youngstown? Closer to a big city," Stan asked, genuinely curious about what lay ahead.

"Well, that's da problem. City folks don't like us that much. Sheriff in Youngstown don't like nobody. Ya almost has to hit the ground runnin and hope he's drinking coffee at the diner," the old man with lifeless eyes continued. He then laid back and pulled an old cap over his eyes.

"How long have I been here? Sleepin?" Stan asked, stretching his arms out then rubbing his face, trying to work out dry wrinkles.

"You was here when we got on this side of Nashville," Jacob replied, eager to make amends. "No one bothered ya for most o' the night. Then ya didn't move nor nothin and we all figured ya was dead. Dead men don't need boots and bottoms o' mine are mostly shot. Didn't think ya would mind . . . being dead an all. Sorry 'bout my mistake." He then settled near the door where he could watch farms roll past.

Stan chuckled slightly at Jacob's explanation. Rubbing the back of his head, he felt a big lump. A big tender lump. "Well, seems I was put on this train. Not sure why and have no idea who. Can't remember what I was doing that might have got me here," he mumbled to himself.

Still not sure who he was and confused as to how he got into this freight car, Stan began searching his pockets. No wallet, no id, no money. Nothing. Recalling that something was inside his boot, he sat and pulled it off. Inside were two cards. One was a business card of Michael Geoffrey Turner, Licensed Private Investigator from Asheville, North Carolina. Two sets of letters and numbers were written on the back. The first set was "KAT - 225", then "TVACUSK - 733". The second card was a mini-menu from Pearl's Diner in Oliver Springs, Tennessee. A woman's name, Siobhan, was written on the back in a sultry, seductive style with lots of curves and loops. A small heart dotted the "i". After pondering the cards for a moment, he dropped the mini-menu back into his boot and put the other in his shirt pocket. He then pulled his boot back on and stomped it a couple times to make sure it was seated properly.

The rhythmic melody of steel rails below the freight car

sang on, hour after hour, changing only briefly when the chariot crossed a bridge. Stan studied his fellow travelers. The old man with lifeless eyes, and three others, slept with caps resting over their faces. Jacob and two others now sat toward the back of the car, playing cards with a deck that was way past well-worn. All were older men, or appeared older, except one. One younger man, possibly early forties, sat alone on the right side of the one open door and watched the scenery roll past. Being early spring, scenery consisted primarily of expansive flat fields waiting to be planted or turned over from winter crops. Trees bore fresh green leaves, not yet the darker summer green they would achieve in weeks ahead.

Stan studied the man sitting in the door for a moment. Younger, that was obvious. His jeans weren't so full of holes and his boots were in good shape, too. He wore a flannel shirt and a mid-weight jacket, a quality wind breaker. Not having his own area to sit, Stan sat in the open door, to the left side, letting his feet dangle like the other man.

"You seem a bit young for this life. You have a story?" Stan asked, politely invading the man's solitude.

He looked at Stan briefly before replying without emotion, "Do I need a story?"

"Guess not. Do you have a destination or just riding?"

"Destination? Hmm. Suppose I'm headin' into tomorrow, like the rest of these gentlemen. Unlike them, I am lookin for something . . . work. Any kinda work that will let me get back with my family. At least they're safe."

Stan looked at the man more closely. His clothes were relatively clean and he seemed in good shape. Beard was a week or ten days old, not too scraggly yet. Couldn't see his eyes; they mostly just followed the fields and buildings beyond the rails. "Let me guess. You lost your job and your family is with wife's parents?"

"Somethin like that." He never turned his head except to see if the next crossroads might bring something a bit more interesting into view.

Stan looked ahead as well, then silently watched small towns, farms, and cars on a nearby highway float past. After about twenty minutes, one of the old men sauntered over and looked up the tracks. Passing through yet another nondescript town, he turned and called out, "Shelburn. Farmersburg comin up!" He then went back to where he had been playing cards and retrieved an old backpack. Heaving a heavy sigh, he plopped down in the doorway with his feet hanging out and scratched his head. Those who had been sleeping woke as everyone else started moving about. The man with lifeless eyes opened the door on the other side of the car and sat, preparing to jump. Neither Stan nor the younger man moved to make room for others as the empty space between them filled with old men.

More sets of tracks appeared on the east side of the car and the train slowed, almost to a crawl, as they passed freight cars parked on sidings. After a few minutes of crawling along, their train began to slowly pick up speed. Moments later they approached a small town. Men began hopping off onto dirt pathways, unobstructed by rows of dangerous tracks. Some stumbled. One man fell and others helped him up. Passing the first street, Stan followed Jacob's example and hopped off, stumbling but not falling. Looking up he saw the younger man still sitting in the doorway, clicking down the tracks.

Stan followed Jacob toward what appeared to be the center of town. Three other men from the train joined them. When the group passed a post office, two men jumped out of a parked car and started yelling. Following others' example, Stan ignored them. These men then looked at a picture one held and started running in their direction. The group of travelers scattered; the two men chased Stan.

Stan ran across the tracks toward two old brick buildings that appeared to have been abandoned. Both were two story red brick with large arched windows on the second floor. Together they spanned the entire block. Hearing a gun shot and ricochet too close to his head, Stan ran into an alleyway between two buildings, stumbling on a pile of loose boards, then around the corner. Memories of being in a middle-east battle zone flashed through his mind. Without thinking, he found a vantage point at the top of an old iron staircase. One of the men crept around the corner, pistol in hand. Stan held his breath and waited until this man was right below him. With highly trained and automatic movements, he dropped and overwhelmed the man. In an instant, the hunter was sprawled out on the ground, unconscious. Stan removed the clip of bullets from the man's gun, emptied the chamber, and tossed the now useless weapon into a nearby barrel of trash. He tucked the clip into his back pocket. Not hearing any other movement, he crept along the back of the buildings, through bushes and trash, toward the far corner. Coming to the end of the building, he crouched down and waited. Seconds later, the second man peeked around from the other side, leading with his gun. Stan reached up and snatched the gun, then slammed his body up into the hunter's chest, causing him to bounce his head against a trash dumpster. The would-be-assailant fell to the ground, motionless. Once again, Stan emptied and disposed of the weapon.

Curiosity filled this man who did not know who he was. Who were these men and why did they shoot at him? He quickly searched the dumpster man's pockets. Finding a wallet with almost five hundred dollars, he removed three hundred and then read the driver's license. He was from Hendersonville, North Carolina. Quickly and silently, he returned to the first hunter. This man carried only two hundred forty dollars and was also from Hendersonville. After helping himself to one hundred forty dollars, he checked for other identification. All he found was a slightly soiled handkerchief, which he took.

Taking an easier path, through the parking lot, back toward town, Stan wiped both gun clips with the handkerchief and wished he had not thrown the guns away before wiping them down. Looking back to where he might have tossed the weapons, the only thing that caught his eye was a child's red baseball cap. After wrapping the clips in the handkerchief, he deposited them in a mailbox outside the post office and kept walking.

Stan now knew he had combat experience and could hold his own in a fight. He also realized he was in trouble. He didn't know what kind of trouble, but armed men were hunting him. Not knowing what direction to go, and too unsure about too much to devise a plan, he walked. Three blocks from the train tracks, passing small brick homes with neat green lawns, he found an excited group of citizens in a church parking lot. Stopping across the street, he considered options. *I can keep walking and likely get found by those thugs or maybe I can get lost in a crowd.* He didn't think long before he crossed the street and started mingling with the locals.

The crowd's excitement, he quickly learned, was centered around a missing boy. An eight-year-old who had not been seen for eight or nine hours, since breakfast, and his parent's had called the community together to search. "How many places can a boy get lost in a town like this?" Stan asked himself, aloud.

A man standing close to Stan looked at him with a stunned expression. "You'd be surprised, mister. He could've fallen into an abandoned well, down somebody's basement steps, or even been grabbed by that riffraff that jumps off the train. And somebody said they heard something like a gunshot not long ago!"

Stan did not respond, but quietly listened to a preacher who was trying to coordinate the search. "When Brad left this morning, he was wearing jeans and a blue and white t-shirt. All of you know him, so let's go find 'im."

"Don't forget his hat!" someone yelled out.

"Yes, thank you," the preacher agreed. "He always wears an old faded red ball cap. Never without it. That should make him easier to spot, if he's anywhere where he can be seen. You all know which areas you know best, so go search there first and come back here in an hour."

The crowd Stan had hoped to hide in disappeared. All but seven folks went off in different directions. Once again, Stan had to consider his options, but it didn't take long.

"Excuse me, did you say a red ball cap?" Stan asked as he approached the small group huddled around the preacher.

"Have you seen it?" a young woman wailed. Stan figured she was the mother of the missing boy.

Swallowing hard, Stan replied, "Yes. Back across the tracks, behind a building with a green awning."

"I'm gonna whoop that boy!" a man at the young woman's arm exclaimed, just like an angry father. "He knows better'n to go around them buildings."

"Will you show us where you found the cap? Please!" the mother pleaded.

Thinking about the men he left behind those buildings, Stan

hesitated. Then, thoughts of an injured boy took over. "Come on. I got nothin better to do right now."

One person stayed in the parking lot to tell other searchers about this new development. As they walked, Stan asked the preacher, "Do you have a library in this town? One with internet access?"

"Son, if you find Brad, you can use MY computer!" The preacher squeezed Stan's shoulder in support. Stan thought his reply somewhat odd as they were about the same age, the preacher possibly a bit younger; possibly about 35.

Approaching the post office, Stan noticed the car used by the two hunters was gone. Breathing a sigh of relief, he picked up his pace just a bit. Rounding the brick building through the parking lot, Stan trotted over to a bush at the corner of the alley between buildings, where the red hat still rested. He picked it up and gave it to the mother.

"That's HIS!" the young woman cried out.

"Okay, folks, search the area. He must be here somewhere," the preacher directed.

As everyone fanned out, Stan recalled stumbling over some loose boards when he ran between these buildings. This alleyway was only about six feet wide and boards were scattered loosely only a couple yards from the end. Seeing a long rusted access ladder leaning against the building, he kicked the boards aside revealing an old rusty iron pipe, about three feet across, going into the ground. Stan looked down into the pipe but couldn't see anything other than dark.

"Hey, anybody have a flashlight or a phone with a flashlight?" Stan called from the edge of the buildings.

One of the men ran up with a small LCD flashlight. "Will this do?"

"Don't know, but we can find out." Stan took the light and stepped back into the alleyway. Shining it down the pipe, he and the owner of the light caught a faint glimpse of something white, possibly blue and white. "BRAD! BRAD!"

There was no response from the pipe, but everyone in the area came running. Stan looked at the group and asked, "Anyone got any rope?"

"I saw Johnson's truck across the street. He should have

some," one of the men called as he ran back toward the rear of the buildings. He returned five minutes later with a length of rope that looked like it could tie up a fishing trawler.

Stan looked around for something to secure the rope to. "Well, looks like three of you will have to hold this rope so I can see if that's Brad down there."

The preacher, Brad's father, and two others grabbed the rope after Stan dropped most of it down the pipe. Flexing his hands and taking a deep breath, he climbed into the pipe and began edging his way down. After descending twenty feet, or so, his hands began to hurt. He braced his back on one side of the pipe and pushed with his feet against the other. Surface rust slid under his back and feet, causing him to flinch but not fall. Stretching across the pipe was uncomfortable and probably not safe, but was an effective way to relax his hands. After a brief rest and stretching his fingers, he continued to the bottom of the pipe. Somewhere around thirty or thirty-five feet down, he found a tunnel-like structure which had caved in on both sides of a space about four feet square at the base of the pipe. Using the borrowed flashlight, which he carried in his mouth, Stan verified that it was indeed Brad at the bottom, curled up and unconscious, but breathing. "He's alive!" he called to the folks above.

"Is he all right?" two men yelled down the pipe.

"Don't know yet. He's unconscious but breathing. I need to see if I can wake him."

Ignoring sobs and chatter above, Stan stepped carefully between Brad's tangled legs. While reviving the boy, Stan discovered he had one broken forearm, a broken leg, and dislocated shoulder. Carefully working around so he could manipulate the shoulder, Stan calmly told the boy, "You do realize this gold mine played out years ago." As the boy started to laugh, Stan popped his shoulder back in place. Brad passed out from the jolt of pain. Stan then fashioned the rope into a harness between Brad's legs, then around his torso and shoulders so that he would hang vertically, with only his head falling sideways,

"Okay, he has several broken bones and has passed out again so lift him gently. I'll guide him up the first part, then you'll have to throw the rope back down to me so I can climb out." Stan held the rope as it went taught, then carefully lifted Brad as he passed him in the confined space. Once the boy was above his reach, he watched fading daylight bounce around him. Feelings of claustrophobia tried to set in, but Stan focused on the light surrounding the boy. As the boy got closer to the top, the pipe grew darker, then disappeared completely when they lifted him out. Light returned as Brad's feet disappeared over the edge of the dark shaft. Moments later the rope dropped down on Stan. He tugged on it, to make sure folks up top were ready, then climbed up using his hands on the rope and his feet on the side of the pipe.

Climbing out the top, Stan saw folks removing gear and tools from the back of an old white pickup he had previously seen parked across the street. They then laid Brad into this makeshift ambulance. The driver called emphatically, "Bill, be sure you coil up my rope and put it with the rest of my stuff. I'll get it after I deliver this young man to the hospital." The preacher waved acknowledgment.

Only the boy's mother and father joined him in the truck. Everyone else gathered around their new hero, patting him on the back and offering him whatever he wanted.

"Well, to be honest, I'm not sure I've eaten today and Reverend Bill, here, offered to let me use his computer."

Everyone laughed and the young man who owned the flashlight put his hand out. "My light? Don't want to lose it now that it's part of history."

Stan chuckled and pulled the light from his shirt pocket. "Nice light, thanks." He handed the lifesaving device back to its owner.

Walking back to the church, the preacher nudged one of the men, saying, "Go tell Miss Betty that she will have a guest for supper and bed tonight." The man immediately split off and entered an old two story Victorian house one block from the church.

"What are you searching for?" Reverend Bill asked as he unlocked his office, making his computer available to the town's new hero.

"Not sure, really. I have some notes on a business card that don't make sense."

"Well, I will leave you to it. " The preacher sat in a big overstuffed sofa and worked on his weekly sermon, using a yellow notepad and ball point pen.

Stan pulled the card from his pocket while the Firefox browser appeared on the computer screen. After pondering for a few seconds, he typed google.com in the address bar. The world's most popular search engine now at his fingertips, he entered the phrase "TVACUSK." Google reported more than 32,000 results in less than one second. Most of the few that were actually displayed were useless, however a few were newspaper articles. They were no help, either. Clicking on images related to this search, the screen was flooded with ads and icons from the Knoxville TVA Employees Credit Union. He then ran the same search on "KAT." This time, Google reported millions of hits. The first page did not help, but an entry on the second page rang a bell, Knoxville Area Transit. Clicking on this result, the letters "kat" glowed in front of Stan. *Two hits from Knoxville. More than a coincidence*, he thought.

Flipping the card over he entered the name, "Michael Geoffrey Turner." Once again, a lot of hits but nothing that made sense. No private investigators. He chuckled when one of the images Google returned was a professor in criminal justice at a North Carolina college. He wrote the professor's phone number on the card below the printed number, just in case he might need it later.

Seeing his guest fold his hands below the keyboard, Reverend Bill asked, "Done already? That didn't take long."

"Nope, not long at all. May I make a phone call?"

"Help yourself."

Stan punched in the number that was printed on the business card. "We are sorry but that number is no longer in use or has been disconnected."

Frustrated, Stan started to get up, then remembered the second card. Whipping back around to the computer he entered the name "Oliver Springs." Google quickly brought up results from Oliver Springs, Tennessee. Clicking on a map link, he saw that it was just more than a stone's throw from Knoxville. "That's number three," he said softly to himself. Turning back to the preacher, he asked, "Do you folks have bus service here?"

"Sorry, no. But we can get you to Terre Haute. You can go anywhere from there." The preacher closed his notebook and looked at his guest. "My stomach's rumbling, you ready for supper?"

"Just a minute, let me see what's available out of Terre Haute." Stan then searched the Greyhound Bus Lines for service to Knoxville. With $440 acquired from the two men who shot at him, he could afford it, but there was a two-hour layover with a change of buses in Nashville. Recalling that the men on the train told him this is where his journey might have started, he was more than a little concerned; however at present, it was his only option.

Before closing FireFox, Stan cleared all history records, erasing any trace of what he had been looking into. He then joined Reverend Bill and they walked over to Miss Betty's. Bill asked a few questions as they walked, hoping he could help this hero just a bit. Other than his assumed name, Stan was unable to provide any answers. The reverend could see tension in Stan's demeanor, his face and jaw growing visibly tighter, and did not press for information.

Supper was served family style in a large oak dining room at a table set for twelve. Three other men joined Stan and Reverend Bill as they enjoyed baked ham, authentic mashed potatoes, green beans, turnip greens, hot rolls, green salad, apple sauce, and iced tea. One of the men tried to engage Stan in conversation, but gave up when Stan replied with only short uninformative answers. Reverend Bill listened and wondered who this hero was, and what he might be running from.

That night Stan slept in a large bed in a modest bedroom on the second floor. There were four other bedrooms on this floor, all served by one bathroom; two doors down from Stan. This bath featured a claw-foot tub, raised tank commode, and ceramic pedestal sink. The floor was covered with small white tiles, accented by an occasional blue square.

Laying his head on an overstuffed pillow, Stan listened to the sounds of night through an open window: crickets and other bugs, an owl, and an occasional passing car. Thinking about his encounter with the gunmen as his eyes closed, he did not sleep well.

          - 12 -

Miss Betty activated the neighborhood phone tree shortly after sunrise. "Anybody going to Terre Haute this morning? Our special guest needs to be at the bus station by 10:00." About 7:35, Brad's father called Miss Betty's to say he was going.

Stan settled into the passenger seat of an old green and white Ford F150 pickup as it pulled away from Miss Betty's, shortly after 8:00 a.m. Looking to the driver, Stan commented, "I thought you would've been at the hospital with Brad."

"I came back last night so I could go to work. Then the boss told me to get my hide back to the hospital, where I belong. They expect to keep him a couple days. Maybe send 'em home on Sunday. Thank you for saving my son's life."

Brad's father was not much of a talker, which was good because Stan didn't have answers to typical questions and was not in a mood for chatter. Stan looked around the cab of the truck. The seats were worn, the AM/FM radio was off, and there were a few cracker wrappers on the floor. The air had a slight odor of gasoline. Seeing a quarter on the floor under the edge of his seat, Stan picked it up and dropped it in the open ash tray. Looking through the back window, he saw an old shovel and a few dried leaves. Otherwise, it was clean and appeared to be a reasonably maintained older vehicle.

The twelve-mile drive up highway 150 was anything but exciting. Flat terrain carrying four lanes of asphalt divided into pairs by a grass median. Businesses were scattered along the roadway, separated by open fields and rows of trees planted as wind breaks. Large tractors turned over soil as they plowed through several of these fields. Service stations seemed to have been placed at a few intersections, as though dropped on a Monopoly Board. Entering the urban scene of Terre Haute, the landscape changed to strip malls, big box stores, auto and motorcycle dealers, restaurants, and more frequent service stations. Civilization had covered this part of the landscape with buildings.

Seeing a blue and white sign for a hospital, Stan asked, "Is that where your son is?"

The boy's father nodded silently and kept driving. He did

ask one question as they arrived at the bus station, ten minutes later. "Where you going?"

"Not sure," Stan replied as he opened the truck door, which was only half a lie. "Don't be too hard on your boy. I bet he's learned why you don't want him messin' behind those buildings."

The father nodded solemnly and pulled away from the bus station.

Walking into the depot, Stan quickly surveyed people in the waiting area. He wasn't sure why, but reasoned it must be habit; there were fifteen to twenty occupants sitting or milling about. Iron benches, such as you might find in a park, filled most of the center of the room and lined the front wall below the window. Vending machines and a small snack bar occupied the right side. Aroma of fresh popcorn wafted from the snack bar, mixing with a lingering hint of pine scented cleaner. Lockers and entry to restrooms lined the left wall. Straight ahead was the ticket counter, baggage check-in, and offices. A hallway leading to bus parking was between the lockers and ticket booth. The floor was speckled concrete with a glossy finish. Well lit and clean, this terminal appeared to be a typical bus station.

Walking up to the ticket counter, Stan noticed two men dressed in khaki slacks and sport coats, their eyes following him. Stan had planned to purchase a ticket on the Southbound to Knoxville, however seeing one of the men coming up behind him, Stan felt the hairs on the back of his neck rise and quickly changed his travel destination.

"One way to St. Louis, please."

"Economy is $32, leaves at 1:40, on-time." The ticket cashier replied and waited.

Stan peeled $40 off the bills he had collected from his would-be assassins, then pocketed the ticket and change. Stepping away from the window, he paused to listen. The man behind him bought two tickets to St. Louis. His partner was talking on a cell phone.

So, they aren't going to shoot me today, but they want to follow me. Stan thought to himself. Examining the departure board he saw that a bus left for Indianapolis at 1:45, five minutes after the westbound bus. *Now, how to get a ticket? Well, I have four hours to figure this out.*

Wandering around the station, he found he could get a snack but not a great meal, buy a magazine or a paperback novel, and even wash his face. Stepping outside he looked for a more relaxing place to wait. The bus station was part of a multi-level parking garage, which stretched down to his left. Brick buildings lined the block to the right, a parking lot sat diagonally to the right, and single large building filled the block across the street. In front of this facility was a statue of a basketball player making a shot and a sign which read "Hullman Center, Indiana State University." *An arena, not a place to eat,* he thought. No signs of a coffee shop or restaurant nearby, Stan turned to go back into the station. He noticed one of his followers standing at the corner, about thirty feet away, lighting a cigarette.

Finding a discarded newspaper in the waiting room, Stan settled in for a long wait. He had just finished reading the first section when he heard a young man screaming.

"What do you mean you lost it? That was my grandmother's ring!" He was about twenty-one, give or take, clean shaven and wore blue jeans, grey t-shirt, and a dark blue Indiana State University Sycamores baseball cap.

"I didn't throw it away! It was on my finger when I came back from the wash room, I checked!" a young woman with him cried.

"It's got to be around here somewhere! Check your purse!"

Both the man and woman searched wildly in her seat and around on the surrounding floor. Stan noticed a sparkle about twelve feet from where they were searching, then casually walked over and picked up the ring. He turned in time to see the young man storm out of the waiting room.

Joining the young man just outside the door, Stan asked, "Where you heading?"

"St. Louis . . . or at least we were!"

"What's changed?"

"My fiance has just lost my grandmother's engagement ring!"

"Here's your ring," Stan said quietly, holding the ring out between his fingers, keeping his elbow close to his body. "It rolled across the floor." As the young man reached for it, Stan closed it into his hand. "I need a favor."

"What?" the young man asked, becoming very defensive.

Stan looked at him. They were about the same build and similar hair color. "I need you to rent me your ball cap and buy me a ticket on the 1:45 to Indianapolis. I'll give you the cap back when you get on the bus to St. Louis." He pulled a $100 bill from his shirt pocket and held it so the young man could easily take it. "Get the ticket and I'll give you the ring in the men's room. Five minutes?"

The young man looked at Stan coldly, not sure if he wanted to get involved. But he did need that ring back. "Sure, five minutes." He then took the $100 and turned to go back into the station.

Before the young man could open the door, Stan looked through the glass into the waiting room. Seeing both men watching him closely, he called to his new partner, "Hey, son. You forgot this . . . oh, and the hat." Stan handed him the ring in exchange for the hat."Change of plan, not in the men's room. You might wait about 15 or 20 minutes to buy that ticket. I'll get it from you before we board the bus to St. Louis. You keep the change." Stan knew the cost of the ticket was only $34.00.

The young man smiled and returned to his fiance, who was sitting on the bench, sobbing. Stan returned to the business section of his newspaper, however he kept an eye on the two men watching him and, now, the young man. His followers stopped watching the young man after about thirty minutes, just before he went to the ticket counter and returned to his seat.

Stan walked around periodically, just to stretch. After the Southbound bus pulled out, to Knoxville, he wandered into the snack bar for a sandwich. Finding the young couple there as well, he joined them and quietly retrieved his Eastbound ticket. They continued to chat and even laughed together, presumably about the cap by the way Stan took it off and examined it.

When the boarding call for the Westbound bus, to St. Louis, came across the public address system, Stan was first in line. The young couple was right behind him. Stan got on the bus and found the first seats on both sides of the isle empty. He sat next to the isle behind the driver; the bride-to-be took the seat across the isle next to the window. The young man ran back into the waiting room, as Stan had instructed him earlier. The men who had been watching Stan took seats halfway back, behind the driver.

As departure neared, the young woman began crying. Stan adjusted his cap as he moved over to the empty seat next to her. He tried to console her, audibly assuring that her fiance had not left her. As luck would have it, a baby began crying loudly at the rear of the bus just as the driver boarded. Stan took advantage of the distraction to slip off the bus. The young man quickly boarded and sat next to his fiance. He was now wearing the cap.

Stan slipped down the side of the Westbound bus and presented his ticket to the Eastbound driver. He found a seat midway back on the isle; his heart racing as he watched the bus in front of them. It pulled out, heading for St Louis, and nobody else got off. Heaving a sigh of relief, he settled back for the ride to Indianapolis, in the opposite direction.

Reaching Indianapolis two minutes late at 3:02 p.m., Stan wove his way out of the station area, bypassing crowds welcoming friends and relatives. He reasoned his ruse would have been discovered long before his arrival and somebody would be waiting for him, even though the couple would have told the men that he was heading for Chicago. He still had no idea who he was or possibly more important, why these men were looking for him.

Escaping the bus terminal area, Stan discovered the train depot, literally on top of the bus depot. Scanning the neighborhood, the trademark blue and white of a White Castle Hamburgers restaurant across the street caught his eye. Wanting to avoid people and make sure he wasn't still being followed, he went for a bite to eat. Finding a place where he could watch the front door and see beyond to the bus terminal, Stan slid onto a white laminate bench after placing his blue tray with two blue and white boxes on the blue trimmed table. Biting into the first dinner roll stuffed with a square of fried ground beef, he settled back and enjoyed his afternoon respite.

A man who was eating with a group at the table next to him left without his jacket. Stan watched for his return, but after fifteen minutes he took the coat and slipped it on as he left. Miss Betty had washed his shirt and jeans, removing dirt from the pipe and boxcar, but the green shirt was easy to spot. The tan wind-breaker covered this target nicely.

He now needed train schedules out of Indianapolis, preferably heading east or south. Not sure who might be hanging around the bus station, he circled the block, arriving at the train depot from the other side. Entering the station, he scanned faces of those waiting and standing around. Not seeing anyone react to his arrival, he studied various schedules while listening to the din of voices and announcements. Eastbound would take him to Charlottesville, Virginia. Charlottesville also had connecting service, by bus, to Richmond. Only $82, this would work and it would keep him out of sight for about seventeen hours. *I should be able to get from Richmond to Knoxville without any problems*, he thought. The train left at 11:59 p.m.; he had seven hours to kill, or be killed.

When finding his way into the train depot, Stan passed the Pan Am Plaza. While this was a wide-open area, there were several buildings around it that might provide cover while he waited for his train. The plaza was a raised open area paved in white and grey brick, bordered on three sides by streets and a building on the fourth, where patches of green grass softened the harshness of all the brick. Walking down the side of the plaza, he stopped twice to see if anyone was watching or following him. Reaching the far side, he entered the building, a shopping mall. He had not spotted any followers, but the mall would be a perfect place to hide, just in case.

Returning to the train station at 9:30, after the mall closed, Stan purchased a book and got comfortable in a waiting area. Every ten to fifteen minutes he scanned other travelers, diligently looking for anyone who might be watching him. Hearing his boarding call, he moseyed out to the platform, boarded the train, and found a seat where he could easily see three-quarters of the passengers in his coach. He stayed vigilant until the train pulled out, five minutes late, and then for another hour. Shortly after 1:00 a.m., he fell asleep.

Waking to the same rhythmic clicking that lulled him to sleep, Stan made his way to the toilet where he refreshed himself, as best he could in the confined space, then went in search of something to eat. Returning to his seat with a cup of coffee and a sweet roll, he watched the landscape slide past his window in predawn light. He could barely make out shadows of low hills on one side and what appeared to be a river on the other.

Stan took inventory of what he currently knew about himself while the train danced alongside the river between changing hills. Most obvious at the moment, he enjoyed coffee and sweets. He had tried the coffee black but found it bitter. Cream & sugar seemed to have a familiar taste. He apparently did not eat many sweet rolls because he was in pretty good shape, physically, for a man in his late thirties or early forties. Thinking of his physical being, he did have several scars, which he discovered in the shower at Miss Betty's. Presumably battle wounds. And there appeared to be a burn on his upper right arm, possibly where a tattoo had been removed? Rubbing his chin, he considered his beard; probably only a couple weeks old. He knew, or at least thought, he had been in a war, most likely the Middle East, because he had connected with a memory that suggested this. But, was it truly his memory? Recalling how he had seen Brad's hat and then spotted the lost diamond ring, he knew he was observant. Was this a trained skill or a natural ability? Maybe a natural ability he had refined?

Thinking about his time at the shopping mall, he recalled young couples wrapped in each others arms rushing into adulthood and older couples holding hands, holding onto deep love. He had also seen a young girl, possibly eighteen or so, arrested for shop lifting. It was not the two officers apprehending her as she left the store that had grabbed his attention, rather he focused on a young man who blended into the crowd yet seemed to direct the officers making the arrest. He had a way of seeing the big picture without missing small details.

Finishing his coffee and wiping the last bit of sweet roll from his lips, he tried to think about what work he must have been doing. His green shirt was somewhat uncommon, however his clothes said nothing. They were free of holes, showing little wear, and reasonably clean when he had awakened in a freight car. And how did he get in that freight car?

Men traveling the rails said they found him when they

boarded in Nashville. Was he dumped into the car in Nashville or further south? Possibly Birmingham, Chattanooga, or even Atlanta? He recognized the names of these cities from a big map in the Indianapolis train station. How did he know to go east to get around to Knoxville? He had no idea who he was, yet he had no problems with maps, directions, and cities. Where was he when he was clubbed in the head and why wasn't he killed? Or was he left for dead?

Questions seemed to be piling up faster than the miles rolling beneath his coach. Watching the landscape slip past did not ease his mind. He kept recalling a memory of being in a war zone. When? Where? What was he doing there? He tried focusing on this one event, presumably from his past, but soon lost it when a scream roared from the front of his coach.

Most of the other passengers jerked to attention when a little girl screamed as though she were being murdered. Stan sat still and listened, then leaned over and looked under the seats. In the back of his mind he recalled that she had been running up and down the isle with an old stuffed bear. Rising from his seat, he walked forward four rows and pulled the lost bear from under a bench. She cried with relief when he handed it to her. Her mother's entire face smiled as she softly said, "Thank You!"

At lunch, Stan succumbed to his nagging emptiness and purchased something the dining car called a "sub sandwich." A hoagie roll with cold cuts. Back in his seat and chewing the first bite, he saw the little girl with the bear staring up at him. Recalling that her mother did not look like she had much in pocket change, he gave the girl a third of his sandwich. She smiled, took a big bite, then raced back to her mother, sandwich in hand. Lunch behind him, he settled back to consider what he might have done to deserve that huge bump on the back of his head.

The train rolled into Charlottesville at three in the afternoon, slightly ahead of schedule. Riders were told a bus was ready to take passengers to Richmond. Walking around the old red brick station, Stan found he was again studying people. Not only looking for anyone who might be watching him, but simply watching the way people interacted, made connections, and stood around. Boarding the bus he relaxed a bit, believing he might have lost the folks who were after him. He did, however, watch every person who got on the bus. Was anyone giving him a second look?

Stan continued to relax and watched the changing blend of spring green filling the trees that lined Interstate 64 as the bus raced down the black ribbon for two hours. Before getting off the bus at the Amtrak station north of Richmond, Stan asked the driver where the Greyhound terminal was. The driver looked at him briefly then offered, "Take a seat, I'll drop you off a couple blocks from there." The "couple blocks" turned out to be closer to a half mile, but still a significantly shorter distance than he might have had walking from the train depot. Three other passengers got off with him, including the girl with her bear and her mother. Having talked with the mother a bit on the bus, Stan wound up carrying the girl on his shoulders most of the way to the bus station, where her mother bought tickets to Williamsburg.

Now close to six o'clock, Stan was dismayed when he found the next bus heading toward Knoxville didn't leave until 4:00 a.m. To make matters worse, there was nothing of interest in the neighborhood surrounding this depot. With ticket in hand, Stan settled into a bench seat in the corner of the waiting room and pulled out the book he purchased in Indianapolis. He resumed reading on page 12.

Buses came and went all evening. About nine o'clock, he noticed an older woman searching the waiting room. Looking much like a grandmother, dressed in a skirt and sweater, she had apparently just arrived, but whoever was to pick her up was not there. Stan watched as she ambled toward the front door, wearily dragging her wheeled suitcase behind her. Three young men dressed in jeans and dark-theme t-shirts followed her. Before she reached the parking lot, one of these boys tried to grab her suitcase. He screamed in pain as Stan gripped his shoulder and pushed him to his knees. His companions tried to come to his rescue, but found Stan's one free arm was more than the two of them could manage. When they ran off, Stan released his captive, who quickly disappeared around the building.

"Do you mind if I wait with you?" Stan asked the stunned lady.

Before she could answer, a maroon minivan pulled up and a young woman jumped out. "I'm sorry, Mom. Mike and I got into a tiff about who was supposed to pick you up." Seeing Stan standing close behind her, she continued, "Is this man bothering you?"

"Oh no, he was just making sure I was not alone while I waited."

The mother turned her head and smiled at Stan with true gratitude as her daughter helped her into the car. Stan returned to his seat in the waiting room, after getting a cup of coffee, which was somewhat bitter from age. A station attendant asked those sitting around after midnight where they were going. He woke Stan at 3:15. "You can board your bus now." Stan grabbed some crackers from a vending machine and found his seat for the next eleven hours. He laughed to himself when he awoke shortly after 6:00 a.m. and saw that they were back in Charlottesville.

Had I known the bus didn't go south, I would have skipped that loop. I need to get a travel agent, he thought to himself, believing his journey to Richmond had been pointless.

Those passengers who had paid more than the basic fare got breakfast at the depot in Wytheville, VA. Stan grabbed a sausage and egg biscuit at The Travel Store, adjacent to the terminal. Returning to his seat he moaned a bit, realizing he now had less than $100 in his pocket. Settling back, he again began trying to figure out what he had done that started this unusual roundabout journey. No matter how hard he tried, his mind was still a blank. Looking at the cards in his pocket, which he had found inside his boot three days before, he began wondering about Siobhan. Up til now he had been focusing on himself, now he wondered who she was and was she important to him? Once again, no answers.

The bus pulled into the Knoxville, Tennessee terminal at 2:40 p.m. Saturday afternoon, five minutes early. Standing outside the bus terminal, which was actually a convenience store in a commercial neighborhood, Stan considered his next move. He had three locations to find in or around Knoxville. His research on the minister's computer back in Farmersburg had given him links to the KAT bus terminal and a credit union. He also had the pocket menu from a restaurant in Oliver Springs, wherever that might be. Knowing the credit union would be closed, he asked a clerk in the store where the KAT terminal was.

"Not a bad walk from here, just cross under the highway to Hall of Fame Drive. Catch the Knoxville Transit there and they'll deliver you to the main terminal in about ten or fifteen minutes."

Stan thanked the clerk, purchased a cold Coke, then started walking. The neighborhood was somewhat run down, with dirt parking lots, and warehouse buildings. Walking beneath a high overpass, Stan marveled at its construction, then had to jog the last block to catch a bus he saw coming down the street.

Arriving at the main terminal on Church Street, Stan looked around. One end of the long building was filled with ticket booths and seats. The opposite end, beyond restrooms and offices, was filled with lockers. Strolling through this area, he pulled the business card from his pocket and looked at the back again. KAT - 225. Intuition told him to find locker 225. It was locked and he didn't have a key. He then studied a route map on the wall in the ticketing area, hoping to find a ride to Oliver Springs. His destination was thirty miles away and unfortunately beyond the Knoxville Area Transit system, actually the other side of Oak Ridge. He did find a route that would take him as far as Cedar Bluff. He'd start walking from there and hope he could catch a ride.

A plan in place, he found the Cedar Bluff Connector and rode around Knoxville, weaving down two lane roads and divided four lane parkways, through established neighborhoods, land yet to be developed into a neighborhood, business districts, and past strip malls, until they reached Windsor Square Mall. He stretched his legs a bit making his way to a McDonalds restaurant, where he got supper.

Eating a burger and carrying his chocolate shake, he began walking south down highway 11, a five-lane highway without sidewalks. Keeping to interconnecting parking lots and grassy areas beside the road, he soon arrived at highway 140. Turning north on 140, he used ramps and luck to get through a massive cloverleaf with Interstate 40 until he reached highway 162 on the other side. This roadway was a four-lane divided highway, but offered wide grassy spaces well off the pavement.

"Five hours to cross Knoxville," he moaned as he trudged

up the highway. "I sure hope this Siobhan is friendly and has a car." An hour later, with dusk fading into night, a local trucker offered him a ride. Stan gratefully accepted and thanked the man for his generosity.

Stan and the driver chatted during the twelve-mile journey. Passing through Oak Ridge, Stan asked if the driver knew of Pearl's Diner. He didn't have time to answer before arriving at the southern edge of Oliver Springs, where the driver let Stan out before turning off the highway to go home. "Just continue down 62. In about two to three miles you come on a ramp of sorts. I think it's labeled 'Downtown,' but don't count on that. Follow that ramp and it'll take you right to Pearl's. Good luck to ya."

Chapter 3

Stan watched the truck's headlights disappear down the road then turned and looked where he was going. Walking down the divided four lane highway, he looked at the fronts of various businesses, each sleeping silently for the night. He had trekked about half a mile before coming up on a service station and convenience store. Being a bit thirsty, he stepped inside and purchased a Coke and two packs of peanut butter nabs. Passing a hardware store, fifteen minutes later, he had just taken the second cracker from its wrapper when a small dog joined him. Stan looked down at the red wire-haired terrier-type dog now trotting beside him like an old friend.

"Guess you smell my cracker . . . here. I'm not sure I want it anyway." Stan then dropped the cracker. The dog snatched it from the air, paused briefly to eat it, then caught up with Stan, who chuckled half-heartedly as he shook his head slightly from side to side.

Every time Stan removed the top from his drink and took a sip, the dog yipped politely as if to say, "I'll take another cracker, thank you." Not knowing anything about this critter, Stan didn't want to encourage him, but he couldn't resist. Their journey passed multiple service stations, a Hardee's restaurant, grocery store, a school, and more sleeping businesses. Traffic was light and diminished as night took control of the countryside. They finished the first pack of crackers as they reached the ramp the driver had told Stan to follow. There was an exit sign that read: "Downtown." The dog stayed right beside him as they walked along the ramp, which circled down and under the highway, becoming a street leading into town.

The two companions walked only two blocks before arriving at an empty parking lot in front of Pearl's Diner. Reading hours posted on the front door, Stan turned to his new friend. "Well, they serve breakfast and lunch. Tomorrow being Sunday, they don't open till 10:30. What say we see if we can find a soft spot around back?"

Barking softly, the dog started around the corner, just as Stan had suggested. They did find a somewhat soft spot to rest beneath a tree; however, it began to rain during the night. With the first drops, Stan hunkered down under his tree branch. When the rain came harder, Stan and his new companion raced back around to the front of the diner, taking shelter under a cover near the front door. Seeing his friend shivering just a bit, Stan opened his arms and took the dog into his lap.

"HEY! Wake up! You can't sleep here!"

For the second time in a week, Stan awoke to someone assaulting his body. This time it was a woman pushing on his hip with her foot. The dog leapt from Stan's lap and shook off his sleep. Stan started to stretch but his wake-up call persisted.

"C'mon, don't take all day. We'll have customers comin' in here soon."

Stan got to his feet and looked at the woman. She stood about five feet eight inches and weighed in at about one hundred eighty pounds. By her attire, Stan figured she was either a cook or manager of the diner. After a full yawn, Stan looked at her and apologized. "Sorry. Had to get out of the rain."

"Well, I'll be. I know someone who'll be glad to see your sorry face. Come inside and I'll get you a cup of coffee and something to eat." She then began walking around the side, but paused and looked at him again. "Beard looks good. You should keep it."

Once inside, this unexpectedly friendly woman made a phone call, carrying the cordless phone with her as she fired up a gas grill and two ovens. After completing her call, she started a pot of coffee. "Help yourself when it finishes. I gotta get biscuits cookin."

While the coffee dripped slowly into a pot darkened by age and use, Stan took inventory of the kitchen. One large grill, about six feet wide and thirty inches deep, surrounded by shining stainless steel work counters. Then a sink with commercial dish washer and a large double door refrigerator. A small freezer stood alone in one corner. The coffee maker, situated close to a door to the dining room, could hold four pots warming and one brewing. A small table sat to one side between the door to outside and the door to the dining room. Peeking in the dining room, before lifting the coffee pot, he counted twenty tables, all covered with clean plastic covers of different colors and patterns held down by sugar, salt, and pepper dispensers with menus stuck between them. A cash register sat near the door on the opposite side from the kitchen.

He had just finished fixing his first cup of coffee, in a heavy ceramic mug, and was heading toward the kitchen table when another woman came through the back door. Dressed in a light-green waitress uniform, she was a medium build and stood about five feet nine inches tall; a very pleasant picture to Stan's eyes. Her soft brown hair just reached her shoulder and framed a warm, friendly, oval face. Brown eyes, a medium refined nose, and oval mouth were accented by a dimple on the left side of her growing smile. Rushing over to Stan, she took his cup from him, placed it on the table, and wrapped her arms around him.

"I wasn't sure I'd ever see you again!"

Stan reacted in the only manner possible under the circumstances. He wrapped his arms around her and held her tight. It all seemed right, but he still had a big problem. Speaking just over a whisper he said, "I sure hope you're Siobhan."

The young lady immediately released Stan and stepped back, examining him from head to toe. "What!?"

"I don't know who I am. I woke up in a freight car, in Indiana, four days ago with a bunch of hobos, a big overgrown knot on my head, and no idea who I am or how I got there."

"How'd you get here?" the waitress asked suspiciously. The cook now stood beside her, glaring at their guest.

"Bend over," the cook interrupted.

Not wanting to cause more suspicion, Stan bent at the waist. The cook felt the back of his head, then turned to her waitress. "Yep, got one whopper of a bump back there. At least that's true."

Raising back to upright, Stan continued. "Look. I found two cards in my boot. One was a menu from here, with Siobhan's name written on it. I was hoping you might be able to tell me who I am and what I was doing that made somebody rather mad at me."

"Mad . . . I suppose that's one way to describe it." She sighed and turned to the cook. "Mary, how long till we can get some breakfast in this good-for-nothin lout?"

"About ten or fifteen minutes. I just put first biscuits in the oven."

Turning back to Stan, the waitress motioned for him to sit. She then fixed herself a cup of coffee and joined him. Sitting across the table, she stared into his eyes while deciding where to begin and how much to tell. "Okay, short story . . . I guess I'm going to have to trust that your memory is like Swiss cheese . . . for now. Yes, I am Siobhan and your name is Stan Winthrop. You're an investigator of some sort. Don't know if you're a PI or cop or what. Just that you have been workin on some big case . . . investigating a politician or public official somewhere. You left here four . . . no, five weeks ago to follow up a lead somewhere around Atlanta, Georgia."

Listening with interest, Stan smiled when she paused. "Stan? You said my name is Stan Winthrop?"

"Yes, does that mean anything?"

"When I needed a name on the train, I pulled the name 'Stan' out of the air. I had no idea that it was really my name . . . just one that came to me."

"Don't get too used to it. I'm not sure it's your real name."

"What do you mean?"

"When you didn't come back after a week, like you said you would, I googled you. Stan Winthrop doesn't exist, at least not on the big web. But then, neither do I. Got a lot of hits on 'Siobhan Thomas' but I wasn't any of them. Looked kinda like one in London, but not me. I thought a man with your background would be somewhere on the internet."

"Might be that I just keep a low profile. Anonymity could be an asset to an investigator." Stan paused to enjoy looking into Siobhan's eyes while sipping his coffee. "Any idea what this big case was I'm supposed to be working on?"

"You're looking into the background of some man . . . a politician I think."

"A politician?"

"Yea, I looked in your briefcase when you were in the shower one morning."

Stan pondered this revelation, one he thought he would really like to remember. "You said I have a briefcase?"

"You did and it was full of papers and maps and

photographs."

"You said 'did'."

"I don't know where it is. The day before you left for Atlanta, it disappeared."

"Did I leave anything with you to hold or take care of for me?"

"No."

Mary slid two country breakfast specials onto the table. Each plate was loaded with two fried eggs, a generous piece of country ham, a bowl of grits with a pool of redeye gravy, and a basket of steaming biscuits. She then refilled both coffee cups. "Eat up, girl. Customers will be here before you know it." She then returned to the grill and biscuit making.

Finding a biscuit that was too dark to be golden, she grabbed it and a couple sausage links and stepped out the back door. The dog was waiting patiently and appreciated the generous breakfast.

"What's his name?" Mary asked when Stan joined them.

"Don't know. He isn't really mine. Joined me on my hike from Knoxville." Sipping his coffee, Stan walked to the back door and looked at the dog. He then squatted down, setting his coffee cup on the ground beside him, and began rubbing the dog's neck. "Seems to be a pretty good companion, though. I guess I'll take care of him as long as he hangs around."

"You better talk with Siobhan about that. I don't know that she's so fond of animals." Mary said before turning to go back into her kitchen, bumping into Siobhan.

"I don't know. If he gets a bath I suppose I could make room for him." Siobhan said as she squatted next to Stan. After rubbing the dog's head for a second, she looked over at Stan. "I seem to have a soft spot for strays." She then kissed Stan on the cheek and went back inside behind another young woman dressed in the same green uniform.

Stan turned his head and watched Siobhan with an admiring eye. Turning back to the dog he remarked, "Well, sir. Looks like Siobhan is indeed friendly and we have a home. Seems my name is 'Stan;' what might we call you?" Stan gently lifted the dog's head so they could see each other eye-to-eye.

The wiry-haired dog looked at Stan, his reddish-brown eyes

wide with alert anticipation. After a few seconds, he stood, shook from head to tail, then sat and placed his head back in Stan's hand.

"You are an odd bird. Kind of remind me of a dog I read about one time. His name was Flibbertygibbet. How do you like that name?" Stan chuckled as the dog lifted his head and rolled his eyes to one side. "Okay . . . how about just 'Flibber'? Or maybe 'Flib'?" The dog sat upright and looked straight at Stan. "Okay. Flib it is then. As long as you want to hang around with me and Siobhan, we'll see that you are fed and have a warm place to sleep. Deal?"

"Arrfph!"

"I'll take that as a yes."

Stan reached down for his coffee cup just as Mary opened the door. "Hey forgetful, do you remember what I taught you about working the grill? My assistant just called in. Say's he's sick but sounds hung over. Either way, I'm going to need help."

"Let's find out," Stan replied as he stood. Looking down at the dog, he concluded their conversation. "Mister Flib, I'll check on you as I can. Be sure to be here when we leave if you want to go with us."

"Wash yer hands and put somethin on yer head," Mary commanded as Stan returned to the kitchen.

Complying, Stan stepped over to the grill as he tied an old apron around his waist. Mary smiled and looked around. "Sylvia, start another pot of coffee. Make it decaf, then another hi-test. Siobhan, go ahead and unlock the front door, I'm willing to bet we have half a dozen out there already. Stan, throw some ham and bacon on the grill. As soon as Old Man Johnson gets here, he'll want three fried eggs. You'll remember how."

Stan did remember, as though he had been working short orders for years. His grill sizzled loudly with sweet aromas each time he dropped ham or bacon on it, and more quietly when he cracked an egg. He quickly got scrambling eggs down to two or three motions and busted only two fried eggs. He found aromas of the grill more than satisfying. The morning flew by with only one break, about 10:40. Stan and Siobhan spent these quiet minutes with Flib. Going back inside, both were commanded to "wash up before the next wave attacks."

Closing time, two-thirty, didn't come soon enough for Stan. While he found working the grill satisfying, his back and legs weren't accustomed to standing for so long. When the last order was finished, he automatically started cleaning and prepping for the next day.

Stepping out the door at quarter past three, he looked around for Flib. The small dog was nowhere to be seen. Following Siobhan to her car, he heaved a sigh. His disappointment was short-lived, however, as Flib jumped into the car before Stan got settled in the passenger seat of Siobhan's Subaru Forester.

Siobhan turned off the highway near Hardee's, about three miles from Pearl's Diner, and followed the narrow road into a small apartment complex. Two rows of single level apartments facing the parking lot, six on each side. She lived in an end-unit, furthest from the road. Parking in the next to last space, Siobhan led her guests down the short walk and inside. A small closet formed a foyer area which fed into a twelve by fifteen foot living room. A dining area in the corner of the living room, behind the closet, merged into the galley kitchen with a back door. A hallway off to other side of the living room led to two bedrooms, separated by a shared bath. Stan surveyed the accommodations looking for something he might remember. The apartment was familiar, sort of, as if it was cloaked by a dense fog.

"What stuff you left is in the front bedroom," Siobhan told him as he wandered about. "I sleep in the back room." She then looked at Stan with a sense of longing. "You, too, sometimes."

Stan tried to smile, but couldn't. His mind was being overwhelmed by that fog that was hiding memories of this apartment. He did not yet remember being with Siobhan, though he desperately wanted to. The apartment seemed familiar, somehow, but nothing absolute. He continued to search for something that might trigger a definite memory.

Flib sniffed from room to room. Completing his second pass, he went into the bathroom and examined a built-in heater with his nose and eyes. Completing his examination, he sat and barked once.

"What'd you find Flib?" Stan asked as he joined his small companion.

"That heater doesn't work. You said you'd fix it, but never did," Siobhan added as she came to see what Flib had barked at. "Not sure we'll need it for a few months, now that spring's here."

Stan squatted down to look at the heater cover more closely, then turned to Siobhan. "Do you have a screwdriver? Maybe a small table knife?"

Siobhan left, then returned a moment later with a small green tool box. Stan opened it to find a collection of common screwdrivers, pliers, and a small hammer. He picked out a flat screwdriver and proceeded to remove the heater cover.

Pointing to a melted wire, he told Siobhan, "Here's why it's not working."

Flib pushed around him and sniffed intently around the side opposite the controls. Stan followed the dog's lead and poked around with the screwdriver. Woven between the vanes of the heater element was a cotton string. Stan fished it out with the screwdriver and gently pulled it to the side.

"A key!" He exclaimed as he retrieved what appeared to be a locker key, tied to the string. Reaching over to the dog, he rubbed his neck warmly. "Good boy, Flib. You're quite the detective." Standing, he smiled at his host. "The bus station in Knoxville."

"How do you know? There's no tag," Siobhan challenged.

Stan pulled the business card from his pocket. "I have the number right here. Do you work tomorrow? Can you take me to Knoxville?" Before dropping the key in his pocket, Stan noticed a series of numbers and letters stamped into it. "3A4C"

"Sure. But right now you and Flib need a shower. I'll get you some clean clothes."

Believing this to be a good idea, Stan proceeded to undress. Siobhan returned with clothes from Stan's room as he dropped his shirt. Placing the clothes on the counter, she stroked his bare shoulders and back. Sighing as though recalling a delightful memory, she closed the door and went into the kitchen. Her coffee pot was empty.

Completing his own shower, Stan coaxed Flib into joining him. The only shampoo available was a generic bottle for babies. No tears variety. Flib stood patiently as Stan scrubbed him, appearing to understand that he either suffered through the bath or went back on the road. Washed and rinsed, Stan tried to get a towel around him but wasn't quick enough. Flib shook water all over the bathroom, including Stan's clean clothes.

Emerging from the bath just a bit damp, Stan found Siobhan in the living room, on a wood frame sofa with brown plaid cushions. The television, an old RCA nineteen inch color CRT on a lightweight tv cart, was on, but she was watching rain fall outside her window. There was also a blue armchair in the corner by the front window and a coffee table in front of the sofa. Flib leapt onto her sofa, jumped over her, then sat on the floor at her feet. She laughed and reached down to pet him.

"AGH! You're still wet!"

"So am I," Stan chuckled. "He sort of transferred the shower from the bath to the bathroom."

"Great!" She exclaimed as she stood. "I'll dry him. You dry the bathroom!"

Cleanup and drying Flib completed, Siobhan and Stan settled back on the sofa. Each with a cup of coffee and nothing on their agenda.

"Miss Siobhan, what should I know about you and our previous relationship?" Stan asked. His eyes were filled with her simple beauty, which was growing with each minute of her company.

"I grew up in Pigeon Forge, but never liked the touristy atmosphere Dolly brought to the town. I was engaged once, but never made it to the altar. He found my maid-of-honor more appealing. They didn't make it either. Couldn't afford to go to college so I have limited job opportunities. I sort of fell into the job at Pearl's. I was eating lunch there one day when a big logging crew came in. She was short handed and I was looking for a job. When they started calling for service, I began taking their orders just to shut them up. Been there for five years, now. No, six."

"How did we meet?" Stan asked, wanting to reach over and take her hand but not bold enough to make the move.

"It was a rainy Sunday, kind of like this one. I went out to start my car and it didn't. You were my last customer and offered to help. You got it started after ten minutes of fiddling in a soaking rain and came back to Pearl's every day for the next week."

"Only one week?"

"One week before I gave into your flirting and we went out."

"Where was I staying then?"

"A Motel 6 in Knoxville, I believe. I never went there, so I'm not completely sure."

Stan pondered for a moment. "How long did I stay with you . . . before I disappeared, or went to Atlanta?"

"Just over a month," Siobhan replied quickly. "We dated for three weeks before I made the offer. You said you couldn't afford the motel any longer. I offered to share this place . . . you owe me for last month's rent."

Stan smiled with a bit of contentment. "As soon as I get my hands on some cash, it's yours." He desperately wanted to explore how close they had been, but decided to just let a new relationship develop, or not. "I must've had a car."

"You did. A very nice Ford Explorer. Green with gold accents. There's a spare set of keys in the kitchen drawer. I had them in my purse for a while, but didn't see the point when you didn't come back."

Looking out the window, Stan suggested, "Looks like the rain's let up. I suppose we should go get some dog food and something for supper?"

Siobhan reached down to where Flib had gone to sleep at her feet and scratched his head. Looking over to Stan she replied, bluntly, "I sure hope that key unlocks some money."

Chapter 4

A Hardee's breakfast special in their stomach's and refilled coffee cups in hand, Siobhan and Stan headed for Knoxville. Siobhan sipped her coffee and glanced over at Stan as they approached the highway interchange west of Knoxville, Tennessee. She was driving and he was holding a full cup of coffee. He simply held his cup; Siobhan hadn't seen him take even a first sip. She was taking them to the Knoxville Area Transit main station on Church Street; he was lost in his thoughts when not watching cars behind them.

Rounding the access ramp onto Interstate 40, Stan relaxed his traffic watch and turned his head to look at Siobhan. She was familiar, or was it simply her natural warmth and spirit? He dug for memories of her but could not find even one.

Flib raised his head as he moaned. Lying on the back seat, he wasn't a fan of travel by car. God had given him four good feet; why did he need to be in this vehicle? Still, odd as these people were, he enjoyed their company. Feeling the car straighten out and accelerate, he rested his head on his paws once more.

Passing through downtown Knoxville, Siobhan swung her Forester onto the Highway 158 exit, then took the Church Street ramp. Turning right onto Church, she slowed down for pedestrian traffic and narrower streets. Reaching the bus station, she continued to the next block and pulled into the left turn lane to enter a parking deck.

"Drive around the block, please," Stan said, a sense of urgency in his voice.

Continuing down the street, Siobhan looked over at Stan. "What's wrong?"

"I thought we were being followed, but they turned off." He continued to watch a car going down another street.

As Siobhan rounded the block, Stan asked, "They don't have parking at the depot?"

"No. This is a city bus and they run all over town so you don't need a car," Siobhan replied with a grin. "Most folks come here just to change buses or get to the coliseum across the street." Completing the loop around the block, she turned into the parking deck.

"Okay. Can we leave Flib in the car?" he asked while watching a car behind them continue to the upper levels of the parking deck.

"Probably better than him running loose around Knoxville. I don't think they'll let him in the depot."

Turning around, Stan addressed his small companion. "We won't be gone long. I'll roll the window down a bit so you'll be okay. Stay put and guard the car."

"Did you just wink at that dog?" Siobhan asked as she closed her door and pressed the lock button on her fob. Stan shrugged his shoulders and began walking toward the depot. Before going too far, Siobhan turned and looked at Flib in the rear window. He seemed to settle before she turned back around. "Do you really think someone's following us?"

"Don't know. Just my nature, I guess."

Walking into the depot, Stan turned left toward a bank of steel cabinets. Arriving at the locker he had visited two days before, he removed his key, inserted it into the lock, and tried to turn it. Nothing happened.

"Items left in lockers more than seven days may be claimed at depot security office," Siobhan read from a sign over the lockers.

Looking around, Stan saw a depot attendant. "Excuse me, sir. Where is the security office?"

The man turned and pointed toward the main lobby area. "Go down to the ticket counters. Just this side is a door marked 'Security'. On the left."

"Thank you," Stan replied and immediately stepped toward his next destination, Siobhan at his side.

Entering the small security office, they found a counter, but no personnel. The standing area between the counter and wall was only about four feet wide and eight feet long. A bulletin board covered with legal notices hung on the wall opposite the counter. The area behind the desk was the same size but included a small desk at one end, with a computer, and the wall was decorated with the 'kat' logo.

Siobhan stepped to the counter and tapped the button on top of a small silver bell. A woman in the typical blue and white 'kat,' Knoxville Area Transit, uniform stepped through a door behind the counter. "May I help you?"

"I am looking for contents of locker 225," Stan replied, becoming a bit anxious.

"You have the key?" the woman asked, holding her hand out.

Stan gave her the key which she examined.

"No tag, how do you know this is 225?"

"I have it written on the back of a business card."

"Okay . . . we'll see." Reading the number stamped into the key, she stepped over to the computer. Leaning over the keyboard, she rapped the keys until a screen appeared where she entered the registration number on the key, 3A4C. After reading several lines of data on the screen, she disappeared through the door she had arrived through. A couple minutes passed before she returned with a black brief case. "That'll be $55.00."

"Excuse me?" Stan replied, a bit flabbergasted.

"Fifty dollars for storage and five dollars for a new key tag. Our lockers are not for long term storage. There are places all over town for that."

Siobhan's eyes opened wide when she saw the case. In a chastising tone she said, "Stop fussing and pay the lady."

"Yes, ma'am." Stan smiled at Siobhan and dug a fold of bills from his pocket. Sighing at the shrinking size of his funds, he peeled off two twenties, a ten, and a five, then stuffed the remainder back into his pocket. "Thank you for keeping it safe," he acknowledged as he accepted the briefcase.

"What now?" Siobhan asked as they left the depot.

"Well, I think I'd like to get back to the car and see what's in this thing."

"Sounds good." Her hair bounced as she almost skipped with delight.

Walking up to the car, both Siobhan and Stan looked through the windows. Flib seemed to be asleep, however as soon as she unlocked the doors with her fob, he was standing, alert and protective. Recognizing his people, he relaxed.

"You're a good'un Flib," Siobhan cooed as she reached back and scratched the dog under his chin.

Stan surveyed the parking deck before getting into the car.

Seeing no one sitting in their car or standing around, he slid into the passenger seat and placed the briefcase on his lap. Simultaneously pressing two release buttons, he found both to be locked. Lifting the case he saw the latches had numeric locks, each three digits. Without thinking, he spun the left set to "237" and the right set to "846." Nothing happened when he pressed the buttons. Without hesitation he reversed the numbers, setting left to "846" and right to "237." Pressing the buttons again, both popped open. He then wondered how he knew those two numbers.

Lifting the lid, he peered at the contents of his briefcase. Two six by nine inch brown envelopes and one ten by twelve white envelope. All sealed. He quickly looked through the folder pockets but found nothing. "Okay, let's see what's in these envelopes," he mused as he looked to Siobhan.

One of the smaller envelopes was thicker, almost bulging. Carefully tearing this one open, he peered inside and smiled at Siobhan. "You said something about finding money in this briefcase?" Emptying the contents of the envelope, they counted three thousand six hundred dollars in twenties and fifties. After stuffing the cash back into the envelope, he lifted the second small envelope and peeled back the closure. "Hmm," he mused as he looked inside, then dumped the contents into the briefcase. A driver's license and a folded note. Looking at the license, he commented, "You're right. I'm Stan Winthrop and I'm from Brevard, North Carolina." Handing the license to Siobhan, he looked at the note. It was a phone number, 1-899-FND-LOST, and a second series of numbers, "98542".

"Shame you don't have a cell phone, I could call this number and have them find me," Stan chuckled.

"Yes, well, phones and rain puddles don't work together."

Taking the driver's license back from Siobhan, he folded the note and put both in his shirt pocket. He then lifted the larger white envelope and peered at it.

"Are you just going to wonder about that thing or are you going to open it?" Siobhan asked, her voice filled with anticipation.

"Yeah, okay." Stan then fumbled with the envelope as he tore it open. Once again he dumped the contents into his case.

He found a Tennessee driver's license, a pad of temporary checks, and a handwritten note. Looking at the driver's license he saw it had his picture but identified him as "Taylor Buncombe," residing in Oliver Springs. The issue date was one week before he left for Atlanta.

"Let me see *that* one," Siobhan giggled, her hand out.

Stan gave her the license. Looking at it she exclaimed, "Hey! This is my address! Who is Taylor Buncombe?"

"That mut have been an alias I used for banking," Stan replied calmly as he read the note, first to himself. Silently. *Take Siobhan to her car and say these words. . . .* Per instructions in the note, Stan looked at Siobhan and clearly said, "Ostrich Conundrum."

Without saying a word, Siobhan reached across the car and opened the glove compartment in front of Stan. Digging to the bottom of the pile of maps, napkins, a flashlight, and assorted salt, pepper, and sweetener envelopes, she retrieved a plastic registration wallet which she handed to Stan before blurting out, "And who said you could use MY address?"

Post hypnotic suggestion. She was programmed to be a key to some hidden information, Stan thought to himself, smiling with a bit of cringe as he opened the thin document holder. Inside were registration and insurance papers for Siobhan's Subaru. Behind an insurance agent's card, stuck solidly in a card slot, he felt something hard. Looking behind the card, he found a small key taped in place. Scraping at the edge of the tape, he finally worked enough of it loose to grab and peel off. Fortunately, the key came with it. Using the tape to hold the key to the dashboard, he closed the wallet and slipped it back into the bottom of the glove compartment.

Peeling the key from the dash, he looked to Siobhan who was staring at him with utter disbelief. "Since you dropped your phone, I think our next stop is a TVA Credit Union."

"Which one? They're all over town?"

"Not sure. I'm thinking South Knoxville, but have no idea where that is. I do recall seeing a sign for one in the shopping area where I got off the bus. Near the intersection of I-40 and the highway to Oliver Springs."

"Yes. I know where you're talking about. It's a place to start.

You know, come to think of it, a package came for Taylor Buncombe . . . but I sent it back."

"You sent it back?" Stan asked as they backed out of their parking place and headed for the bank at Windsor Square. He watched to see if any cars pulled out behind them. Not seeing any, he relaxed.

"I had no idea who this 'Taylor Buncombe' was and you weren't around to tell me. What was I supposed to do?"

Stan chuckled softly and took a sip of his coffee. It was now lukewarm. Looking at the cup he thought he saw a slobber mark across the top. Looking to the back seat, he asked, "You like coffee?" Flib cocked his head and licked his lips.

Siobhan waited in the car when they arrived at the credit union fifteen minutes from the kat bus terminal. She rolled her windows down, calling to Stan, "Don't be too long." Flib stuck his head between the seats. Siobhan responded by gently stroking his head.

Walking up to a customer service desk, he asked, "Excuse me, can you tell me which of your branches have lock boxes?"

A pert young brunette looked up with a smile. "We don't have any here, but several branches do. Are you trying to locate a specific box or are you trying to secure one?"

"Just shopping. Do you have a branch with boxes around South Knoxville?"

"Our South Knoxville branch does have safe deposit boxes available."

"Do you have an address for that branch?"

Reaching into her desk drawer, the young lady pulled out a brochure which listed all Knoxville area branches, complete with addresses and a small map. Pointing to the South Knoxville entry, she said, "Easiest way to get there from here is to take I-40 into town, then go south on 441, toward Chapman. It's a bit of a drive but not so bad."

"Thank you for your help." Stan then folded the brochure and turned to leave, but stopped and returned to the young lady. "If I have lost my credit card, do I need to go back to the branch that issued it or can I request a replacement at any branch?"

"The easiest way is to access your account online, but I would be glad to handle it for you."

"No, thanks. I have one more place I need to look first. Have a nice day."

"You as well, sir."

Stan returned to the car. Climbing into the passenger seat, he looked to Siobhan. "Let's go get you a phone. There's bound to be a carrier store somewhere in this shopping complex."

"I don't have the money for that right now!"

"Yes we do," he smiled, patting the brief case.

Siobhan stared at Stan. He had a generous nature before he disappeared, but not quite this generous. She wanted to say something, but wasn't sure what. Swallowing, she found her voice. "Tell you what. It's getting warm out there and I know Flib doesn't want to wait in the car for as long as it would take to get a new phone. Why don't we head back to my apartment and let Flib run for a while. We can see about the phone at the store in Oliver Springs."

Stan looked back at Flib, who sat up when he heard his name. "Well, fella, looks like someone likes having you around." Turning back to Siobhan, he agreed. "Sounds good."

Once they left the shopping area and were back on the highway heading home, Stan asked, "So, you said I had a room at the Motel 6, but you never went there. What did I tell you about what I was working on? Why was I here in Knoxville?"

Siobhan replayed everything she had told him at Pearl's the day before. This time she was more convinced he really could not remember. But she wanted him to.

Chapter 5

Flib jumped from the car as soon as they pulled up to Siobhan's apartment. He had business to take care of. About thirty minutes later, Siobhan heard a polite bark at the kitchen door and stopped making lunch to let their four-footed friend inside.

The small dog watched as Stan took a sandwich into the living room, but the man was reluctant to share. This hefty collection of meat, lettuce, and pickles was his. Flib's persistent stare, however, won him over and Siobhan laughed aloud as Stan surrendered the last two bites.

"He's got your number," she snickered with delight.

Looking around, Stan changed the subject. "Do you have a computer and access to the internet?"

"It's old but it'll get out there," she replied and retrieved an older Sony notebook from her bedroom. After turning it on and seeing it immediately shut down, she went back for the power adapter.

Windows 7 finally booted up without any fanfare and little promise. Stan looked for a web browser, ultimately clicking on Internet Explorer. It struggled for five minutes before slowly displaying the MSN homepage.

"How do you get email?"

"On my phone . . . before it took a bath."

"And you use your phone for all your web stuff?"

"Sure. I don't go out there much. Never found a need to."

Stan pondered for a moment, thinking about puzzles he had encountered that morning. "Okay, let's go get you a phone."

Flib followed them outside but showed no interest in getting back into the car. Stooping down where he could rub the dog's neck, Stan told his small friend, "It's nice out, enjoy the sunshine. We'll be back in a couple hours." Flib sat by the front door and watched them drive away.

"Okay, Miss Thomas, we do have a phone like yours in stock, but you didn't have insurance on your previous phone that 'went swimming,' as you put it. You'll have to purchase the new one for $225.00." The clerk at the phone store looked at Siobhan with apologetic eyes.

"Do you take cash?" Stan asked, standing behind Siobhan.

"Err . . . yes, sir. We normally bill it to the account, but yes, we can accept cash for the phone. I see on your account that you were not using our cloud backup. If you have your old phone, we might be able to retrieve your contacts and other data."

"No, like I said, it took a dive into a mud puddle. I tried the rice trick, but it never came back on," Siobhan replied with a shrug.

"Yes, ma'am. We can get that replacement and have you back online shortly." The young man turned to go to the stock room, however Stan called him back.

"How much to add another line to this account and make it unlimited data?"

The young man smiled. "An additional line will be $9.99 per month and the upgrade to unlimited data will be an additional $20 per month. What phone did you have in mind?"

"What's the smallest and fastest phone you have?"

"By 'fast,' you mean for web access?"

"Yes. And I do need a good camera, but I don't like big phones." Stan frowned at the thought of a bulky phone.

"Well. Samsung has the best cameras, but Google Pixel is possibly the smallest. Apple Mini is just as small, but its camera isn't near the quality of Samsung. Not near the price, either. The key problem is smaller phones don't have better cameras. Under six inches, the best camera you'll find is only twelve megapixels. In the six-inch range we can get you sixteen, possibly forty-eight megapixels. At six point eight inches you can get over 100 megapixels, but that one costs a thousand dollars."

"Okay, that six inch, sixteen. Do you have one?"

"I'll check sir."

The young man smiled and turned again for the stock room. He returned after five minutes with one box. Looking at Siobhan, he told her, "Your phone will be ready shortly. They are setting it up now." Turning to Stan, he opened the box. "You're in luck, I hope. This model has been discontinued but is forty-eight megapixels and only six point one inches." Lifting the phone out of the box, he handed it to Stan. "Because it has been discontinued, the cash price is only $360.00."

"Okay." Turning to Siobhan, he asked, "Do you mind if I ride along on your account?"

"What? You mean I get a say in this?"

"I'll give you the cash up front for six months of the added cost. Deal?"

Siobhan looked into Stan's eyes. "Sure, add it to my account." Behind her acceptance she thought, *Of course. This will keep us in touch and maybe help you remember. Do you remember anything yet? Anything about us?*

The young man pulled up a new screen on his terminal and began asking Siobhan questions required to add the new line. Stan looked into the mirror behind the counter, staring into Siobhan's eyes and thinking, *This is one exceptional lady. I'm not sure what we had, but I think I might like to build something new with her.*

Walking out of the phone store, thirty minutes later, Siobhan stopped and looked around. Spotting a sign for a men's store at the end of the next block, she grabbed Stan's hand and tugged. "The man I knew did not carry cash wadded up in his pocket. You're going to get a new billfold!"

Walking past several brick buildings built so close they merged as one, Stan looked absently into each store window, paying no attention to any of them. Waiting to cross the street to the next block, Siobhan drew a deep breath and looked down the street to the right. Stan noticed a tall heavy set man with red hair and beard leaving a shop ahead of them. This man crumpled a piece of paper and dropped it on the ground, then proceeded to count bills in his hand. Passing at the edge of the street, Stan noticed the bills were all $100s and he had quite a stack. Seeing the litter the man had dropped, Stan picked it up and looked for a trash can. Not finding any receptacles on the street, he tucked the paper in his back pocket.

The men's store had a varied selection of wallets. Siobhan offered several elegant suggestions, however Stan zeroed in on one of simple style. Leaving the men's store en route to the car, Stan ducked into a hardware store and purchased a Swiss Army Knife and a pocket flashlight similar to the one he had borrowed in Farmersburg. Even though it had the same incredible power, this new light was smaller and fit his shirt pocket like a writing pen.

Driving back to the apartment, Stan directed Siobhan to pull into a parking lot at a small grocery store. "You want steak for supper?"

Siobhan's eyes lit up. While Stan talked with the butcher, she picked up some potatoes, fresh asparagus, and makings for a salad. As they approached the cash register, Stan paused. "You still have charcoal?"

"Only what you bought last time," she replied, smiling ear to ear. *He found a memory!*

Arriving back at the apartment, they found Flib waiting at the front door. The spring sunshine had been replaced by clouds and a chilling wind. He was ready to get back inside.

Siobhan put potatoes in a pot on the stove, medium heat, and sat on her sofa with her new phone. After entering Stan's number and linking it to speed dial 1, she began the arduous task of entering phone numbers from an old address book she carried in her purse. Sitting next to her, Stan woke up his new phone and began customizing it by entering Siobhan's number, linking it to speed dial 3. He then went exploring on the internet. After retrieving the pad of temporary checks from his brief case, he tried to log into his bank account. Good news was web access had not yet been setup for this account. Bad news was he needed an email address to continue.

Siobhan suggested he set up a gmail account. Once he completed the registration process, she added his email address to his contact information in her phone.

Armed with a new gmail account, he returned to the bank site. Gaining access presented another stumbling block. After entering his account number from the checks and new email address, he needed the last four digits of his social security number. Pondering the problem, he mumbled numbers softly to himself. "237 . . . 846. No, it couldn't be that easy. No, but close . . ." He entered "8732" and held his breath.

A new prompt came across his small screen: "Enter new username . . ." Remembering this account was in the name Taylor Buncombe, he entered "taylor." The screen responded, "That name is already in use. Please enter new username."

Seeing warnings about using familiar names for usernames and passwords, he thought, *The username doesn't mean anything, just a tag to id the account.* Tapping the keys quickly, he entered, "flib." Accepting the new username, the bank site responded, "A confirmation email has been sent to the address you provided. Follow instructions in this email to set your password."

Exasperated with this too-many-steps process, Stan put his phone on the coffee table and stood. "You want a cup of coffee?"

Siobhan considered his offer before replying, "No, I'm good."

"Well, I need a cup before I set that blasted phone up for email so I can get into this bank account. Gettin there, but it's slow." He then went to the kitchen and fixed his coffee. Returning to the living room, he noticed Siobhan was running email on her phone and solicited her assistance to get his working. Minutes later he opened the email from the credit union and proceeded to reset his password, per instructions in the message.

Gaining access to the account, he immediately went to the summary screen. Seeing a balance of $44,255.21, he gasped and looked at the transaction summary below the balance. This summary showed only recent transactions; there were none. Seeing a tab for transaction history, he tapped it and waited. Seconds later a complete history of this account appeared. It was established less than two months ago with a deposit of $50,000. Clicking on a link to the deposit he saw an image of a certified check from MG Turner. Then there was an immediate cash withdrawal for $5,000 and three credit card charges. The first was $28.71 for gas at an Oliver Springs self-serv station. The second was $40.87, for gas in Cartersville, Georgia, and the final charge was $675.21 from a Motel 6, in White, Georgia.

Looking for a link to cancel and request a new credit card, he asked, "Siobhan, please see if you can find a Motel 6 in White, Georgia?" Finding a link to a phone number for lost cards, Stan pressed it and raised the phone to his ear. Seeing Siobhan had found the motel, he raised a finger and began speaking with an operator. "Yes, I would like to report a lost card and see if I can get a new one. . . . no, I don't remember the card number. It was linked to my account, number 0004239251 . . . . you need my security pin for verification? I don't have one . . . yes, the last four of my social are 8732 . . . there has been no activity on the card? . . . good. And you can have a new one sent to the address of record? . . . yes, those checks were returned by mistake. It would save me a stop by the bank if you could have them reissued, as well. . . . order them from my account on the web? . . . No, that will be all. Thank you very much for your help."

Completing his call to the bank, he turned to Siobhan. "Yes, what did you find?"

"White, Georgia is a spot near Cartersville . . . wherever that is. Do we need a reservation?"

Stan smiled at "we" and replied, "No. Not yet, anyway. Thanks." He then located account services on the credit union's website and clicked the button to order checks, electing to take the automatic order rather than select something himself. Closing his online session, he pondered what he had learned.

"What'd you find out?" Siobhan asked, placing her own phone on her lap.

"It appears Michael G. Turner paid me to find something or do something for him."

"What?"

"I have no idea. All I have is a deposited check and his business card with two references on it. The bus station, where we found the briefcase and what I believe is a safe deposit box at a TVA Credit Union branch office. Since my memory is a great big hole, I would say any ideas you have on the subject would be better than mine." Looking into her eyes, he felt an urge to lean over and kiss her. Taking a gulp of coffee, instead, he noticed Flib licking his lips.

Both relaxing on the sofa, with Flib now curled up at Stan's feet, Stan broke the silence. "I guess I should go check out that safe deposit box tomorrow. May I use your car?"

Turning her head, she found Stan looking at her. "You'll have to get up and take me to work first, but sure. I trust you. . . . Shouldn't we start fixing supper?"

Stan nodded and stood, extending his hand to assist Siobhan. Both standing, they looked into one another's eyes. "Supper!" Siobhan stated plainly.

Stan found a small barrel grill outside the kitchen door and charcoal in a small aluminum trash can. After cleaning ashes from the grill and scraping remnants of the last cooking session from the grate, he stacked the charcoal briquettes and soaked them with lighter fluid, then stepped inside to get matches. Reaching into the cabinet closest to the door, he retrieved a box of wooden magic sticks and returned to the grill. Striking the first match caused a sudden and brief explosion from lighter fluid vapor rising above the coals. Stan stepped back, feeling his face to make sure his eyebrows were still intact. Seeing fluid flames dancing on the briquettes, he went back inside to find his coffee and prepare the steaks and asparagus for grilling.

Stan didn't have to ask for anything. He seemed to know where everything he needed was. Siobhan smashed up the potatoes and mixed the salad fixings, feeling comfortable with the way things were progressing. Dinner was a delightful success. Flib especially enjoyed the leftover steak and potatoes. He didn't eat any asparagus.

Chapter 6

Siobhan usually ate breakfast at Pearl's on days she was working. Tuesday was no exception, so Stan followed her into Pearl's kitchen.

"Know who you are yet?" Mary asked, taunting Stan and unable to keep a bit of laughter from her voice.

Stan proudly removed his new wallet and produced a driver's license with his name and picture on it. "Stan Winthrop, just like Siobhan told me."

"So, Stan Winthrop, what are you doing here in Oliver Springs?" Mary continued, this time with a bit of challenge in her tone.

Returning the wallet to his back pocket, it was his turn to laugh. "That, Miss Mary, is the million-dollar question."

Thinking she recognized the phone in the holster on his hip, she commented, "You found your phone, I see."

"No. New phone. New phone number. Can I get some breakfast without fixing it myself?"

"After Sunday, you're good for a few more freebies. Fix yourself some coffee and have a seat." Mary cut her eyes across to Siobhan who was smiling with delight. Nodding slightly, Mary drew a deep breath, letting it out with a long low sigh.

"Car keys?" Stan asked as he and Siobhan finished breakfast.

Handing them over, she reminded Stan to pick her up. "Three o'clock. If you're late, you won't use it again." Lifting their plates from the table, she paused. "You taking Flib with you?"

Stan thought briefly before replying. "Yeah, I guess so." He then left.

Sitting at the table in the apartment, with Flib snoring at his feet, Stan reviewed what papers he had. Picking up the slip with a phone number on it, which he had found inside the brief case, he realized he had not called it. Without hesitation he dialed 1-899-FND-LOST.

A recorded female voice, generic, yet pleasing, answered.

"We cannot help you find your car keys or misplaced cell phone, however if you have lost something near and dear, please leave your name, contact information, and a brief description of what you have lost. We will be in touch as soon as we are able." Beep.

Without thinking, Stan pressed the star key twice then entered the number from the paper, 98542.

"That pass code is invalid." Beep.

Stan pondered for just a second and entered 8542#.

"Press 1 for general mailbox. Press 3 for private mailbox."

Stan quickly pressed 3 and heard another beep. Looking at the slip of paper, he entered 985#.

"You have ten private messages. Your mailbox is almost full. Press 1 to hear most recent. Press 5 to hear oldest."

Thinking he would prefer to start at the beginning, Stan pressed 5 on his phone and begin listening. Shortly after the first message began, he set the phone to speaker and laid it on the table. Hearing a distorted voice, Flib jumped up and stared at Stan with a quizzical look. Stan scratched his companion around his ears while listening to the messages. "Don't worry, boy, this is just a trick to conceal the identity of the person speaking. We used to do it to share intelligence between operatives."

Stan immediately paused the message. Once again he remembered working in intelligence services, but which one? Where was he? This was the second time he reacted to something he knew but could not remember. After unsuccessfully struggling to identify where this knowledge came from, he resumed listening to the distorted voice. One question plagued him, "Did I know MG Turner from intelligence work?"

Each of the ten messages was recorded at 9:00 a.m. on Saturday, for ten consecutive weeks and was between five and fifteen minutes long. The last message was three weeks ago. As he listened, Stan recognized them as an audio diary, a log of discoveries. Their content led Stan through an investigation into corrupt politics funded by an organization in northern Georgia and reaching all the way to Washington, D.C. The person under most intense scrutiny was Albert David Cunningham, a councilman in Asheville, North Carolina. Cunningham was being groomed for the North Carolina Senate, with plans leading to the U. S. Senate, and ultimately the White House. All he had to do was follow instructions and he would be President someday, possibly in the not-too-distant future. The money backing Cunningham was rooted in a large clandestine organization seeking control of drug, sex, and other illegal markets along the entire east coast of the United States.

Closing the phone session, Stan asked a new question, "Why wasn't this handed over to the FBI?" Then answered himself, "The answer has got to be in that safe deposit box."

Before heading out to the car, Stan used his phone to look up the address of the South Knoxville branch of the TVA Credit Union and tapped a button sending it to his GPS app. By the time he and Flib got into the car, he had turn by turn directions to the far side of the city.

Driving toward Knoxville, Stan kept his eyes out for anyone that might be following him. Traffic was heavy on I-40 and he had no sense of a tail until he turned south on highway 441, toward Chapman. Congested business traffic quickly faded as he continued to suburban Knoxville. This suburban five-lane highway was dotted with fast food restaurants, used car lots, gas stations, other well established businesses. Trees filled spaces between and around establishments as the highway rolled gently up and down small hills. Watching his rear-view mirror, Stan thought he recognized a white Lexus swapping out with a blue Toyota and a green Dodge. One would follow a few blocks or a mile then disappear and another would show up. One of the three seemed to always be behind him.

Feeling the hair rising on the back of his neck, Stan turned right, into a middle-class neighborhood and stopped midway down the second block. None of the cars followed. After waiting fifteen minutes, he circled right through the neighborhood until he was back on the highway. Two blocks before arriving at the bank, he again noticed a white Lexus in his rear-view. Casually pulling into a Burger King restaurant next to the bank, Stan asked his companion, "You feel like a burger, Flib?"

When Stan opened his window at the order station, the smell of hamburgers flooded the car. Flib was in Stan's lap before he could place the order. "One whopper, one burger, one medium order of fries, and a coke." He had a bit of difficulty driving around to the pick-up window with Flib standing in his lap, but they made it. After receiving their order, Stan pulled into a parking spot where he could eat and watch both the bank next door and the highway.

Stan gave the burger to Flib and began opening his own sandwich. He stopped when he noticed a white Lexus parked in front of the bank. A young woman dressed in a business suit exited the bank and was about to get into the Lexus when Stan felt Flib reaching for the whopper in his left hand.

"Excuse me! This one's MINE!" Stan growled. "Here, have a fry."

Stan continued to watch the bank while eating his burger and sharing fries with Flib. He then returned to Oliver Springs without additional stops.

That afternoon, Stan picked Siobhan up as planned. They talked at length about the phone messages and cars Stan believed were following him. The more they talked, the more concerned Siobhan grew for Stan's safety, as well as her own.

"You haven't seen anyone following you around Oliver Springs or anyone watching around here, have you?" she asked.

"Not that I can tell. And I have been looking."

"What about you, Mister Flib? Have you seen any dastardly strangers lurking around our apartment?" Siobhan asked the dog, who seemed to be following their conversation. Rubbing his neck she added, "Besides Stan, I mean."

Stan repeated the trip to the bank Wednesday morning. Even though he did not detect any followers, he decided to play it safe and stopped at Burger King, where he could watch but not go into the bank. Being earlier in the morning than his previous visit, he got coffee for himself and a sausage biscuit for Flib.

On Thursday, he waited until Siobhan got off work and they went together. She drove and he watched traffic. Satisfied nobody was following, he told Siobhan to pull into the bank parking lot.

Stan rolled his window down a couple inches to allow fresh air for Flib. Flib immediately caught scent of the burgers and sat very alert, licking his lips as his people went into the credit union together, without him.

Stan glanced back to the car and seeing Flib's reaction, suggested, "Maybe we should get our guard another burger before we head back?" Siobhan just shook her head.

Walking over to the customer service desk, Stan said politely, "Excuse me, I need to access my lock box."

The young lady smiled and pointed toward another desk. "Mister Browne will be glad to help you."

Continuing to the next desk, Stan read the name plate and greeted the assistant manager. "Mister Browne. My name is Taylor Buncombe. I need to access my lock box, please."

"Certainly, Mister Buncombe. Do you have your ID with you?"

Stan removed a driver's license from his wallet and handed it to the gentleman. Mister Browne, a managerial type in his mid thirties, looked at the license and then at Stan. Satisfied, he entered information from the license into his computer.

"I'm sorry sir, but we don't appear to have a box leased in your name. Do you recall the box number?"

Stan thought for a moment, recalling how numbers on the card were not in the proper order. "No, the box was leased by my employer, Mister Michael Turner. He said he had approved me to gain access."

"One moment, please." Mister Browne rapped his keyboard again and examined several screens of information. "Yes, sir. You are approved. I will need you to sign here." He then pointed to a signature tablet.

Stan signed the electronic terminal device with the provided pen, whereupon Mister Browne compared this signature to his driver's license. Satisfied they were the same, he recorded the image from the signature tablet and the Taylor Buncombe driver's license for future verification. Looking to Siobhan, he asked, "Will your guest be entering the vault with you?"

"Yes," Stan replied, smiling at Siobhan.

"Okay, I will need to see her identification, and if she will also sign, we can go to your box."

Siobhan retrieved her driver's license from her purse, which Mister Browne scanned into his system. Returning her ID, he then had her sign on the same signature pad Stan had used. "Okay. You will need your key."

"Got it," Stan replied with a renewed confidence.

The assistant manager then led them into a vault of safe deposit boxes and inserted his key into box 373. Stan inserted his key and allowed Mister Browne to open the door and retrieve his own key. Stan then removed the large box from its cubicle and set it on the table.

"Take as long as you need. When you finish, you can return the box to its cell. Your key will be released as soon as you close the door. I'll be at my desk if you need anything." Browne then left the vault, closing a privacy door behind him.

Stan and Siobhan looked at one another, then looked at the box. Apprehensively, he lifted the lid. Papers on top were a lease agreement for a post office box in Oliver Springs. The contract included two keys, however only one key was clipped to it. Setting that aside, Stan next pulled out an expandible folder, one with a fold-over flap and a rubber band closure. Opening this folder he found clippings from newspapers, photos that looked liked they were printed on an inkjet printer, two USB memory sticks, and three six by nine paper note tablets.

Flipping through the news clippings, Siobhan chuckled, "You really know how to pick 'em. This Michael Turner is wanted by police. Something to do with campaign corruption in Asheville."

"Yes, according to these notes, and what I heard in Turner's phone messaging system, he was investigating political corruption in Asheville and links to family holdings outside of Atlanta."

Lifting one of the white tablets, Siobhan scanned several pages. "Yep, that fits with these notes. Hard to read but what I can make out, this politician he was investigating has links to white collar crime in northern Georgia and likes married women."

"Married women?" Stan repeated. He then stepped next to Siobhan and looked at what she was reading. After scanning the page, he commented, "What a character. Fooling around with Turner's wife and now Turner is missing. Makes you wonder what we have here."

Stan then picked up another tablet and flipped through it. "Look. That money we found in the bank account appears to be a retainer. I was hired, under an alias to keep tabs on Turner's activities. . . . We often used aliases in intelligence operations to confuse or hide paper trails. Protect your true identity." Stan paused to consider this new realization from some distant memory slipping into his consciousness. Looking back at the tablet, he continued, "Some kind of partnership. Guess I didn't do such a good job."

Siobhan began flipping pages on one tablet. "His scrawl isn't any better than yours. Lots of dates and locations. Some dollar signs. I hope you can make sense of this stuff."

"Possibly, but I don't dare take it all out of here. I need to figure out what's most important to helping me regain my memory and leave the rest here." He then sat and began rapidly checking three other folders.

Siobhan continued checking out the paper tablets. "HERE! This one. These notes are dated the two months before you went to Atlanta! Let's take just this one and the post box key. Maybe he mailed you something from Atlanta."

Taking the most recent tablet from Siobhan, he recorded the safe deposit box number and the number of the post office box in Oliver Springs, then slipped the PO Box key into his pocket, with the two memory sticks. Handing the tablet back to Siobhan, he put everything else back into the safe deposit box, checked to make sure nothing was left on the table or floor, then slid the box back into its cubicle. After closing the door, he removed his key.

Leaving the vault, Stan stopped at Mister Browne's desk. "Thank you for your assistance."

"Any time Mister Buncombe."

Walking toward the door, both Siobhan and Stan stopped when a young woman at the tellers' counter cried out, "What do you mean you don't have it? I gave it to you right before we left!"

"No, you didn't!" a young man with a thin, scruffy beard and long hair retaliated.

Both were dressed in old, naturally faded, jeans and t-shirts. She wore cheap cross-trainer style shoes. He wore open sandals, which showed feet in need of washing.

The woman ran over to the work desk, where she had completed a deposit ticket. Repeatedly pushing her shoulder length amber brown hair back, she looked around the counter, behind brochures, the desktop calendar, and all around on the floor. Her companion looked with her, but with far less energy.

Seeing a bit of cash sticking out of the young man's back pocket, Stan went over to help and unobtrusively retrieved the cash; smooth as a professional pickpocket. Fluttering the cash with one hand, he could see it was more than $1,000 in hundreds and twenties. Pressing the young man on the shoulder with a painfully firm grip, he whispered to the young woman, "Is this what you are looking for?"

Seeing the expression on her friend's face, she exploded, "YOU HAD IT ALL THE TIME?"

As he stuttered in reply, Stan and Siobhan slipped out the door, finding Flib with his nose to the car window facing the Burger King, next door.

Chapter 7

Flib made his burger disappear almost before they pulled out of the Burger King parking lot. After devouring his treat and searching the carpet and back seat for crumbs, he poked his head between the seats, looking from Siobhan to Stan as if asking, "More? That was good! More?"

Stan rubbed Flib's head affectionately, chuckling, "That's all for now, boy."

"So, how did you know that guy was holding out on his girlfriend?" Siobhan asked as she drove toward Oliver Springs.

"She was in a panic, but he wasn't. That told me to look at him. As luck had it, the money was sticking out of his back pocket," Stan replied nonchalantly.

"No. I looked at him, too. I didn't see any money sticking out."

"The fact that you looked shows you have good instincts. What you must have missed was the bulge of the folded money and the corner of the bills sticking out."

"Okay, mister eagle eyes, if his jeans were tight enough to show the bulge of money, how did you get it out?"

"Not sure, must be a talent from my past."

"You were a pickpocket in your past?"

"I do know I did some kind of intelligence work. Is being a pickpocket so far fetched?"

Siobhan smirked and drove on in silence. Stan pondered what they had left behind in the safe deposit box. Passing through Oak Ridge, he reminded her, "Don't forget to go by the post office."

"It's one block from Pearl's; why don't you go there tomorrow after you drop me off?"

Stan curled his lip and sighed as he considered the option. "Yeah, okay. I have enough to look at this evening." He then looked around at cars passing them, wondering why he had not been watching for a tail on their return home.

Entering the outskirts of Oliver Springs, Stan looked behind them in time to see a white Lexus sedan pull into a parking lot just as a green Dodge pulled out. He tried to recall how long the Lexus had been behind them, but couldn't. *How could I be so relaxed that I quit watching?* he chastised himself. Seeing the Dodge closing the gap to just over one block distance, hairs on the back of his neck stood up.

"I feel like chicken for supper. Anyplace to get good fried chicken around here?" he asked, speaking calmly to not alarm Siobhan.

"I think there's a chicken place across town, but when I want fried chicken I usually stop by Hardee's. They're just up the road a piece."

"Sounds good. Dine in or take home?"

"I bet Flib would prefer we take it home. He's been in the car for a while."

"Take home it is then."

Stan watched the green Dodge pass by as they pulled into the drive-thru at Hardee's. While waiting for their order, he watched cars going both directions. He continued to watch traffic and searched parking lots as Siobhan drove back home.

"Do you have a gun?" Stan asked as Siobhan turned the car off at her apartment.

"No. Why?" Her voice became tense with concern.

"Atlanta. When I go find this Michael Turner, I might want to be armed." He then watched the street as he and Siobhan went inside. Flib did not follow the others inside, instead took off on his own. Minutes later, he barked gentlemanly at the kitchen door, before his people got settled at the table.

With chicken and fixin's on their plates, Siobhan looked at Stan, studying his face. "You aren't thinking Atlanta; you want a gun right now. Why?"

"On the way home, just now, I thought I spotted two of the cars I saw following me Tuesday morning. From what little I read in Turner's papers at the bank, these people aren't nice. I just want to be ready." He then bit into a juicy chicken breast made twice its size by crispy fried batter coating. Flib reminded them that he was hungry before Stan took a second bite.

Returning to his seat after giving Flib a proper meal, Stan asked, "May I use your computer after supper? I want to see what's on these memory sticks."

"Sure. I'll do cleanup while you go exploring." Siobhan winked at Stan, who chuckled at her sense of sharing household duties.

Still smiling at Siobhan's comment, Stan booted up her computer and inserted the first memory stick. Seeing the index that appeared automatically, Stan was initially disappointed. There was nothing there; the stick was apparently empty. Looking at the stick itself, he read "16 GB" printed on the side. Looking at the computer screen he saw the device had only four gigabytes available. Without a second thought he went to Windows folder properties and selected "show hidden and system files." The directory of the memory stick instantly refreshed showing one hidden folder. Double clicking this folder revealed more than one hundred files of assorted types with dates ranging from one year to three months old.

Not sure where to start, Stan ordered the folder by date and clicked on the oldest JPG file, then followed the trail of twenty-three images. None of these pictures made much sense beyond seeing the same three men, one of them with several different women in not-so-public places and one in a private, richly appointed, bedroom.

Finding a spreadsheet titled "Time Line," he clicked on it. An older version of Excel slowly opened the file. Reading its contents, Stan quickly appreciated Mister Turner's organization. The spreadsheet was actually a database, with columns labeled "Date," "Contact," "Contact Type," and "Event." Rows were color-coded to differentiate between political activities, meetings with criminals, meetings with business owners, and encounters with women. Beginning at the top of the displayed spreadsheet, sorted by "Date," he followed the discovery of questionable practices, clandestine meetings with known criminals, and verification of links between one of the men in the photos, Asheville councilman Albert David Cunningham, and organized crime. Many of the entries were underlined, indicating they were linked to another entry, file, or picture. Curious about the criminal activities, he clicked on a name labeled "known criminal." Another spread sheet opened, listing names of individuals and documentation of their criminal activity, including the source of this information as FBI, local, or media.

After closing both spreadsheets, Stan clicked on a folder titled "News Clippings." Once again he ordered the directory by date and clicked on the oldest file, a PDF. He read the opening line of the first paragraph written in the Asheville Citizen-TImes newspaper. "Local business owner Albert D. Cunningham exploded onto the political scene this weekend with a rally that shows he is a serious contender for the Asheville City Council seat held by twenty-year veteran Michael Spencer. . . ."

Looking back at the contents of the "News Clippings" folder, he quickly realized what he had at his disposal. "Siobhan, do you recall that big folder filled with news clippings?"

"Yes, why?"

"Turner has downloaded every news story about the man he was investigating and saved them as PDF files on this memory stick."

"Is that all?"

"No. Detailed logs of everything this joker has done since he entered politics. And I mean EVERYTHING, including stuff he wouldn't want anyone to know about."

Siobhan put down the book she had been reading and stepped over to the table where Stan was working. When he backed out of the news folder, she pointed to a recent audio file. "What's that file?"

"Let's find out." Stan double clicked a file labeled "201113.wav" It was a recorded phone call between two men. Both Stan and Siobhan looked at one another in total disbelief of what they were hearing.

Voice1, deep, coarse, and gravely: "Yeah, you've done fine there in Asheville. Time to move you to Raleigh. Whatcha want, the Govenor's seat or a spot in the senate?"

Voice2, smooth, masculine, and commanding: "Governor undergoes too much scrutiny. I'm not sure we're ready for that just yet. Besides, the local senate seat comes open next year. They just elected the governor; something would have to happen to him and then there would have to be a special election called."

Voice1: "We can make that happen, Mister Cunningham. Just say the word and it's yours. No problem."

Voice2: "Senate. Let's go to Raleigh next year. Stay under the radar, for now."

"HOW did he record that conversation?" Siobhan exploded.

"Wonders of modern technology," Stan chuckled as he

closed the playback window.

"You've GOT to hand this stuff over to the FBI!"

"Not yet. I need to look at his notes . . . see if I can find out if he has or *why* he hasn't already done that and possibly more important, who hired him? Who's paying for this investigation?"

"We already know Cunningham was fooling around with Turner's wife, could it be personal?"

Stan pondered a few seconds before replying. "Possibly. But he's put in a lot of time and the gizmos he's using aren't cheap. We know somebody put up at least $50,000. It's in the bank. Who? And why?" Stan then pushed the computer aside and picked up the notepad they took from the safe deposit box. After getting a cup of coffee, he settled down on the sofa and began reading.

Two hours later, Stan placed the notepad on his lap, swallowed the last gulp of cold coffee, and looked over at Siobhan. Her book was open on her lap and she slept peacefully. Flib looked up from his nap when Stan sighed deeply.

"It's been a tough day. You need to go back out before we move sleeping beauty to her bed?" Stan asked his golden haired friend.

Flib got up and trotted over to the door. Stan followed, let his friend out, then returned to the sofa. After placing a bookmark in Siobhan's book, he gently lifted her in his arms. Without waking, she wrapped her arms around his neck and snuggled into his shoulder. After placing her on her bed, he removed her shoes and pulled a blanket over her, which woke her up.

"What'd you find out?" she asked, more asleep than awake.

Chuckling slightly, Stan replied, "Regional Director of the FBI is on their payroll. We're on our own if we want to find Turner."

Rolling over to her side, Siobhan moaned, "Okay, that's nice."

Chapter 8

"What do you mean you couldn't wake me up? How hard did you try?" Siobhan railed at Stan as they got ready to leave early Friday morning.

"To be honest, I didn't try that hard. You were asleep and I didn't see any reason to wake you," Stan replied, smiling at her tirade.

"If it EVER happens again, wake me up! I hate waking up in my street clothes."

"You got a shower didn't you? What's it matter?"

"It just does." Siobhan closed the conversation and began sulking. Her pout continued as they drove to Pearl's, ultimately ending when Mary asked how the trip to Knoxville went.

"We found a slew of papers, some notebooks, and newspaper clippings. Seems whatever this guy was into, he wanted it fully documented," Stan replied.

"Any clues as to your background? Who you were before you came here?" Mary asked, renewing an old subject.

"Nope. Stan Winthrop. No solid memories beyond last week."

"And he can really cook steak," Siobhan added, finally breaking into a smile.

Mary chuckled a bit and returned to her grill to check on morning preparations.

Stan didn't say anything else until he finished breakfast and carried his dishes to the wash area. "I'm going to the post office. Be back in a bit."

"I'll be on tables by then. You going to need the car today?" Siobhan replied.

"Not planning to go to Knoxville, if that's what you're asking." He then winked and stepped out the back door.

Stan walked around to the front of Pearl's and crossed the street. Sweet aromas of the first morning batch of fudge wafted from the candy store across from Pearl's. Licking his lips, he continued one-half block up Spring Street to the U.S. Post Office. Being a small facility, it took him only a minute to locate the box and begin moving its contents to a counter behind him. Sorting out the sales notices and other junk mail, he found only one item of interest, which he set aside. Looking through the dozen plus pieces of unwanted mess once more, he started to drop it into the trash can provided for this and stopped. He wrapped the junk up in a sales circular, picked up the one piece of mail that carried a first class stamp, and returned to Pearl's. Dumping the unwanted mail into Mary's kitchen trash, he sat at the server's table and looked at the parcel he had saved. A plain brown lightweight cardboard mailer, measuring about four by six inches. It was hand addressed to the post office box number, without a name or return address. The post office cancellation stamp was zipcode 30067 - Marietta, Ga.

"Boy. I haven't seen one of those in a decade!" Mary exclaimed, looking at the mail Stan turned over in his hands.

"What do you mean?" Stan asked.

"Cardboard disk mailers. Media mailers, actually. Company I used to work for, ages ago, bought 'em by the gross. That was back when folks were sending computer diskettes through the mail. Ours even had a lining to protect the disks from those postal x-ray machines. Nobody uses diskettes anymore. They just email data around the world." Mary then returned to her grill, watching Stan out of the corner of her eye.

Seeing a pull tab to open the cardboard envelope, Stan grabbed it and opened the parcel. Inside he found a small plastic case which held a black card measuring about one and a quarter inches by one inch, and one-eighth inch thick. The only printing was in its upper right corner: a white triangle and the number "256." He recalled seeing a rack of similar cards at the phone store; memory chips. Looking into the envelope to see if there was anything stuck inside, he noticed a foil lining.

When Siobhan came back into the kitchen with a new order, Stan called her over. "I'm going back to the apartment to see what's on this thing and check on Flib."

"Keys are in my purse," she said, sticking an order slip on a wheel and picking up plates ready to deliver.

As Stan pulled the keys, he heard a man scream. Turning around, he saw Horace, Mary's assistant cook, holding his hand. Mary grabbed the wailing man and shoved his hand under the sink faucet, turning cold water wide open.

"You're done for today and maybe the weekend," Mary

commented as she pulled his hand out of the water and looked at it. Horace's palm was bright red and blistering. Looking down, she noticed his shoes had come untied. "Shoulda taken time to tie yer shoes." Looking around she called to Stan. "Don't go anywhere, I need you on the grill. NOW!"

Dropping the car keys and the cardboard mailer into Siobhan's purse, Stan grabbed an apron and paper hat, washed his hands, and picked up where Horace had left off. He grabbed a cup of coffee during a lull, around 9:45, but it got cold before he could finish it. The transition from breakfast to lunch was marked by an order from a late morning regular: cheeseburger with fried egg on top. Curious about this flavor combination, Stan fixed himself one before cleaning the grill at closing.

Returning to the apartment, Siobhan found Flib waiting at the kitchen door, soaking up sunshine. Once inside he quickly devoured a small pile of french fries leftover from the lunch shift.

"Not sure that salt is good for him," Stan commented as he turned on Siobhan's computer.

"Not salted," she replied as she disappeared into her room to change clothes.

When she returned to the living room, she found Stan holding the black memory card in his hand and staring at the computer. "What's wrong?"

"No slot for this card," Stan replied with frustration. "I think my old computer had a card slot and I prefer to look at the file listing before opening anything. I suppose I could use my phone."

"You remembered something, that's good. Use your phone and stop fretting about it."

Stan reluctantly picked up his phone from the kitchen table and started turning it around. Finding a tiny mark next to a bar on the side, he pushed the end of the bar. A card holder popped out. It had two slots and only one card. Stan carefully oriented the card to fit the slot and pushed it back in. His smartphone then registered the card and opened a window showing a half-dozen files, each about a month old. He quickly realized he could see everything that a computer might show him. Tapping the oldest file, a window opened which offered options for play, stop, speaker, delete, next, and previous. Stan tapped the speaker, then play, and listened. He immediately recognized the first voice from the recordings he had played the previous evening.

Voice1, deep, coarse, and gravely: "Yeah, did you find Turner?"

Voice2, male, a bit squeaky, slurred as though speaker was chewing gum: "He's hold up in one of those interstate motels. Why you want this guy?"

Voice1: "Cause he stole half a million dollars from me. Go get 'im and bring 'im to me. In ONE piece!"

Voice2: "Sure thing. By the by, so I know who else might be watchin, how'd he get the money?"

Voice1: "His wife owns one of them high-end dress shops. She was running money for Cunningham. Shouldn't be anyone else involved."

Voice2: "Sure thing, I'll pick 'im up this afternoon."

"That's pretty high-end if somebody took off with half a million dollars," Siobhan commented, leaning on the table next to Stan.

"Somehow I don't think the dress shop was doing that level of business. I'm thinking these guys are using Cunningham, in Asheville, to launder money through the dress shop. But I don't recall seeing anything about Cunningham being married. We may be heading for Atlanta soon."

"You have grill duties tomorrow and Sunday."

"I know. Besides, I need to check this dress shop out before we go any further."

"You do that, I'm going to check the mail," Siobhan replied. "Flib! You wanna go check the mail with me?"

Flib was at Siobhan's side before she had the door open. They went out together and strolled side by side to the end of their parking lot. After pulling several pieces from her box, they strolled back to the apartment. Flib attentively watched the scenery as they walked.

Punching play on the next file, Stan tapped the speaker icon and put his phone down as he turned to the computer. The voice on the recording reported that Turner was not at the motel but somebody was now watching for him. Stan brought up Internet Explorer and went to google.com. While the third recording complained that Turner had not been apprehended, Stan scanned through the results of a search for "asheville dress shops + cunningham," finding multiple entries linking Cunningham to an establishment named "After Six Limited - attire for the discriminating lady." Exploring "After Six," he discovered this shop was owned by Gwendolyn Turner, a shapely blonde always elegantly dressed and adorned with glittering jewelry. Gwendolyn Turner was married to Michael G. Turner, however there was no information about him, nor any pictures of him.

While reviewing information about Missus Turner and "After Six," Stan noticed an image in a pop-up from a local news feed which he recognized as the red-bearded man he saw leaving the pawn shop earlier that week. The way this man carelessly tossed his pawn ticket on the ground had stuck in Stan's mind. After clicking on the picture, he read with growing interest. According to the news story, this man acted as a courier for his family and had been asked to deliver three diamond broaches to an uncle in Memphis. Knowing the value of the jewelry, an estimated $40,000, the courier says he never let them out of his sight. He reports that he did have them in his hands when he left the men's room at the Johnny Cash Rest Stop near Dickson, Tn. "There was a commotion as I left the men's room and I must have dropped them when I got knocked over a bench. I remember stumbling back to my car." On further questioning, he simply couldn't remember for sure if that was the stop he used. The box for the broaches had been found in the rest area trash, but none of the jewels were recovered. A substantial reward was offered for their return. Stan saved the link to this story in his Favorites folder and went to his room in search of the pawn ticket he had picked up as discarded trash.

Finding the ticket crumpled up on his dresser, Stan smoothed it out and read aloud softly. "'Eight thousand dollars.' They are supposed to be worth forty grande...." He then began pondering silently. *I have money in the bank but no way to access it without drawing attention. How long does it take the bank to print checks or issue a replacement credit card?* Looking back at the pawn ticket, he read the details once more.

"You got mail!" Siobhan called out, dropping two envelopes on the keyboard. "Any idea what you want for supper?"

Stan carefully placed the pawn ticket in the center section of his top dresser drawer, then joined Siobhan in the kitchen. "Supper . . . only thing that comes to mind is flapjacks."

"That's because you made a hundred of 'em for that crew of kids that came in this morning. Come up with something better. . . . Oh, you got two pieces of mail."

Stan looked on the table and found two envelopes. Before opening either, he knew what was in them. "Checks and . . ." he paused while opening the longer of the two deliveries. "A new credit card." Confirming the name on the card and address on the checks, he pondered. "I need to go to that pawn shop downtown, near where we got the phones. You want to join me?"

"Since it's my car, I guess I had better. Why the pawn shop; you have something to sell?"

"No. Something to recover and tomorrow we can collect a healthy bounty. I might even see about a better computer."

"Mine too slow?"

"It has seen better days. Let's go jump into an adventure."

Seeing Siobhan's eyes light up, Stan retrieved the pawn ticket and all three headed for the car. Flib arrived first and sat patiently by the passenger door while Siobhan locked her apartment.

"Sorry, Mister Flib. You can't go this time," Stan responded, scratching his friend on the head. "We won't be long."

Seeing that he was not invited into the car, Flib returned to the apartment door and sat, watching his people drive off without him.

Walking up to the pawn shop, Stan looked for familiar icons. Seeing MasterCard and Visa logos adorning the window and front door, he relaxed somewhat and confidently entered the shop, scanning the displays. Jewelry was to the left, computers and electronics to the right front, power tools in the center, and musical instruments to the back right. Casually strolling to the right, he checked the specs on three notebook computers before continuing to the desk in the back. Pulling the ticket from his wallet, making sure the clerk saw his cash, he said, "I would like to collect my broaches."

"I don't recall seeing you in here before," the skinny scruffy man responded.

"Here's the ticket," Stan replied before looking around and seeing Siobhan gazing into a jewelry display.

The clerk took the ticket and disappeared through a curtain behind him. Returning with a cardboard box, he told Stan, "Eight thousand, three hundred dollars. Cash."

After looking inside the box and verifying that there were three broaches as pictured in the news article, Stan challenged the clerk, respectfully. "Your door says you take MasterCard."

"That's for purchases, not redemptions. You want it or not?"

"Tell you what, Add another hundred, to cover the MasterCard fee, and I'll take that top end Dell notebook, as well. I'll even pay cash for the notebook."

After rolling his jaw for a minute, the clerk agreed. "Yeah, sure. My brother was an idiot to take these things in anyway. We'll never be able to sell 'em here. So that'll be $8,400 on your card and $1,284 cash for the computer."

While Stan pulled cash and the new plastic card from his wallet, the clerk retrieved the notebook. Five minutes later, Stan and Siobhan were heading back to her car with a new computer and a box of jewels.

"Your money won't last long if you keep spending it like that!" Siobhan chastised as she started the car.

"Not to worry. We should have the money back by tomorrow evening, plus a handsome finder's fee." Stan winked at Siobhan who returned his growing smile.

Flib was still at the front door when they returned, alert and welcoming. While Siobhan fixed a pot of spaghetti and heated a can of meat sauce, Stan got his new computer humming and activated the 30-day trial of Norton 360 security included with the system. He accessed the Internet on his second try, stumbling over the password for Siobhan's router, and went hunting for the owner of the jewels. While his phone was great, the larger screen of the notebook made searches much easier. Finding the news article he had seen previously, he located the owner of the jewels in nearby Kingston, Tennessee and pulled a phone number and address from anywho.com.

"You going to call them?" Siobhan asked as she put supper

on the table.

"No, I don't think so. I think I would rather drive by and either call them from the street or just knock on their door. Can we go after work, tomorrow?"

"Only if Flib gets to join us. I don't think he likes being left alone."

Flib was waiting by Pearl's kitchen door when Stan and Siobhan finished Saturday afternoon. All three piled into the car and Stan found their destination in his phone's GPS app while Siobhan headed west on highway 61, toward Kingston. Stan watched traffic diligently for the first fifteen minutes. Not seeing anyone following them, he wondered if leaving from Pearl's, rather than the apartment, had made a difference.

Following GPS instructions, Siobhan turned onto Bluff Road, thirty minutes later. Stan began to wonder if this was the right place. Houses lining the street were strictly middle class, close together and not of the caliber to own this type of jewelry. After passing a wooded section, the nature of the homes changed dramatically. Stopping at the address, Siobhan asked, "Well?"

The house before them was a large two-story Tudor style construction. Real stone adorned the entire first story. Its upper half of the structure was tan with dark-brown timber accents. A high ceiling carried the entry way to the top of the second story. This small area was built primarily of stone framed with rough-hewn logs. The patio area at the door was natural grey stone. Dark stained glass lined both sides of a heavy oak door. Lush green grass filled the front yard which was richly appointed with ornamental and native trees and sculptured bushes.

"Let's go knock on the door," Stan replied. "Put the box in your purse. It should fit."

"Just barely," Siobhan complained, but did as requested.

Flib waited in the car as Siobhan and Stan walked to the house. Stan smiled inwardly when he recognized the hefty red-bearded man who opened the door. "I am looking for Mister Oliver Winston."

"Yeah, just a minute," the man replied and went back into the house, leaving the door open.

After a moment, a much older man, in his seventies, muscular build, wearing slacks and a sweater came to the door. "Yes?"

"Sir, my name is Stan Winthrop and I have something I believe you are looking for."

"Yes?" His tone was somewhat disinterested and annoyed at the interruption.

Stan looked to Siobhan who pulled out the box of jewelry and handed it to Stan, who removed the lid, displaying the contents to the man at the door.

"Come inside." His tone was now interested but suspicious.

Stan closed the box and followed Siobhan into the house. Their host closed the door, then led them into a large room with a wall of windows overlooking a hillside and lake below. The red-haired man sat at a bar to the side, drinking a beer.

"Please, sit down," Winston offered with his hand pointing toward a sofa as he sat with his back to the windows. "How did you get those broaches?" When he asked this question, the red-bearded man shifted on the stool where he was sitting, straining to improve his view.

Seeing the red-bearded man growing visibly apprehensive and nervous, Stan began explaining how he came into possession of the jewels. "Last week, Monday, we were walking down a street in Oliver Springs. I noticed a man coming out of a pawn shop counting a considerable amount of money. When he got to the pawn ticket, at the bottom of the stack, he balled it up and tossed it aside. I hate seeing litter on the street so I picked it up and stuffed it in my back pocket. Figured I'd toss it in the trash later. Then, a couple days later, I saw a picture of this same man in an Internet news feed. After reading the story, I located the pawn ticket and redeemed it."

The bearded man breathed heavily and gulped the last of his beer, nervously turning the empty bottle in his hands.

"You didn't find them in a box in a rest area on Interstate 40?" Winston asked, calmly.

"No, sir. Though I do understand that they found an elegant case that was made to hold these broaches."

After taking a deep breath, Winston turned to the red-bearded man. "Jerry, go get the case." Turning back to Stan and

Siobhan, he added, "The state police returned it yesterday." When Jerry returned, Stan noticed how pale he was as he carefully placed the case on a table, avoiding eye contact with their host.

"Let's see if what you have fits the case," the host suggested.

Stan opened the box he was holding and transferred the broaches to the case, one by one. The first one did not fit the first space but did fit snugly into the second. Each space was crafted to hold a specific broach. Lined up in their velvet case, the broaches sparkled radiantly.

Winston lifted the case and examined its restored contents. "My insurance has offered a reward of twenty thousand dollars for the return of these baubles. How much did it cost you to redeem them from the pawn shop?"

"Eight thousand four hundred. Fifty percent of value is a hefty reward."

"You read they were worth 40K. Insurance told me to say that. They're worth a bit more," Winston responded with a twinkle in his eye. "Will you accept my personal check or would you prefer to wait for the insurance company?"

"As long as it's good, I'll take your check," Stan chuckled softly.

Winston then stood and left the room. He returned a moment later, glaring at Jerry, and handed Stan a check for $28,400. "You can fill in the payee name . . . Stan Winthrop, correct?"

"Yes, but it will be deposited into another account. Do you mind if I verify it?"

"No, go right ahead."

After entering the name "Taylor Buncombe" as payee, Stan opened a banking app on his phone and took a picture of the check. Before touching "Deposit," he ticked "Verify Check Before Deposit." Seconds later the screen responded, "Funds have been verified and will be available within 24 hours." He then folded the check and put it into his shirt pocket.

"Thank you, sir. Your check is good." Stan then stood to leave, lifting Siobhan by her elbow.

As they walked to the door, Oliver Winston asked, "Stan,

do you have business card? In case I need your services again?"

"No sir, but you can find me most mornings at Pearl's Diner in Oliver Springs. Thank you, again." He and Siobhan then returned to her car, where Flib eagerly welcomed them back. They could hear Jerry screaming inside the house.

As they pulled away, Stan smiled at Siobhan. "Looks like our Taylor Buncombe account now owes me twenty grande . . . guess it's time to open my own account."

Chapter 9

"So, you are going to open another bank account. This one in your name?" Siobhan asked as she sat down on the sofa next to Stan. She could see he was browsing local banks on his new computer. "Not going with the credit union?"

"No, they already know me as Taylor Buncombe. I'm thinking I want an account in my name at a small local bank. Still want the online access but something more personal. Where do you bank?"

"Around the corner. Putnam County Bank."

"Around the corner?"

"Yes. That's why I bank there. Less than a mile from here. I can stop and use their teller machine on the way to work or deposit my check on the way home. Easy. Convenient."

"Sounds good. We can go there on Monday."

"That check Oliver Winston gave you won't clear by Monday."

"Funds have been verified, but you're right, they won't be available till midweek. There is other money in the account I can draw on." Closing his computer, Stan turned toward Siobhan, who was sitting on the sofa, flipping through a magazine. "What's on television?"

Siobhan picked up her remote and with Stan settling close to her, they began flipping through channels, ultimately settling on an old western movie.

Horace showed up for his shift Sunday morning. Seeing the burn was not as bad as expected, Mary allowed him to work. In less than five minutes he dropped the spatula twice and heat from the grill caused his burned hand to throb. Stan, who had been enjoying a cup of coffee at the kitchen table, took Horace's shift. Throughout the morning, Stan tried to mentally organize what he had learned about Michael Turner. Distracted by his thoughts, he overcooked an order of soft-fried eggs. Mary threatened to fire him if he ruined another order. Realizing his data analysis was too comprehensive to be done mentally, he decided he needed a white board. The rubbery eggs were set aside until he and Siobhan took a break outside, when their favorite four-footed-dispose-all enjoyed them without hesitation. Seeing the three together inspired Mary, who quietly stole several pictures with her smartphone.

After closing Pearl's, the couple dropped Flib off at the apartment and drove to Walmart in Oak Ridge to purchase a white board. On the way back they picked up hamburger fixings for that evening. Once home, Siobhan prepped ground beef for burgers, adding a splash of Worcestershire, a few select spices, and a bit of bread crumbs. She then shaped them into patties and stored them in the refrigerator.

Stan spread his notes on the table. After glancing over the spread of information, he began cataloging it on his new white board, set up next to the table. Without referring back to the table, he listed everything he knew in two columns: essential and trivial. His board now filled with assorted details, he began reviewing what he had written, moving some items to the other column, then further ordering the essential list with numbers and letters.

"What are you doing?" Siobhan asked as she read the massive list of facts.

"Oh, it's easy," Stan replied, obviously somewhat proud of his accomplishment. "These items on the right are trivial but might need to be considered, so I keep them in front of me. This list to the left is what I consider most important. Those with letters are 'need to know' and the numbers are what I expect to encounter in Atlanta."

"You have the dress shop as 'trivial'? Losing half a million dollars is trivial?"

"No, the money is essential, see … I have it over here. The dress shop itself is trivial. It's merely a vehicle, a means to an end. It could just as easily be a hamburger stand."

"Why do you have a star by Cunningham?"

"As near as I can determine, he just arrived on the scene in Asheville. We know he's being backed by organized crime, but why him? Where is he from? My gut tells me Turner found something and *THAT* is what took him to Atlanta. There is nothing directly linking Cunningham to Atlanta in these notes, which also bothers me. Why Cunningham and why Atlanta?

And of course the twenty-million-dollar question, where is Michael Geoffrey Turner?"

"Well, I hate to interrupt your scheming, but you need to start the grill if we're going to enjoy burgers tonight."

"I'm not scheming, just analyzing." Stan, now filled with excitement and purpose, capped his marker, kissed Siobhan smartly, and went out the kitchen door to start the charcoal. Siobhan stood delightfully stunned, a smile spreading across her face.

Siobhan fried up sliced potatoes and fixed a mixed green salad while Stan cooked burgers. Looking through the window, she could see he was still puzzling on a plan of action. His eyes glassed over staring into the distance, while he absentmindedly turned the spatula handle in his hand. When Stan returned to his duties and flipped the burgers, Flib showed up at his feet and stayed close by until the meat was taken inside. Siobhan finished putting condiments on the table while Stan crumbled a large grilled meat patty into Flib's food bowl, spreading juicy morsels across an otherwise dry dinner.

Conversation while eating was light, though Siobhan was about to burst with curiosity. Seeing Stan fold his napkin onto the plate, she broke and asked the question he had not addressed. "When are we going to Atlanta?"

"You're off tomorrow, Monday, but can you take the week off?"

"I'll make the call as soon as you let me know."

"Tomorrow. I want to open a local checking account. Now that we have a bank card and checks, we can use the Taylor Buncombe account and get some of those funds moving to a new home. Then we can hit the road. I'd like to get cash for expenses, too."

"Why not just use the card?"

"Don't want to leave a trail for anyone to follow. Cash is anonymous."

Siobhan looked at Stan with a new satisfaction and longing in her heart. Analyzing all that data and developing a plan seemed to have changed him. As she thought about it, she realized he had the same energy while pursuing the broaches, just to a lesser degree. The shadow of his missing past was fading and their future looked promising.

"You clean the table while I call Mary. Are we taking Flib?"

"Without a doubt!" Stan replied, picking up empty plates.

"Mister Winthrop, your driver's license says you are from Brevard, North Carolina; what brought you to our bank in Oliver Springs?"

The assistant manager of the Putnam County Bank hesitated as she held Stan's license. A young woman in her early thirties, her confidence showed experience in banking and customer service. He wanted to open a "Super Now Checking" account and had placed a $3,000 personal check from Taylor Buncombe on her desk, for deposit.

Stan answered calmly with a cordial tone. "I'm finding more work in this area than in the North Carolina mountains and think I might like to settle here. Is there a problem?"

The assistant manager looked to Siobhan, who was now beaming with delight. "Well, as Ms. Thomas is a valued customer, I see no problem. Do you have a local address or should we use the Brevard address for this account?"

"He can use my address," Siobhan offered without hesitation.

Seeing Stan nod, the assistant manager completed opening the account. Stan was impressed when she gave him a temporary Visa debit card with his account papers. "Please keep in mind that only $200 of your funds will be available for seventy-two hours. After that, you will have full access to all funds in your account. You should be receiving a golden Visa debit card and checks for this account in about ten days. Is there anything else I can do for you today?"

"No, I think this will do quite nicely. Thank you." Rising from his chair, Stan offered his hand to the young woman. Their business completed, Stan and Siobhan returned to the apartment and packed their bags.

An hour later they pulled into a TVA Employees Credit Union in west Knoxville. Stan withdrew $1,000 cash from their teller machine, using the Taylor Buncombe account. He had to press a button to acknowledge knowing he had reached his daily maximum withdrawal. Siobhan reluctantly yielded the driver's seat of her Subaru Forester, believing Stan knew where to go. He confidently headed west on I-40 then south on I-75 toward "The Big Peach." Atlanta, Georgia.

"We don't have a motel room reserved!" Siobhan exclaimed suddenly, half an hour down the road.

Flib woke up from napping on the back seat and lifted his head to an alert position. Stan chuckled at Flib and took a swallow of cool water from a bottle beside him. "Don't want one. I want to check out the motel where I supposedly stayed last time. I think this is where Turner was staying, as well. It's our best starting point to find out what's going on."

"Do you remember how to get there?" Siobhan asked, a smirk on her face implying a bit of doubt.

Handing his phone to her, Stan replied, "Here. Find it in my phone and let the GPS take us there. Probably better than wandering around. I think the name was . . ."

"Motel 6, in White, Georgia. I remember. You have a thing about Motel 6?"

"Cheap and clean. What more do we need?"

"Oh, I don't know . . . . maybe a swimming pool, spa, exercise room? Something besides a TV to fill time when nothing's going on?"

"When I'm out on a job, there is no time 'when nothing's going on'," Stan chuckled. "I'm always in surveillance, research, or in motion."

Siobhan smiled at his description of a life he did not remember, then reported on their estimated travel time. "Two hours, ten minutes. One hundred forty-two miles, according to your phone."

When they reached Cleveland, Tennessee, Stan turned unprompted south onto highway 60. The GPS quickly tried to redirect them back to I-75, but relented when he turned onto 74, giving new directions using US-411.

"Why this way?" Siobhan asked, casually.

"Tired of interstate scenery. Besides, I seem to recall something of import on this route. Not sure what." His voice betrayed another puzzle he was trying to solve.

"Well, before you take us too far off the beaten path, I could use a rest stop. I'm sure Flib wouldn't mind stretching his legs, too." She sighed and looked back at their four-footed companion sleeping on the back seat.

Moments later Stan pulled off at an old country store with gas pumps. Siobhan went inside while Stan gassed up the Subaru. When she returned with a late morning snack of crackers and drinks, she took Flib for a walk on a leash. Stan paid for the gas with cash and they continued south along the rural highway.

While the scenery was more pleasant than what the interstate provided, Stan saw nothing of importance. Trees grew almost to the edge of the road, with modest brick homes interspersed with fields of crops. Occasionally they would see an older home tucked in the trees on a hillside that opened onto a large field. Mobile home parks were identified by clusters of mailboxes. They passed few cars as the rolling landscape repeated itself over and over again.

Approaching Rydal, about ten miles from their destination, a sign for Cunningham Dairy caught Stan's eye and he slowed down. What he could see from the highway was an unimpressive dairy farm, not much larger than other family farms in the area. Passing through the community of White, he noticed a Cunningham Dry Cleaners. Not a modern facility, rather more like an old cleaners building that forgot to close. The building was made of cinder block and covered with paint that was faded and peeling. A few miles farther, just before reaching I-75, they passed Cunningham Farm Equipment and Cunningham Bakery, both of which backed up to railroad tracks.

Feeling his curiosity rewarded and heightened at the same time, Stan grinned as he looked over to Siobhan. "I'm feeling a bit peckish. How about the Waffle House?"

"Sure, I'm a bit 'peckish' as well."

Seconds later they went under the I-75 interchange, passed the Motel 6 on the right, and turned into a Waffle House restaurant on the left. Getting out of the car, Stan checked his phone. "Three hours, door-to-door. Not so bad."

Concerned for their four-legged companion and the

possibility of rising late-May temperatures, Siobhan rolled her window down a bit. "Mister Flib, we won't be too long and will bring you a treat. You watch the car for us." She then scratched his head and closed the door, putting her hand out to take the keys from Stan. Once she had them, she pressed the remote fob, locking the doors.

Inside, a waitress dressed in a Waffle House uniform greeted them. "You folks can sit anywhere you like. I'll be with you in a jiff."

They barely had time to settle into a booth before the waitress slipped two menus onto the table. "I'll get you some water while you decide." Her voice was shrill with a bit of southern twang.

When the waitress delivered their water, Stan asked, "So, what would you recommend for a pair of weary travelers?"

"It's too early in the day to be weary, young man. But looking at you, I'd suggest the Texas Sausage sandwich. It'll fill you up and chase those wearies away. For the young lady, I'd suggest one of our tasty everyday sandwiches. We have several, depending upon what your taste buds like."

Siobhan looked at the sandwich listings and quickly ordered. "I'll take a toasted BLT with chips."

"I kinda like your suggestion. I'll take the Texas Sausage," Stan responded.

Siobhan quickly added, "And would you please bring us a grilled cheese, wrapped to go. Thank You."

"Yes, Ma'am. It'll be just a few minutes." The waitress smiled and sashayed behind the counter.

"So, what's the plan?" Siobhan asked Stan after the waitress left with their order.

"Lunch, then drive across the street and check out the motel. According to bank records, this is where I stayed when I was here before. I'd like to find Turner in residence, but that's really a long shot."

"How long ago were you here?" Siobhan asked, trying to establish a time frame.

"A bit over a month ago, as I recall."

"As you 'recall'?" Siobhan asked, wondering if this was a trustworthy memory.

"According to the bank records, I charged my room on a card and bought gas near here just over a month ago." Stan sipped his water and gazed out the window, at the motel across the highway. Siobhan watched Stan, wondering what was going on in his head.

Stan's silent gaze was interrupted after a few minutes when the waitress delivered three plates. Siobhan reminded her that the grilled ham and cheese was "to go."

"My apologies. Our cook is half asleep today. I'll take care of it myself."

Stan and Siobhan wasted no time waiting and began eating their lunches as soon as the waitress left. When she returned with the wrapped sandwich, Stan looked at her more closely. She was mid-fifties, had a friendly face, and her uniform showed off a pleasant mature figure. This time he also noticed her name tag.

"Excuse me, Sharon, who is Cunningham? The name seems to be everywhere," Stan asked, casually.

"Old family, been here since forever," the waitress replied.

"What do they do besides the bakery and farm equipment? That's pretty diverse." Stan prodded for more information.

"Yeah, the great-grandmother started the bakery back in the 1920s. Rumor has it that they did more than bake bread. That's a big plant for no more bread than they turn out. Then about forty years ago, one of the boys got into farm machinery; he liked tractors. They got their hands in near everything that happens around here . . . not all of it above board, if you know what I mean. I remember hearing my granddaddy say that back in the days of prohibition their dairy made the best whiskey in the south. Y'all need anything else?"

"We're good. Thank you very much," Siobhan replied, smiling appreciatively.

Finishing lunch, Siobhan got a cup of water to go and they returned to the car.

Flib jumped out as soon as Siobhan opened the door and shook himself from nose to tail. Feeling heat coming from the car, Siobhan offered him the water and sandwich. He ate only half the toasted treat but lapped every drop of water from the cup.

"We need to get him a water bowl," Siobhan declared as she

signaled Flib to get back into the car. "We can get cool water almost anywhere, but he shouldn't have to drink from a small cup. His nose barely fits to the bottom." She then slid into the passenger seat and handed the keys to Stan.

"I thought we were going to the motel," Siobhan remarked as Stan drove north, under the interstate.

"We will, but first I want to check out this bakery and farm machinery place."

"What if somebody recognizes you?"

"Good thought. Why don't you check out the bakery and we'll just drive past the machinery lot. See what's going on."

A mile past the I-75 interchange, Stan turned left on a narrow road that ran between the bakery and farm equipment dealership. Coming to railroad tracks, he paused. Siobhan followed his gaze as he looked at both properties. A boxcar was being unloaded at the bakery dock and several freight cars were parked at loading docks for the farm machinery building. Stan noted that one siding served docks at both buildings. There was a second siding where a dozen or so boxcars were parked, then the main line. After crossing the three sets of tracks, Stan continued down the road, roughly a quarter-mile, turning around at a private driveway.

"Nice to be a Cunningham," Siobhan commented. The name adorned elaborate brickwork which supported iron gates sitting across the corner of iron fencing extending out of sight in both directions. Behind the gates, lush grass filled a front yard large enough to hold a soccer field.

"Yep. Makes you wonder," Stan agreed as he completed his turn and began their return to the highway.

Crossing the tracks, Stan looked at the collection of trucks parked in the lots of the two Cunningham businesses. Seeing several vehicles of various sizes, he felt everything was normal enough. Neither building was protected by a security fence and neither building seemed familiar. He found it humorous, however, that trucks for both companies were painted black and yellow.

Pulling around the front of the bakery, they found an outlet store. Siobhan sighed nervously as she got out of the car and walked toward the entrance. Stan's eyes followed her, then focused on a sign above the building. "CUNNINGHAM BAKERIES - *enriched breads for healthier living since 1923*" Looking across to the farm machinery facility, as a cloud passed overhead, the building's appearance in shadow sent shivers down Stan's spine.

Siobhan returned after a few minutes with a black and yellow plastic bag. Getting in the car, she reported. "Nothing unusual. They have pastries, donuts, and bread. Not a great variety, but it all seems fresh. I bought a loaf of bread and some snacks for later."

"Good enough for now," Stan replied. He looked back at the tractor building once more and headed for the motel.

Pulling into the parking lot of the Motel 6, Stan looked at the two story cinder-block building, painted white with sections of stone facade. A few room sections were painted a muted orange, presumably to give it some appeal. Parking at the motel office, Stan suggested, "Open the windows a bit more. No shade here and I don't know how long we'll be inside." He then slipped the keys into his pocket and joined Siobhan on the other side of the car, taking her hand as they walked into the office.

"Mister Winthrop, so good to see you back again." A neatly dressed man in his early thirties greeted the couple as they approached the desk. "Will you be staying with us long?"

"I'm not sure," Stan replied with some concern. "I take it you remember me from when I was here before?"

"To be honest, sir, it is a bit of a parlor trick. I try to always remember a guest, though they do occasionally get jumbled together. The reason I remember you is your unusual check-in and the uproar your friend caused."

"Can you explain a bit?" Siobhan asked. "Mister Winthrop suffered a major head trauma and we're trying to piece fragmented memories into an understandable picture."

"Certainly, ma'am. Mister Winthrop checked in for himself and one other guest, a Mister Turner, as I recall. He requested rooms across the court from one another. We are 'L' shaped, all rooms facing our pool, so I gave him two rooms on different wings and on different levels. Mister Winthrop then paid for his room with his card and paid for Mister Turner's room with

Mister Turner's card. That is what I thought somewhat odd; he signed Mister Turner's name and initialed it. Not unheard of but a bit unusual."

"And this uproar?" Stan asked, trying to keep the conversation going.

"Yes, sir. The night after you checked out, there was a brawl in Mister Turner's room. The police were called. By the time they arrived, however, the room was trashed but otherwise empty. The police put crime tape across the door, which I removed the next day . . . my manager felt it gave us a bad image. He doesn't like police hanging around the motel. Besides, they seem to have forgotten the incident."

"So, you are saying that Turner's room is just as he left it?" Stan affirmed.

"Yes, sir. Fortunately, we're not running near capacity or it would have been cleaned long ago . . . with or without police consent. They told us to not touch it. However, with a recent rise in tourist bookings, I imagine our manager will ask the police chief to complete their investigation, so we can start renting it again. That is a popular wing."

"Is the room Mister Winthrop had before currently available?" Siobhan asked, before Stan had a chance to pursue this same thought.

"Yes, ma'am. Should I register you for that room?"

"Please," Stan replied, smiling at Siobhan.

After rapping the keys on his computer, the clerk returned his attention to the couple before him. "That will be $60 for the night. I gave you the returning client rate. Do we charge the same card?"

"No, I'll pay for two nights in advance with cash." Stan handed the gentleman $120.

"We still have your card on file in case there are any additional charges. Here are two keys. The easiest access is from the back parking lot, up the stairs and half way down the corridor. Will there be anything else?"

"One thing. May we borrow a key to Mister Turner's room? Maybe jog a few memories." Siobhan smiled seductively with her request.

The clerk looked at Siobhan for several seconds. Seeing Stan slip a folded hundred dollar bill across the counter, the clerk accepted it with a smile. "I shouldn't, it being a crime scene and all, but if you promise to not upset anything, I don't see why not. After all, you did pay for it the first time." He then prepared an electronic key for this room, as well, handing it to Siobhan.

Returning to the car, they found Flib lying on the ground in the car's shade. He stood and greeted his people, his tail flashing side to side rapidly. Driving around the motel, Stan noticed a green and gold Ford Explorer parked in the shade of a large tree at the opposite end of the lot.

"That looks like your car," Siobhan commented. Stan did not reply.

Wanting to get the lay of the place, Stan parked at the entry between two buildings and they went to their room. After climbing concrete steps with a metal railing, they continued down an exposed walkway of the same concrete and metal to get to their room. As the manager had said, the motel was in an "L" configuration. They were in the longer side, opposite a kidney-shaped pool surrounded by a six-foot black chain link security fence. Siobhan looked at another feature not far from the pool with wonder, a round concrete pad about twenty-five feet across with a fire pit in the center. Eight or ten pool chairs provided seating. Grass struggled to grow around this meeting area and the pool.

Stan had not chosen this motel for the amenities and proceeded to open the door to their room. Heat poured out the door so they quickly turned the air conditioner on full cold and returned to the balcony. Flib turned back into the room and sniffed around the single king bed and every corner.

"Turner was in room . . ." Siobhan offered, turning the key case over and looking for, but not finding, a number.

"Second from the far end, lower level. Easy to watch from here." Stan completed her statement. "Might even be able to see it from inside this room." He then entered the room and stood before the large window, looking toward Turner's room. It was clearly visible from inside, where he could watch without being seen.

Feeling apprehensive and a bit uneasy, Stan took a deep breath and looked at Siobhan. "Let's go see what's in Mister

Turner's room."

Siobhan smiled in support and called to Flib. "Come on Mister Flib, we may need your expert nose."

A minute later Stan opened the door to Mister Turner's room. It was a mess. Lamps were knocked over, the table on its side, the night stand closest to the door was also knocked over, and bed covers and clothes were strewn around the room. There had clearly been a violent struggle.

"See what you can find. Get a hand towel or wash cloth from the bath and check the drawers. Don't leave any fingerprints or proof that we were here," Stan directed as he began searching the floor for blood stains.

Flib put his nose to work and began examining nooks as he had in Stan's room. Coming to the night stand on the far side of the room he stopped, sat, and yipped politely. Stan stepped beside his companion and looked at the night stand. Borrowing a cloth from Siobhan, he opened the drawer. A Gideon Bible and phone book. Stepping back to look at the furniture itself, Stan saw that panels went to the floor on all sides of all the bed, dressers, and night stands.

"Nothing could have gotten kicked under there," he thought aloud.

"What?" Siobhan asked, looking at the small table.

"Flib is interested in this night stand. Nothing out of the ordinary in the drawer and no way anything could have been kicked under it. But . . ."

Stan lifted the table and set it a couple feet to the side. Hidden beneath was a ring of keys and a cell phone. Picking them up, he first checked the phone. "Battery's exhausted. Will have to be charged before it tells us anything." After slipping the phone in his shirt pocket, he inventoried the keys. "Remote fob and ignition key for a Ford product, house key, padlock, and post office box." Looking to Siobhan, he asked, "Did you find anything?"

"Nothing in the dressers, but this watch was in the desk drawer. Looking at the clothes thrown across the room, he dressed a lot like you." Siobhan held out a watch, but Stan didn't seem interested. Shrugging, she dropped the watch back onto the desk where she found it.

Smiling, Stan chuckled, "That's more than we had. Now, we just need to find someone who dresses like me, and half a million other men. Let's go check out the Explorer."

Walking out to the vehicle, Siobhan asked, "Why would he have keys to your car?"

"Who said he had them? True, we found them in his room, but as you recall I suffered a blow to the head. I might have been involved in the scuffle or I may have loaned them to him. I don't know."

Extending his hand with the key fob, he began to press the unlock button but his thumb froze in place. Slowing his pace, he approached the car cautiously. It was backed into a parking space, neatly parked in the shade of a large oak tree. Flib circled the car twice then stopped near the driver's side front tire and barked, politely.

"I agree, Mister Flib. Let's proceed with caution." Stan then unlocked the door with the ignition key and popped the hood open. In plain sight were two sticks of dynamite wired to the ignition system. Looking at Siobhan, he asked, "Do you have pliers in your car?"

"I do. My father taught me to always carry an emergency tool kit. This will be the first time I have ever opened it. Be right back." Siobhan walked briskly to her car, retrieved a bundle from the back end, and returned just as quickly.

Stan smiled as he watched her journey to her car and back. He also checked out the parking lot, but did not see anyone else around.

Unrolling the bundle of tools on top of the engine, Stan smiled and removed a pair of pliers, which he used to loosen the battery terminal and pry it off the post. Successfully disconnecting the battery of the Explorer, he removed the explosive package. Tossing the dynamite to the ground behind the car, he called to Flib. "Okay Flib, you seem to have a nose for what doesn't belong; see what else you can find."

Flib was already sitting at the rear of the Explorer and barked in response.

Joining his trusted companion, Stan unlocked the rear hatch and looked. An equipment case, resembling a large silver brief case, laid to the right, where it apparently belonged, but something wasn't right.

"You kept a clean car," Siobhan complimented as she looked. She then leaned forward and picked up a writing pen that had rolled to far edge, against the back seat.

"Step back, both of you," Stan warned as he lifted the equipment case to the ground. He then lifted the panel covering the spare tire. Tucked into the spaces beside the spare were blocks of plastic explosive. Wires led from each block to a box resting near the jack. Stan immediately recognized this device.

"What'd you find?" Siobhan asked, stepping next to Stan.

"Motion sensor with timer delay. When the car starts to move, the motion sensor turns the timer on. Then, when the timer ticks down . . . boom."

Considering that there were only two wires going to each block of explosive, Stan looked into the equipment case and removed a pair of wire cutters. After disabling the bomb, he carefully lifted the switch and gently put it on the ground near the dynamite. He then removed the plastic explosive and started to close the spare tire compartment, but stopped. Reaching into the equipment case he removed an odd looking device. It had a metallic loop about eight inches long and three inches wide attached to a black plastic box with a single dial. Stan turned the dial and this device began beeping erratically. As he adjusted the dial, the beeping sound became slow and regular.

"What is that thing?" Siobhan asked, watching Stan wave the loop around the spare tire.

"A bug detector," Stan replied. Suddenly the beeping became a buzz. "My own design and very effective at close range . . . has to be within about three feet."

He put the detector down and examined the top of the spare tire. After a few seconds he pulled his knife from his pocket and pried a black bead from the tire. Smiling, he handed the bead to Siobhan and resumed scanning. Using the detector, he found three more "bugs" of various descriptions. One in the engine compartment, one over the passenger visor, and one under the driver seat. Taking all four from Siobhan, he stared at them, pondering. When Siobhan began to speak, he put his finger to his lips, hushing her.

Looking at this uncommon young woman who had become

a significant part of his life, Stan noticed a hamburger bag two parking spaces behind her. Without a word, he signaled her to retrieve this trash, which she did with a quizzical expression. When she opened the bag, they found several wrappers and a cup. Seeing Stan point to the cup, she took it from the bag and removed the lid, revealing an inch or so of water. Stan then dumped all four bugs into the cup, put the lid back on it, and carefully returned it to the bag. Winking at Siobhan, he placed the bag on the curb near the rear of the Explorer. Pondering his next move, he felt the hair rise on the back of his neck and shivers chilling his spine. Looking back at the bag of trash he realized the bugs had done their job. Whoever had planted those bugs had probably heard their conversation, up to the time he dumped them into the water.

Stan quickly collected Siobhan's emergency tool kit and walked purposefully back to her car. She and Flib followed. Handing the kit to her, he said emphatically, "Get in your car and drive home. Take the interstate, NOT highway 411. Go NOW! I'll be leaving in just a few minutes but will be returning by a different route." He then quickly kissed her politely and started back toward the motel rooms.

"My keys!" Siobhan called.

Stan stopped, checked his pocket, and hurried back. As he placed the keys in her hand, she reached up and pulled him down so she could kiss him. Planting her lips firmly across his, she opened just a bit. He could not resist her invitation, yet had to. Both hearts began to beat in sync. Siobhan got her message across, now Stan had to regroup.

"Go! Now!" Stan urged, panting just a bit. He then ran toward Turner's room, pulling the keycard from his pocket as he ran.

Bursting through the door, Stan was hit by a wave of memories exploding in noise and chaos. Men, six or more, shouting at one another. Tables getting knocked over. He recalled wrapping bed linen around someone and tossing them aside, then nothing. Staring at the room, the memory of his abduction washed over him like cold water from a fire hose.

Gasping for air and heart pounding, he said to no one, "I don't have time for this right now!" and grabbed a bath towel.

Seconds later he returned to the Explorer, dropped the hood, and quickly wrapped the explosives in the towel, then placed them behind the front passenger seat. Seeing the back end still open, he went to close it, stumbling on his equipment case. Taking a breath to collect himself, he closed the case and returned it to the back of the Explorer, closed the tailgate, and slid behind the steering wheel while inserting and turning the key. The Explorer failed to start.

Nearing panic, heart now pounding in his ears, Stan popped the hood and looked at the engine - the battery was still disconnected. Breathing deeply, he pushed the connector over the battery terminal. It was loose, too loose. Without pausing a single painful heartbeat, he raced to the trash bag with the electronic bugs and pulled out the straw. After looping the straw two times through the metal terminal hoop, he smashed it over the battery post. It sparked as it made contact. Wiggling it, Stan found it a bit loose but tight enough for now. Closing the hood, he returned to the driver's seat.

When Stan turned the key this time, the engine fired off, sputtered a bit, then purred. Pulling out of the motel parking lot, Stan turned right, away from the interstate, Oliver Springs, and all things Cunningham.

As Stan squeaked through a yellow light, two blocks from the motel, a black and yellow pickup truck turned into the Motel 6 and continued toward the rear parking lot.

Chapter 10

Monday morning, Mary sat in her apartment, adjacent to Pearl's Diner, and listened to Siobhan's message for the fourth time. Sipping her coffee, she made a decision but was reluctant to act on it. Holding the coffee for another three minutes, she contemplated the implications of acting on her decision. Finally resolving that Siobhan's safety was more important than her own privacy, she put the coffee cup down, climbed stairs in need of painting, and went into her bedroom.

Opening a closet door, she moved the clothes aside. She had hoped to never come here again, yet action was required. Forcing her arm to move, she pushed a panel on the side wall. A door popped open, revealing a hidden safe. After punching in six digits on a number pad, she turned the handle and opened the door. Hesitantly, she reached in and removed a cell phone and charger. Holding the device in her hand, she considered her actions once more, then closed the safe and returned to her kitchen table, where she plugged the charger into the wall and began bringing a dead phone back to life.

Opening her personal smart phone, Mary located the pictures she had recently taken of Siobhan, Stan, and Flib. *They make a handsome family*, she thought to herself, then selected one showing just Stan. A clean head shot of this man she trusted, intuitively, but history and reason dictated serious doubts. Ready to commit to her decision, she hit the send icon at the base of the picture. Her phone presented three options for sending, or sharing, the image. She pressed "Select another option," and jumped through her list of apps, selecting one she had not used in years, "Security Messaging."

Picking up her old cell phone, she turned it on and went to her contacts list. She carefully considered two names, then selected John W. Barnes. After copying his contact number into the security messaging app on her smart phone, she entered a complex string of letters and numbers, "IUXtpr8362124552771PXH." Pondering what message she should send with the image, she opted for simplicity. "Is he one of yours?" Once more she considered the implications of her actions, then pressed "TX" before she lost her resolve.

Her heart began pounding as she watched the screen. "Transmission Initiating" then "Transmission Completed - Message Accepted".

Now, she had to wait.

Not wanting to be far from her old cell phone, Mary postponed morning errands while the old device completed charging. Once serviceable, she stuffed it into her jeans pocket and headed for the grocery store.

Supper time was looming and Mary stood at her pantry, pondering what to fix. Life was easier on days when the diner was open; she could always have lunch leftovers for supper. Pearl's was closed on Mondays, however, so no lunch leftovers. Finally deciding cornbread would be best with pork chops she had purchased that morning, she pulled out the cornmeal. She had no sooner opened another cabinet, retrieving a mixing bowl, when she felt a silent vibration in her pocket.

"Yes?" she responded after pressing "Answer."

"We have got to get you on the new protocol," the base voice on the other end replied.

"Hey, Jack. No, you don't know how hard it was to open this can of worms. I am not coming back in any way, shape, or form. What'd you find out?"

"Not one of mine, but I did a quick search. He was one of Max Buster's charges."

"Max died last year; what can you tell me?"

"Well, I need to know why you need to know."

"He stumbled into my place several months ago and hooked up with one of my waitresses."

"Waitress? You got that diner you always wanted?"

"Sure did, in a nice quiet out of the way town. Anyway, he disappeared for about a month then reappeared with amnesia. Yes, before you ask, it's real amnesia. Before he disappeared he was cocky, overly self-assured, and almost seemed to be putting on an act. When he returned, he was softer, warmer, more real to life. Much more likable. In this more relaxed state, he unknowingly revealed some practices we used at the company. Not everyday stuff, high level stuff. Either he, or the guy he's working for, is company. Now, he's gone and got my girl involved in some investigation and I'm not real happy about it."

"Okay, good enough. He left the company for reasons unknown. Reading through Max's notes, I gather he was a finder. One of the best. Sent into hot spots to retrieve assets and valuables, if you know what I mean. This guy could find that proverbial needle in a haystack, even when the haystack is a middle-east war zone. What alias is he using?"

"Stan Winthrop."

"Yeah, that's him, or one of him. Any idea what he's working on?"

"No, but I did hear him mention the name 'Cunningham,' in Asheville."

"Okay, I'll look into it and get back to you."

"Jack, where are you now?"

"Funny you should ask; I left the company shortly after you did. Now with the U.S. Department of Justice. Investigations supervisor in D.C. Watch for my call."

Chapter 11

"What is he thinking?" Siobhan asked aloud as she followed the loop onto northbound Interstate 75 at White, Georgia.

Sitting in the back seat, behind Siobhan, Flib watched an eighteen-wheeler whiz past as they merged into traffic. Ever her guardian, he remained alert to everything that was happening. After looking at the empty passenger seat several times, the dog turned around and watched traffic behind them. When Siobhan began crying, he gingerly crept to the empty front seat and watched his driver and companion.

Looking over at her new copilot, Siobhan could not help but laugh. His face was a furry portrait of concern. Reaching over to pet his head and scratch his ear, Siobhan assured her friend, "He'll be okay. Probably be home when we get there."

Pulling into the drive-up at Hardee's near their apartment in Oliver Springs, at 6:35 p.m., Siobhan ordered a Frisco Angus Burger for herself, a Steakhouse Thickburger for Stan, a double cheeseburger for Flib, three orders of fries, and two chocolate shakes. She had not heard from Stan since he told her to leave the motel but was confident he would be home when she got there. Her cell phone rang as she pulled away from the pickup window.

"Where are you? I just picked up burgers for supper," she answered.

"Do NOT go back to the apartment," Stan replied, with an emphatic tone. "See if Mary will put you up for the night. I'll explain when I see you in the morning."

"Stan! What is going on?"

"Go to Mary's, I'll explain in the morning!" He abruptly ended the call.

Five minutes later, Siobhan knocked on the door of an apartment on the left side of Pearl's. Getting no response after a minute, she knocked again, more emphatically. Mary opened the door with a brusque question. "Are you okay?"

"Yes, of course. I just need a place to stay for the evening. Can we use your sofa?"

"Sure, come on in." Seeing the large bag of food, Mary added, "Good, you brought food. My supper plans were interrupted and I'm starving."

Flib sat outside the door, even after Siobhan went through. Mary held the door and stared at him. "Well, you coming in or are you going to sleep outside?" Without further ado, Flib followed Siobhan into the apartment. "Prima donna!" Mary growled impatiently.

The trio passed through Mary's dark living room. Shades were pulled on the windows, for privacy, and only one light was on. A floor lamp stood next to a chair Mary used for reading. Her sofa was covered with newspapers and the tv on the opposite wall was a bit dusty. A dining area separated the living room from the kitchen, which featured a large gas range and restaurant grade refrigerator, both polished to a reflective gleam.

Siobhan distributed wrapped burgers and fries around the table. She then unfolded the paper around Flib's dinner and placed it on the floor; a meal on a mat. He wasted no time making it disappear. As the two ladies sat and pulled their chairs to the table, Mary asked gruffly, "Okay, what happened? I thought you were going to be gone all week, if not longer."

"We got to the motel where Stan stayed before and even checked out the room where Turner had been staying. It was a mess. There were clothes and bed linen strewn around the room, furniture knocked over. Looked as though there had been quite a brawl and nothing had been cleaned up. Something about police tape and it being a crime scene. Anyway, we found Stan's Explorer and he's driving it home."

"Where is your super sleuth?" Mary was concerned, however her tone was a bit abrasive and sarcastic, almost as though she feared his return.

Not registering Mary's attitude, Siobhan replied, "He found electronic bugs in his car and is coming home a different way. He called while I was getting supper and said he'll be here in the morning."

Mary listened to what Siobhan was not saying. Thinking about the conversation she had earlier that day with Jack, she remembered working with men like Stan in her prior life. Many of these operatives considered their objective as justification for any action, including execution of their opponent. She thought briefly about an encounter with a U.S. Congressman who found out what was happening in a middle-east war zone. He called it "murder." She justified it as "acquiring needed intelligence." Intelligence that saved the lives of U.S. servicemen. She now wondered about Stan; what was his background and how far would he go to achieve his objective? Where did Siobhan fit into his plans? Concerned about what she did not know and what Siobhan was not saying, Mary decided to not pursue the untold story. Not just yet. She also wondered, but did not ask, why Siobhan had not gone back to her own apartment.

Tuesday morning, Pearl's diner was buzzing with comments about a local event.

"You drove in from Knoxville this morning; did you see it?" one patron asked another at the next table.

"Yeah, what was left of it. Might have been a Buick LeSabre. Nice car that LeSabre."

"Yep, Buick still makes a nice car," a guest at another table joined in. "This one wasn't local, though. Had Georgia plates, only part of the car not charred black as coal, the license plate. Three of the tires were flat'ern a pancake. Speaking of which, where're my cakes?" He looked around for a waitress who might be bringing his breakfast.

"How'd it happen?" the first man asked.

"Nobody seems to know for sure. I had my police band on, at the shop, and they've been talking about it all morning. Lot's of chatter but no information. One guy did say it looked like it was bombed, from the inside."

Siobhan didn't hear any of the talk about this blown up car on the highway to Knoxville. She was preoccupied and on edge all morning. When waiting tables, she watched the front door, ignoring remarks about a burned up car and even missing several customer requests. When in the kitchen, she kept an eye on the back door. As the morning shift began to fade into lunch, she sat outside, in a chair by the kitchen door, and put her head in her hands. Flib rested his head in her lap.

"You two look mighty glum."

Both Siobhan and Flib jumped at the sound of Stan's voice. Wrapping her arms around his neck and squeezing with all her might, she began to sob. "I was afraid you wouldn't come back."

"I told you I would explain everything when I saw you this morning. Am I too late for breakfast?" After a tight embrace with Siobhan, Stan knelt down to acknowledge Flib. "You're supposed to keep her spirits up; what were you doing?"

Flib wriggled and yelped politely under Stan's scratching and rubbing.

Hearing the commotion, Mary stepped outside. "Good, you're back. Maybe now she'll treat the customers better."

"Got any country ham and eggs left from breakfast?" Stan asked, following Siobhan into the kitchen.

"Sure, help yourself to coffee. I'll get you a plate. I think we have a few biscuits left, too," Mary offered, concealing her own sigh of relief.

Placing a plate with two fried eggs, a slab of country ham, and two biscuits in front of Stan, she sat and demanded an explanation. "Out with it, what's going on? Why did Siobhan spend the night with me and please tell me you didn't have anything to do with that car explosion last night."

"Can I help it if a couple nosy spooks don't know how to handle explosives? Nobody was hurt . . . well, 'cept maybe for a headache this morning."

"What are you two talking about?" Siobhan asked, confused about the explosion.

"Nothing to worry about, now," Stan replied to Siobhan then resumed answering Mary's question. "While I was driving back, I got to thinking those Georgia folks might have figured out where Siobhan lived. That's why I called her and told her to go to your place. Sure 'nuff, when I got back, a little after midnight, I saw two goons trying to break into the apartment. I suspect they got her address when we registered at the Motel 6. I doubt that clerk keeps many secrets. Anyway, I 'gently' put them to sleep and drove their car down the road a bit."

"Wait," Siobhan interrupted. "You 'put them to sleep'?"

"When I drove up to the apartment, they were trying to pick the lock. Earlier, I had found a taser under the front seat of my car, so I used it to immobilize the larger of the two. Then, as the other one turned and reached around his back, I used my version of the 'Vulcan Nerve Pinch'."

"Nerve Pinch?" Siobhan challenged, finding Stan's story difficult to believe.

"Yeah. Pinch the shoulder real hard and the victim drops his shoulder, makes it real hard to pull a gun with that arm. Then, you follow with a right cross. Works most of the time. Any way, I took their car down the road, a mile or two toward Knoxville. As I happened to have a timer and some dynamite in my car, I left it in their vehicle after dumping them in nearby ditch. I'm hoping they got the message to back off. I also made certain their phones, wallets, and shoes were in their car when it went boom."

"Where'd the dynamite come from?" Mary asked, chuckling just a bit.

"Somebody had generously wired my car for a short trip. Thanks to Flib, we found two bombs and I returned one of them to its original owner. I also saw what happened to me in Atlanta, well, White, Georgia."

"You remembered?" Siobhan asked, making no effort to conceal her excitement.

"Only part of it. After checking out, I had gone to Turner's room. Apparently the Cunningham crew was there and we had a bit of a tussle. You saw the condition of the room. I was knocked out and apparently loaded into a northbound freight car behind the tractor store. I do vaguely recall being driven behind that place and then dumped into a freight car on the siding."

"What about Turner?" Mary asked.

"Don't know. But we found another cell phone and it may have answers once we recharge it," Stan replied, with a new and growing confidence.

Mary felt a shiver run down her spine as Jack's words came back to her. *This guy could find that proverbial needle in a haystack, even when the haystack is a middle-east war zone.*" Stan was a finder, one of the best. Again she wondered how far Stan would go to achieve his objective. How much danger was Siobhan in?

"What took you so long to get back?" Siobhan asked, squeezing Stan's hand.

Echoing her squeeze, Stan continued his story. "I left the motel only a couple minutes behind you. I borrowed a towel from Turner's room to provide a bit of cushion for the explosives. Instead of coming straight back, I headed south. I checked my rear-view a couple blocks away and saw one of their black and yellow trucks pull into the Motel 6. My battery light came on as I reached Marietta, so I stopped to reconnect the battery and get more gas. We forgot to put the cable back and I had to 'jimmy' it to get out of there. While at that service station in Marietta, I found another bug behind the license plate, which I transplanted to an RV that was covered with hunting and fishing stickers and seemed to be heading west. A couple of fishermen were talking about some tournament in Kentucky and they had Texas plates. After that, I just kind of wandered around. Spent an hour, or so, in a rest area on I-85 near Spartanburg. Once I was satisfied that nobody was following me, I shot up Interstate 26, to 40, then across the mountain to Knoxville. I thought about checking out Brevard and Hendersonville, since I was going right past there, but realized what I really wanted was to be right here, with you folks. Especially a specific waitress in an out of the way diner."

"What about that golden four legged guardian outside? You didn't want to see him again?" Siobhan jabbed, smiling ear to ear.

"Flib? Yeah, kinda wanted to see him again, too."

"So, you never found Turner and almost got yourself in an even bigger pickle. What now?" Mary asked, bringing the conversation back into focus.

"I need to charge up that phone we found and see what, if anything, is saved on it."

"Finish your lunch and get to it," Mary commanded, rising to resume her kitchen duties.

"What's with her?" Stan asked Siobhan as he bit into a biscuit loaded with country ham.

"She's Mary; what do you expect?" Siobhan replied. "I better get back to work, too." She kissed him quickly, then returned to her own duties.

"I'll see you back at the apartment!" Stan called, finishing his eggs.

When Stan stood to leave, Siobhan, her arms loaded with an order, called out, "Would you please take Flib with you?"

"Sure," Stan agreed, an unaccustomed, yet welcome, warmth filling his soul.

Flib preceded Stan, trotting to Siobhan's car, but when Stan unlocked the Explorer, Flib sat and stared at him and the car. Stan chuckled, opened the door, and called, "Come on, it's safe now." Flib sniffed his way around the vehicle, stopping several times for more intense examination, then carefully climbed in through the driver's door. Sliding behind the steering wheel, Stan shook his head, then petted his companion and started the engine.

Siobhan returned home shortly after three o'clock. Entering the apartment, she found Flib sleeping in the center of the living room floor and Stan sitting at the kitchen table. He had the found phone to his left, his computer in front of him, and a note pad to his right.

"What've you learned?" she asked, wrapping her arms over his shoulders.

"First, and most important, this is NOT a cell phone. It IS a wireless listening device. Turner was eavesdropping on the phone of whomever is calling the shots. This gadget recorded calls for three days after I was abducted. One conversation confirmed that I was abducted and dumped into the boxcar, just as I vaguely remembered. Part of that conversation, and the next two, tell me they never found Turner. He apparently gave them the slip when they were grabbing me and hasn't been seen since. Nobody knows what kind of car he has nor where he might have gone. Simply vanished. Then the last call, before the phone died, indicates they think he might have gone to Hendersonville, North Carolina. That seems to have really upset the boss!"

"What's in Hendersonville?" Siobhan asked, now sitting at the table.

"Only thing I can say for sure is that it's close to Asheville and Albert David Cunningham. Also, those first two henchmen, who attacked me in Indiana, were both from Hendersonville."

"What now?"

"Not sure. I went through all Turner's info too fast. I think I need to spend a few days reviewing everything we have, again, and really pay attention to what I missed. Maybe even tie some names to these recorded voices. Turner collected a lot of information that appears to link Cunningham with organized crime, but no evidence that will stand up in court. We need one 'iron clad' piece of evidence so we can take him down and shut down his crime family. One solid piece of real evidence."

Chapter 12

Stan and Flib watched Siobhan leave for work early Wednesday morning, turning left out of their parking area, then continuing toward the highway. When her car disappeared from view, they returned to the kitchen where Stan prepared his own breakfast of fried eggs on toast. After cleaning the pan and his plate, Stan went to his room to retrieve the small SD memory card, which he had found at the post office, and settled to the table with his computer. As he inserted the SD card into his computer, his phone alerted him to a new message. Putnam County Bank (PCB) reminded him that his new account could now be accessed via computer or smart-phone.

Five minutes after receiving that text message, Stan had established his online identity and logged into the new account using his notebook computer. PCB actively promoted their mobile banking app for smart-phones, so Stan took a moment to look into it. One benefit that caught his eye was an ability to immediately send money to another bank. After reading about this feature, he logged into his TVA Credit Union account, using his phone, and checked to see if they had a similar feature. Before he finished his first cup of coffee, Stan completed the transfer of $17,000 from the credit union to PCB. Two hundred dollars from the balance of this reward from Oliver Winston appeared as instantly available in the PCB account, yet his initial deposit of $3,000, to set up the account, still showed as "pending." Looking back at the credit union status, he could see where the check had been deducted last night.

"I like this electronic transfer business," he said to himself, contentedly. "But, I have a lot of research to do."

After closing all banking apps, Stan fixed a fresh cup of coffee and returned to the data-rich SD card. He found reading the folder contents much easier using the larger screen of his notebook computer than when he first examined this card with his phone. Pulling up the main directory, he recognized the audio files he had listened to previously, but also saw a subdirectory he had missed before. Clicking on the icon, he found a folder filled with document and text files. Opening the oldest, he discovered MG Turner's personal notes on this investigation. Jubilant, as though he had just won the MegaMillions lottery, he began reading.

Feeling a paw push against his leg, Stan looked down and saw Flib with a desperate look on his face. "Sorry about that, boy. I guess I got lost in somebody else's work." Picking up his coffee cup, he stepped to the kitchen door. Flib shot out as soon as the door was opened wide enough. Chuckling, Stan stepped outside as well and took a sip from his half-full cup.

"AAGGGHH, cold!" Stepping back into the kitchen, he placed the cup next to the sink, retrieved his phone, and returned to the fresh air outside.

Drawing a deep breath, he stretched and shook off stiffness from sitting, then looked to his phone. "Egad! Eleven o'clock. I've been at it over three hours." Seeing Flib returning from around the corner, he asked, "You want to drop in on Siobhan?"

Flib pranced expectantly around Stan.

After shutting down his computer and hiding his notes and SD card in his bedroom, where he believed they would be safe, Stan and Flib went out the front door to the parking area. Flib immediately circled the Explorer, sniffing for what might not be right. Satisfied the car had not been tampered with, he yipped approval and waited for Stan to open the door.

Shaking his head with wonder and delight, Stan opened the door and slid behind the steering wheel, forcing his four-footed companion to scoot over just a bit. Turning left out of the parking area, he followed the same route Siobhan had earlier that day.

Moments later, looking in the back door to Pearl's, Stan paused. The kitchen was hopping. Mary seemed to be directing a full concert with Horace fumbling on the grill and three waitresses shuffling back and forth between delivering new orders and picking up those ready to enjoy. Not wanting to cause a breakdown in their symmetry, Stan turned and went around to the front door.

Entering the diner, Stan found the room three-quarters full. Spying an empty table near the kitchen door, he slipped quietly between crowded tables.

"Someone will be right with you, sir," a waitress greeted as she pushed into the kitchen with a bin of dirty dishes. "New customer at table nine!"

"Hey, Stan!" Sylvia, a familiar waitress, greeted as she approached his table. "You want me to get Siobhan or will this ole gal do today?" She was sassy and friendly, but respectful that Siobhan already had a claim on this man.

"You'll do fine, Sylvia. Thanks." He couldn't help but return her flirtatious grin. "I just want a BLT on wheat toast and tea. Where's the crowd from?"

"They're running exercises over at Oak Ridge, again. It happens two or three times a year. Most of these folks are returnees and know not to eat at their Army dinning facility. I'll bring this right out. Sure you don't want Siobhan to drop by?"

"If she has time. Thanks."

Stan watched the crowd, unconsciously analyzing each face. His review was interrupted after about five minutes.

"So! I get busy for a few minutes and you take up with another woman!" Siobhan chastised Stan as she leaned over, delivering a quick kiss, with a promise of more later. "I hear you're flirting with other women?"

"Like you're worried! How long before you get a break?"

"No break today, not with this crowd. You're lucky to be getting fed at all." Siobhan stole another quick kiss when Sylvia returned.

"You two need to either get a room or get married. Your sandwich, sir. Will there be anything else?"

Stan looked into Siobhan's eyes, thinking, *A minister would be nice*, but replied. "No. Thanks, Sylvia." He then watched as both women returned to the kitchen. Siobhan looked back and winked. Stan's thoughts rambled around his relationship with this lady. *I've known her for what . . . two weeks? . . . no, ten days. Yet, I feel as though we've spent a lifetime together. She's known me longer, suppose that helps. . . . a lifetime together . . . I have got to find out who I am and if there is anyone else I need to be worrying about! The answer must be out there; I just have to find it. . . . Maybe Turner can help. . . . Find Turner and get on with life.*

Half-hour after Stan arrived, the surplus of patrons began leaving. Mary kept looking his way between helping customers as the cash register sang its song. When all had left and the checkout line disappeared, she stopped by Stan's table. "Any progress?"

"A bit. A few answers and new questions. Typical, I suppose."

"Well, keep at it and keep me posted. This search of yours is intriguing; a lot better'n the novel I'm reading." Mary then turned to go back into the kitchen, however was distracted when a man in his mid-fifties came in and stood at the door. Mary approached him with a smile. "Sorry for the mess, we just had a large party leave. It'll be cleaned up right away. We do have several tables ready over here."

"Actually, I'm just wondering if I might post a flyer. I was told you get a lot of local traffic here."

"What's the flyer about?" Mary asked and reached out. She was always willing to help locals with fund-raising and special projects.

The man handed her a flyer, which featured a full color picture of an old touring roadster. "My car seems to have wandered off. I was hoping someone might have seen it."

"Wandered off, huh? Sure, post the flyer on our community board, then you might want to talk with that gentleman sitting near the kitchen door. He's good at finding things that 'wander off.' Can I get you anything?"

"A cup of coffee, if you don't mind. Thank you."

Mary walked toward the kitchen, shaking her head. Pausing at Stan's table she whispered, "We got a live one!" Chuckling softly, she continued back to her kitchen duties.

Stan sipped his coffee as he watched the gentleman tack a flyer to the wall, then turn and stroll his direction. Wearing creased khaki slacks and an open-collar striped short-sleeve sport shirt, he walked with an air of confidence, yet not assuming or overbearing. Reaching Stan's table, he offered a flyer.

"The hostess said you might help me find a car that has gone missing."

Standing, Stan offered his hand, which was graciously and gratefully accepted. "My name is Stan Winthrop. Please, sit down and tell me about your car."

Sylvia delivered the gentleman's coffee as both men sat down. Stan covered his cup with his hand, signaling he did not want another refill.

"My name is Brad Ferguson. My father and I restored this beauty when I was a teenager; my first car. A British Salmson S4C Open Tourer. It has become rather expensive to service so I don't take it out too often. Parts were difficult to come by when we restored it."

The flyer featured a color photograph of a cream colored open two-seater roadster, or touring car. Its fenders were brown, matching a leather interior.

"Excuse my ignorance, but except for the color, it looks like an old MG Roadster."

"You're not the only one who thinks that. Morris Garages is still around. However, Salmson made cars in Britain for only four years, prior to World War II. Their parent company made airplane engines in France. My car was authentic Salmson except for the front bumper, which I had made fifteen years ago. On a recent business trip to England, I located an authentic bumper and had it shipped home. When I returned, however, the bumper had arrived but the car was missing. I started searching by contacting a local car club. Several of the members were in love with this sweetheart. But, no luck. I reported the loss to the police but have little hope of help there. So, I'm now posting flyers in hopes that someone might see it somewhere."

"You do realize, Mister Ferguson, that this car could be anywhere in the world. It might even be in several different places."

"Yes, except for one thing, classic car enthusiasts won't generally touch a Salmson. Parts are too hard to come by and the aero-based engine is very temperamental."

"Aero-based engine?" Stan asked, stumped by this reference.

"As I said, the parent company was a French manufacturer of airplane engines. They used this foundation when designing the British Salmson. Not smart, but nice when it runs."

Stan thought for a moment. "And you have no idea who might have taken it? Children, relatives, friends, neighbors, business associates?"

"No. I've checked with everyone I know. My son's more upset than I am because he was looking forward to showing it in a rally this weekend."

"Where?"

"Waynesville, North Carolina. It's primarily a show, held at the Smokey Mountain Event Center, but they also run a road rally. Beautiful scenery. We were going to drive it together."

"Have you contacted the sponsors of the rally?"

"Yes. They weren't a lot of help, either, but said I could post flyers. They don't like the darker side of classic cars. Not good for their image."

"I understand." Stan hesitated, thinking about finding Turner. *I really don't have time right now to take on a stolen car, yet this guy seems sincere. I could get on up to Asheville and come back by Waynesville, no real investment of time that way.* Looking back at the flyer, he pointed to it and asked, "Can you be reached at this phone number?"

"24-7."

Stan gulped the last of his coffee and stood, extending his hand once again. "Mister Ferguson, I'll do a bit of research to see what there is to learn about this car and thefts in this region. You should hear from me in a couple days, but if you don't, watch for me in Waynesville."

Stan couldn't help but notice the hope Ferguson had in his eyes as they stood and shook hands. He watched as his new client dropped a five-dollar bill on the table and left the restaurant. Stan then turned to go into the kitchen. He hadn't taken three steps before he was nearly knocked over by Siobhan and another waitress coming from the kitchen to clean tables.

"You want to bus tables, young man? Could earn a free lunch!" Siobhan teased.

"No thank you, ma'am. I just had a delicious BLT. I was hoping for a spot of desert. You have any recommendations?"

"Hmm. You want something sweet or real sweet?" Siobhan rocked her eyebrows, suggestively.

"I think I like the thought of r-e-a-l sweet."

"Sorry, that's only served to select customers after hours. But I do have a sweet treat." She then reached up and kissed Stan, who tried to grab her. Turning away from his grip, she chastised, "Sweet only, for now. I have work to do. Speaking of which, aren't you supposed to be mining?"

"Yes," Stan replied, dejected. "A friend and I were hoping

for a bit of a break. I guess we'll be headin' back home . . . to the mine."

Dropping her dish tub on a table, Siobhan raced past Stan, into the kitchen, then to the back door; grabbing a bit of country ham as she passed through. Flib was relishing her attention, ham and rubbing, when Stan caught up. Siobhan stood, a moment later, and poked Stan playfully as she turned to go back to work, snickering, "Good to see ya. Be home when I get there."

Looking down at his satisfied friend, Stan moaned, "I guess we know who she really appreciates. Come on, let's get back to work."

Having stayed near the car while Stan ate lunch, Flib didn't inspect it before jumping in through the driver's door.

Returning home, Stan spent twenty minutes reviewing available information about Salmson roadsters. There wasn't much, but what he found peaked his interest. He also ran a few dark web searches to see if Ferguson's car was being sold. He didn't find an S4C Tourer but did find a Salmson GS8 Roadster in California. Frustrated with this search, he returned to mining Turner's data card.

Siobhan rescued Stan from deep research shortly after two o'clock. "What have you found?"

"In short, I need to run to Hendersonville and nose around a bit. Turner located several properties in Hendersonville and Asheville. One warehouse was apparently used for bootlegging during prohibition and then liquor distribution before Henderson county voted in liquor sales. He seemed to have a few other theories, but nothing we can take to authorities. Some law enforcement might even be part of their operation. There is also a family owned estate in Asheville, which gave Cunningham entry into local politics. He apparently moved up there a year before he got elected to city council. There are links to other businesses and properties not in the Cunningham name but with ties to the family."

"When do we go?" Siobhan asked, getting excited about another road trip. Having Stan home, she had already dismissed her concerns over his disappearance.

"Don't think this one will be a joint venture," Stan replied cautiously. "I have more questions than leads and don't want to put you or Flib in harm's way. Thought I might drive up tomorrow afternoon or early Friday morning to poke around Hendersonville then go to a classic car rally on Saturday."

"A classic car rally?" Siobhan asked, sincerely intrigued.

"A gentleman came into Pearl's this morning. His classic roadster was stolen. Might be able to find a lead while I'm in the area."

Siobhan studied Stan with mixed feelings. She knew she had no hold on him, not till he unwrapped his past. She had done all she could to help with that, or had she? She definitely did not want to lose him again, not to this search or something else in his past. Especially not someone lurking in the shadows of yesterday. Something Mary said earlier nagged her, "*Stan is not the same man he was before he left. We all like the new Stan better, but what if he reverts and disappears again? Are you ready to deal with that? CAN you deal with that?*"

Her hand on his shoulder and her eyes fixed on Stan's upturned face, Siobhan took a deep breath and sat at the table with him. "Have you remembered anything else since you got back? Besides the brawl in the motel room. Have you remembered anything else about us?"

Stan pushed the computer away and turned toward Siobhan. Taking her hands in his, he drew a deep breath and responded. "I have been picking up pieces, here and there, but nothing to do with you and me. Our time together seems as though it was meant to be and I don't want to lose that, or do anything to jeopardize it. I was wondering today if there wasn't someone out there who was looking for me - other than the Cunningham thugs. I've been so wrapped up in this search for Turner that I completely forgot about not having a past. You've done that for me. You've given me a life I enjoy and look forward to. I don't know what I lost, but I do know that I look forward to time with you . . . and Flib. Speaking of that devil, where is he?"

"I let him out when I got home. He looked as though his eyes were beginning to float. About you going to Hendersonville. I don't want you going alone."

"I would love your company, but I just plan to follow up on Turner's notes. He raised questions about some properties in

Hendersonville and Asheville. With an ounce of luck I can find what I need to put more pieces together. If I trip something up, this excursion could get a bit rough. We don't really know who we're dealing with, but after the trip to Georgia, we do know they don't play nice. I'll be able to move faster and react more efficiently if I don't have you or Flib to worry about."

"I don't like it!" Siobhan looked down at Stan, doing her best to hold back tears.

Recognizing her worry, Stan took Siobhan's hands and spoke with true concern in his voice. "Tell you what. I'll turn on my GPS tracker and you can follow me on your phone. You won't be able to see what I'm doing, but at least you'll know where I am. Maybe I can program a hot key to send you a text if I get in trouble and you can notify the police to come save me. Sound okay?"

"Not OKAY, but I'll accept it. Just keep in touch . . . please." She squeezed his hands, as though that might bind her safely to him.

Standing, he lifted her to a stand, then wrapped his arms around her in an embrace and kiss that assured her he was not planning to disappear again. When their lips parted, she buried her head in his chest and held him tightly.

Releasing her grip, she looked into his face and began another confession. "Mary said something today that I need to talk about with you."

"Yes?"

"First, we both really like you the way you are now, however, you changed while you were gone."

"What do you mean?" Stan asked. Bewildered, he led Siobhan to the sofa and sat where they could talk while comfortably facing one another.

"When you were here the first time, you were a bit arrogant and always on guard. It took quite a while to warm up to you because you seemed to be putting on an act . . . playing a character in a grande play. Even after you moved in with me, into the front room, there were times I felt as though you were using me. You were, and I knew it at the time, but it was nice having you around. Since you came back, you've been a lot more relaxed and I haven't seen you play your character role except once, at the bank in Knoxville . . . when we opened the safe deposit box. You were acting then, but you were playing a different person. I'd like to keep you just as you are, if we can make that happen."

Stan didn't move, he simply looked at Siobhan and mentally returned to his puzzle from earlier that day. *I pray there is no one out there I need to be worrying about.*

Chapter 13

Wanting to make the most effective use his time in North Carolina and minimize exposure to the Cunningham clan, Stan spent Thursday morning doing his own research from home. After verifying Albert David Cunningham's residential address, he shifted his online search to the Buncombe County Register of Deeds website. Researching Cunningham's residential address, he located its history as well as two other properties in his name.

Cunningham's residence had been in his family since the original owner died, more than seventy-five years ago. The family originally purchased it at auction and it had been handed down from one family member to another. It was transferred to AD Cunningham two years ago. Since moving to Asheville, he had purchased a warehouse in west Asheville and a building just off downtown, which contained offices and several small retail shops. Turner's wife rented one of these shops under the name "After Six Limited." Scant results from researching the warehouse address increased Stan's curiosity about this facility.

Content with targets in Asheville, Stan followed Turner's earlier research and ran similar searches of the name Cunningham on the Henderson County Register of Deeds website. He found only one property, the warehouse he already knew about. Checking records on this warehouse, he found a co-owner listed, JWX Enterprises, which was owned primarily by Xavier Johnson. A wider web search revealed Johnson owned multiple commercial properties, one at an address adjacent to the Cunningham warehouse. He also found a list of criminal indictments against Johnson including illegal sale of alcohol, drug marketing, unlicensed tobacco sales, and tax evasion. Stan became even more curious when he discovered that not one of eleven indictments had gone to trial. Five had been dismissed without prejudice and the remaining six had simply died without any follow-up. None included any reference to Cunningham or his properties.

Thinking he might need pictures of these properties, Stan retrieved the silver equipment case from his car. Opening the case, he found two digital cameras and three interchangeable lenses. Both cameras needed charging, so he plugged one into his USB phone charger and the other into a port on his computer. He then considered what else he might need for a weekend excursion to the North Carolina mountains and started packing.

At 10:45, Stan was ready to go, but his cameras weren't even close to fully charged. Frustrated, he considered options, then raced to his car. Digging in the center console, he found a three port USB adapter for the cigarette lighter. Plugging it in, he smiled at the little blue light shining on its surface. After retrieving his bag, computer, and cameras, which he plugged into the adapter, he went in search of Flib.

Finding his companion sleeping outside the kitchen door, Stan squatted down and began scratching his furry friend behind the ears. "I'll be gone for a couple days. You need to keep an eye on Siobhan and keep her out of trouble."

Flib stood and shook a bit. He then looked up at Stan as if to say, "Go? I'm ready. Let's get moving!"

"No, not this time. It's more important that you keep an eye on our lady. She's important and will need you around this evening when it gets quiet. She's going to worry; can't stop that, but you can keep her from getting lonely. I'll check in when I can." Stan then stood and went back through the apartment to his car, locking doors as he passed.

Flib barked once and ran around the apartment building, arriving in front as Stan started the engine. Sighing, Stan backed up and left. Looking in the rear-view mirror he saw Flib standing at the front door watching him leave.

Stan arrived at Pearl's just ahead of a fleet of cars adorned with US Army logos. By the time he reached the kitchen door there was a parade of uniforms heading to the front door.

"You got customers," Stan called, opening the kitchen door. "Siobhan, see you a minute before you get too busy?"

"Sure. You heading to Asheville?" the sullen waitress asked as she joined Stan outside the kitchen. She still did not like Stan leaving on his own.

"Yeah. Just wanted to say bye. I should be back late Saturday, if all goes well."

"And your tracker is working. I saw you leave the

apartment and head this way. Knew you were coming and fixed you a burger. You'll text me from time to time and maybe call to talk?" She then reached over to a shelf and grabbed a bag and drink, which she put into his hands. "Fries, too."

"I will, but please don't call me. Especially after hours. I'll be turning the ringer off, anyway. Don't want the phone to give away my snooping around."

"Be safe and get back here as quick as you can. PLEASE!" Siobhan pleaded, then reached up for a kiss as Mary called from the kitchen.

Kissing Siobhan with an unexpected, though brief, intensity, Stan drew away and caught his breath. "I'll be back. There's something I want to talk with you about as soon as we put this Turner problem to bed."

"SIOBHAN! LET'S GO!" Mary called, for the second time.

Stan winked and turned toward his car, letting his hand linger in Siobhan's just a second longer. Siobhan's eyes sparkled through welling tears with an alluring glow.

The drive to Asheville was uneventful, which was good because Stan was busy trying to mentally review everything he knew about Turner, Cunningham, and possibilities for his own future. He had programmed his GPS for Cunningham's residence as the first stop and at 1:51 p.m. his private thoughts were interrupted when its voice directed him to take the 240 bypass around the north side of Asheville. He didn't expect to learn anything, but felt he needed to at least make a drive-by. From I-240 he traveled north on I-26 then took the Merrimon Avenue exit.

The first mile of Merrimon Avenue was mostly commercial and offered little to impress the curious investigator. Then a lake appeared to his right and the terrain changed to indicate a more affluent neighborhood. Turning into Lakeview Park, Stan felt as though he had turned into a forest. Indeed, he was driving on a parkway, one-way lanes separated by narrow strips of forest. He chuckled to himself as he drove through Cunningham's neighborhood. This area represented wealth and comfort, not to mention power. Driving deeper, the lots grew larger in size, houses more distant from one another and more impressive. Reaching Cunningham's address, Stan found a locked gate. He could, however, see a significant brick mansion rising from luxuriant manicured greenery on the hill above. Getting out of the car, he snapped a few pictures of the gate, house, and immediate neighborhood. Surrounded by trees with lush foliage, Stan looked back to the house and imagined the valley and mountain scenery that might be visible from patios and balconies above the tree line. Satisfied, for now, with what he could see from street level, the *Lost Finder* worked his way down the hill. Stopping at the highway, he programed his next destination into his phone GPS.

A professional female voice, with a touch of seductiveness, directed him south on Merrimon, past the Grove Park Inn, all the way to downtown Asheville. He identified a tall brick building just off the heart of downtown and boldly labeled with Cunningham's name, as retail and office space. Blending with other buildings in the area, it appeared to be clean and well kept. Its architecture was an older style, in keeping with the image of this Southern Appalachian city. Unable to find a convenient place to park, he wandered around until he made his way through Beaucatcher Tunnel. Pulling off in the parking lot of the old Tunnel Road Shopping Center, he programed the GPS to take him to Cunningham's Asheville warehouse.

Stan's personal navigator directed him back through Beaucatcher Tunnel, through the heart of Asheville to Patton Avenue, then down Clingman Avenue to the River Arts District. Continuing past old warehouses converted into arts studios, he arrived at a cluster of these low buildings nestled between railroad tracks and the French Broad River, which flowed peacefully, almost lake-like, around logs and trees lodged against its banks. The investigator could not help but smile as he drove past one story buildings covered in colorful graffiti and images. He took several pictures to share with Siobhan.

When his GPS announced that he had arrived at his destination, Stan rechecked his location on the map. He could not see any numbers on buildings. Eventually finding the number he sought, hidden in the headdress of an Indian maiden and below a notice prohibiting painting on the building, Stan parked and walked up to the door. At just past three o'clock, he expected to find it locked, and sighed with relief as someone left the building, holding it open for him.

Stan thanked the person holding the door, and apprehensively stepped inside. Half expecting to find a typical space crying out for cleaning, he was surprised to find a tidy and near immaculate network of hallways leading to commercial storage units. The air was dry and comfortable, though he could not see evidence of an air-conditioning system. As he wandered around, he noticed names of local businesses, stopping when he read "After Six Limited." Curiosity carried his hand to the handle on the garage style roll-up door, but it didn't open. Checking his pockets for something to pick the lock, he reconsidered when he heard voices approaching and quickly found his way back outside. Satisfied that this warehouse was essentially a storage facility for commercial clients, he discounted thoughts that it might hold some evidence of illegal activity.

Returning to his Explorer, he checked notes on his phone and programmed his GPS for the Cunningham warehouse in Hendersonville. Expected arrival time 3:52 p.m., about 36 minutes.

Turning south, continuing in the direction he had come, Stan wondered if, and what, secrets might be hidden in the warehouse he had just left. He quit wondering when he saw a truck racing up behind him. Curving to the left as he climbed a bridge to cross multiple railroad tracks, he checked his rearview mirror and saw the distinctive black and yellow bumble bee pattern of Cunningham trucks in Georgia.

"It seems there might be secrets waiting to be discovered in that warehouse, after all," he said to himself.

With the truck riding his bumper, Stan pulled off into the parking area for the Habitat for Humanity ReStore and casually strolled inside. When he came out, forty-five minutes later, the truck was nowhere to be seen. Continuing toward Biltmore Village, per GPS instructions, Stan noticed a black and yellow pickup parked at a bar just beyond the ReStore. Turning south on highway 25, he realized how thirsty he had become. The burger and fries Siobhan had provided were tasty but that was more than five hours ago. Pulling off at a Shell station, Stan went inside for a drink and pack of crackers. When he returned to his car, five minutes later, he saw no sign of the bumble bee truck and relaxed.

Listening to his digital navigator, Stan drove south on highway 25 into the Hendersonville area. With an adjusted arrival time of 4:45, it then directed him west on a small two-lane gravel road, shrouded by trees, then north on a narrow one-lane dirt road that seemed to go nowhere. Moments later he actually arrived nowhere. The GPS announced he had reached his destination, however there was nothing there except an old dirt path disappearing into the forest, overgrown with low weeds which betrayed frequent, though light, traffic.

Stan considered his situation for only a few seconds before slipping the Explorer into four-wheel-drive and followed the tracks. After a quarter mile, the forest opened onto what appeared to be a fortified compound. A ten foot, heavy gauge chain link fence with a curl of barbed wire on top surrounded two old nondescript warehouses. A motorized iron gate, which slid sideways on rollers, controlled entry. Stan could easily see security cameras mounted on gate posts and the front of the warehouse to the right, where five vehicles were parked. Two were older black panel trucks, like bread delivery trucks. There was also one large white SUV type vehicle, one small bus that might seat twenty or so passengers, and one bumble bee pickup truck.

Satisfied he had found his destination, Stan backed down the mountain pathway, about one hundred yards, until he could turn around. He then drove into Hendersonville and called Siobhan to let her know everything was okay.

"No, nothing too exciting, yet," he assured her.

Hearing his calm voice and knowing he was okay eased some of her tension, but her voice betrayed her heart. "Just don't do anything stupid. Do you know anyone up there who might back you up?"

"What? I'm not even sure who I am; who would I know to call for backup?"

"Sorry, I forgot. Just do what you need to do and get back here. Flib misses you."

"Flib misses me?"

Hearing the unspoken question, Siobhan chortled pleasantly, "Yes, I miss you, too. What was it you wanted to talk with me about?"

"Not now and not on the phone. Look, I'm going to find something to eat. Maybe I can get out of here tomorrow. Make my way to Waynesville. Don't forget to feed our friend." Stan paused briefly, continuing in a softer voice, "Talk with you in the morning." He slowly lowered the phone and pressed the red icon to end the call.

Walking downtown Hendersonville, Stan found a local bistro where he enjoyed a hot pastrami sandwich and a cold locally brewed beer. Passing storefronts and groups of people sitting at outside tables, he made his way back to his car, thinking only about the conversation he wanted to have with Siobhan. *She is one special lady and I believe we could make it a go, long term. I just need to make sure there is nothing in my past that will cause trouble down the road. Maybe I can run by Brevard tomorrow, after I finish poking around here. Visiting that address on my driver's license could trigger some memories or something. But, that is a maybe for tomorrow. Tonight, I need to visit that warehouse again. See what goes on after dark. . . . I've got to be out of my mind!*

Driving to the warehouse, Stan listened to a voice in the back of his swiss-cheese mind, a warning from memories filled with holes, and did not turn up the first dirt road. Instead, he stayed on the gravel road, continuing past the turnoff, turned around, and parked where he could watch the dirt road without being seen. As dusk faded into dark, three cars turned up the road, one at a time but all within fifteen minutes. Stan waited until there was no traffic for at least thirty minutes, checking the time before continuing to the warehouse. 9:05 p.m.

Once again, he drove past the path into the woods, turned around, and parked close to the dirt road but still where his vehicle would not be seen. Grabbing his jacket and the better of his two cameras, he affixed a night lens, then slipped the camera and a telescopic lens into a protective carry bag. Hanging the camera bag across his shoulder, he walked cautiously up the road to the warehouse, pausing when he heard a helicopter arrive. Twenty-five yards up the path he noticed a thin red beam of light crossing the road. Looking into the trees he saw a camera trained on the roadway. Looking to the trees behind him, he found a second camera. Seeing no lights on either camera, he thought to himself, *Well, safe this time, but I'm getting too careless. At least I now know they are probably aware that I was here this afternoon. I have got to be more careful!* He then continued through the woods, about twenty feet to the side of the road.

Arriving at the warehouses, Stan found the gate closed. Building lights shown down on the three cars he had seen earlier. Four of the trucks he had seen that afternoon were still there, plus a small helicopter in front of the second warehouse. The bumble bee truck was gone. He followed the fence down to the darkened warehouse to the left and climbed over, using his jacket to cover the barbed wire at the top.

Once inside the compound, Stan crept back to the lighted area and used his phone to snap images of the helicopter and cars with their license plates. He then went looking for a way into the building. He knew using the front door would not be smart, and had already seen there were no lights showing on the left side of the building. Continuing to the right side, he could hear muffled voices. Moving more quickly, he slipped around the corner. In front of him was a warehouse wall about ten feet high and one hundred feet long. No windows, no features of any kind, and the only visible lights were coming from a crack near the roof at the back. Not willing to give up, the lost finder silently made his way to the back of the building, all the while doing his best to keep an eye on both ends of the warehouse. Peeking around the corner, his heart leapt, a door was open and light poured out. Definitely an invitation to answers; or possibly trouble.

Stan paused in the shadows before reaching the open door and listened. Hearing only faint voices, he cautiously looked inside. The first room was a large open area with a few boxes and wooden cases, then another open door to a hallway. Tight spacing of doors on the hallway seemed to paint a picture of cells rather than offices. Voices came down the hall from the other end of the building. Not sure he wanted to go down that hall, but certain he wanted to see what was going on, Stan removed the night lens from his camera and snapped on a telescopic lens. Creeping forward, he lay on the floor behind the door such that he could see down the hall, like a sniper hiding in shadows. Using the telephoto lens on his camera, he saw a comfortable, even plush, lounge area. While he was looking, a man came down the hall, dragging a young woman in a neglige. Her stumbling manner suggested she might have been drugged. Stan could not help but notice a sheer modesty panel in the shape of a "V" on the front, which really did not conceal anything. Without looking at his camera, purely by reflex, he began recording their approach. They stopped at the third door on the left, where the man forced the young woman into the room. He then locked that door and opened the next door. Going inside, he emerged with another young woman, also clad in a flimsy pastel neglige. A firm grip on her arm, he led her down the hall. Shifting his attention to the handler, Stan saw he wore a shoulder harness, suggesting this man carried a pistol in an underarm holster.

"Gently, Jimmy, don't damage the merchandise," someone snickered in a rich baritone voice. Stan thought he had heard that voice sometime in the past, but his heart was pounding too hard for him to recall when, where, or who it might be.

This girl must have been popular, because vulgar compliments were audible and two men crossed in front of the hallway, presumably for a closer look. The girl shouted obscenities, and the men laughed. She then screamed violently, followed by a muffling sound, as though something was stuffed into her mouth to quiet her. More laughter.

"Careful, gentlemen. You can do what you want after you buy; till then, it's eyes only," the baritone voice cautioned.

Stan wanted to rush down the hall to the girl's rescue. Instead, he put the camera away and quietly slipped out the back door. Feeling sick at what he had witnessed, or rather heard but did not see, he paused to draw a deep breath.

SUDDENLY MEMORIES OF A MISSION EXPLODED INTO HIS BRAIN. HE WAS TO LOCATE AND RETRIEVE INFORMATION FROM A COMPUTER, HE WAS OVERWHELMED WITH NAUSEA AS IMAGES OF DISMEMBERED BODIES IN A WAR ZONE FILLED HIS MIND. COMPLETING HIS RETRIEVAL, HE FOUND THE PATROL THAT ACCOMPANIED HIM EITHER DEAD OR MISSING. SLIPPING

Snapping back to the present, Stan slipped into a combat state of mind. Every muscle in his body went taught and he scaled the fence near the rear of the Hendersonville warehouse with ease, disappearing into the dark woods on the other side. Using incredible stealth and speed, he made his way back to his car. Coming out of the bushes just behind his vehicle, Stan froze as a man stabbed his right rear tire with an eight inch hunting knife. The tire hissing, Stan, still in a combat mode, placed his equipment on the ground and picked up a stick about the size of a baseball bat. Filled with anger about again leaving someone behind yet in full control, Stan swung the stick forcefully.

Unfortunately for Stan, the man saw him in time to raise his arm in defense. There was a loud crack as the man deflected the bat with his arm. Not yet feeling pain from broken bones, the man lunged forward with his knife. Stan jumped back, but not before the blade sliced through his jacket and shirt. Without thinking, Stan caught the assailant's arm, spun him, and grabbed his chin, yanking upward and to the side. There was a loud snap and the man fell to the ground. A few quick convulsions passed and he lay still.

Stan removed the knife from the dead man's hand, as well as a gun he found in a shoulder harness inside the man's coat. After rolling the body behind the bushes, Stan tossed the knife into the woods and retrieved his equipment. As he placed the camera bag in the back of the Explorer, his sense of combat readiness faded, allowing his muscles to relax. Instinctively, he drew several deep restoring breaths then checked how many tires had been cut. Fortunately, only the two rear tires were flat, but he had only one spare.

Pondering his next move, Stan's thoughts were overcome with a sense of wonder and remorse. *How could I have killed that man so easily? Every move was deliberate, training for hand to hand combat. But how could I take a man's life without hesitation? I have been trained to gather protected information, retrieve guarded objects, and kill. Who am I?*

Feeling something wet on his stomach, Stan's mental self-examination ended. Sitting in his Explorer, where he had light, he dropped the gun on the passenger seat and lifted his shirt. The assailant had sliced cleanly through his jacket and shirt. A cut about four inches long across his mid-section was just deep enough to bleed freely and required attention.

Digging into his travel bag, Stan retrieved a clean sock. He then looked in equipment bags kept in the back of the Explorer and found a small roll of duct tape. Folding the sock in half, he ran a strip of duct tape to hold it on the cut. "This will have to do for now," he sighed.

While putting the tape away and closing his bag, he heard a beeping from the bushes. Returning to the body of his assailant, he found a cell phone in his pants pocket. "They'll be looking for him when he doesn't answer," Stan told himself. "I've got to move."

After turning the phone off, he tossed it farther into the bushes, just to be rid of it. Then, looking at his car and the road, he began to assemble a plan to get through the night. After making sure he had not left anything on the ground, he slipped behind the steering wheel and began backing down the road, away from the warehouse access and Hendersonville.

Driving slowly, his rear tires plopping as they rolled, he found a hole in some bushes about thirty yards from where he had been parked. He backed into this area as far as he could and still view traffic using the warehouse access road. Bushes pushed against both sides of his car, further concealing his presence. Turning the engine off, he waited and pressed on the sock still soaking up blood seeping from the knife cut.

Just over an hour after he settled into the bushes, Stan saw lights coming out of the forest on the access road. Three cars left in quick succession, all heading out of the forest. Fifteen minutes later the bus left. Stan believed he saw young women on board but could not be sure. Two delivery trucks followed the bus, then the SUV came to the end of the access road and stopped. The driver rolled his window down and using a hand-held search light looked up and down the road, toward where Stan was hiding. A passenger did the same on the other side, with a second light. Not seeing anything, they turned away from Stan and continued down the road slowly, searching the forests on both sides as they passed. While the SUV continued its search, Stan heard the helicopter leave, flying toward Asheville.

"Well, that's all of them," Stan said to himself. "Still, I'd better wait a bit longer." Tapping the screen on his phone, he checked the time. 12:35 a.m. Feeling the knife cut sting just a bit, he drew a gasp of air, put his phone on the passenger seat, and pressed on the sock.

Stan waited for an hour before starting his vehicle. He had recalled seeing a flatbed tow truck at a service station, down the road toward Asheville. Knowing he could not make the entire distance on two flat tires, he reasoned he could move to a more accessible location, away from the warehouse, and walk to the service station. He rumbled down the dirt road then another quarter mile down the two lane gravel road. Finding another unused narrow lane, he backed up the path twenty - thirty yards, parked, and checked the time. 2:16 a. m.

His GPS told him the distance to the service station was just over four miles, a good two hour walk. Wanting to be at the station early, he set an alarm for five o'clock and settled in to sleep. Before he could settle, his injury notified him that it wanted attention. Using water in a partial bottle, from another trip, Stan soaked the sock to soften dried blood and peeled it off. Droplets of blood appeared along the slice. "Well, one sock won't do me any good," he mumbled to himself as he pulled the second sock from his bag. Securing the second sock across the cut with fresh duct tape, he figured he was good until he could get to a store and settled back to sleep.

Awakened at five o'clock by the alarm on his phone, Stan tucked his assailant's gun under his shirt at his back and began walking. Not a single vehicle passed him until he reached the Asheville Highway, where he turned north-east. Knowing Siobhan would be waking and would hear distress in his voice if he called, he texted her as he walked.

= = = = = = =

Eight o'clock slipped past as a tow truck driver hooked chains to Stan's car. "What were you doing up here?" the driver asked as they secured the Explorer on the flatbed.

"Would you believe a friend sent me on a 'snipe hunt'? Part of a ritual for joining a secret organization," Stan lied, convincingly.

"Yep. Not sure I've seen any snipe in these woods for nigh on twenty years. That was when we sent my little brother up to this neck-o-the-woods. We 'stole' his car, though. In addition to tires, you may need two wheel rims, as well. I looked at 'em while I hooked up the chains. Shouldn't drive on flat tires. I sure hope I got what you need."

"You and me both, sir. I do appreciate you taking the time to get me back on the road. I need to start gathering some revenge."

"Does revenge come with a knife blade?" the driver asked, pointing to Stan's shirt and the rough made bandage poking through.

"It could, I suppose. Not sure when fooling around got to be so dangerous."

"Yeah, I've had days like that. At least you had duct tape, I remember times I didn't have that. That's gonna hurt when it comes off. We get back to the station, I'll give you a proper bandage. We use a lot of 'em working around cars."

Stan and the driver swapped stories all the way back to the service station, where the owner gave him a bottle of hydrogen peroxide and a big adhesive bandage. "Turn it caddy-corner, it should fit." He then went to work on the Explorer.

Stan retrieved a clean shirt from his bag and went to the bathroom to tend to his cut. Feeling the immediate danger had passed and not knowing the history of the gun, he disassembled it and threw the pieces in a dumpster before checking on progress with repairs. He kept the clip of ammunition.

"You were lucky, young man," the owner told Stan when he showed up in a clean shirt. "Both wheels were okay . . . just barely, but okay. And I had two decent tires. Didn't have to use your spare. Should always have a good spare, you know. You'll be ready to go in just a bit."

Stan added a cold drink and packaged sandwich to his tab

at the service station. While eating, he programmed his smartphone GPS with the address from his North Carolina driver's license, which he had found in the brief case at the bus station in Knoxville. After settling with the service station owner, Stan climbed back into his vehicle. The cut on his belly twinged with pain as he scooted behind the wheel. On examination, Stan could not see any fresh blood, so he started the engine and headed for Brevard. He hadn't gone far when his digital navigator directed him to take the next right onto highway 64. Glancing at his phone he noticed the time was 10:41. Thinking Siobhan would be on break, he punched her quick-dial icon.

Chapter 14

Siobhan read Stan's text about six-thirty Friday morning, before getting dressed. "Slept in woods. Need to fix flat tire. All's well." Calling up her locator app, she saw that Stan's phone was moving. Slowly, but moving. "He didn't have a spare?" she asked herself. "Something's not right here." Looking down at the fuzzy face in front of her, she continued. "Flib, he's lying about something so I won't worry. Okay, he slept in the woods. I'll bet he has more than one flat, too. But this 'All's well' business, that's a lie. Still, he's moving so he must be okay. I can tell he's on the edge of trouble! . . . You need breakfast ."

After fixing a bowl of food for Flib, Siobhan got dressed, wondering all the while about the trouble Stan was in. She then let Flib out the kitchen door and went back through the apartment to her car. Flib ran around the building, arriving before she got the engine started, so she let him in. He was used to hanging out behind the diner.

During a brief break in the morning rush, about quarter past eight, Siobhan gave Flib a ham biscuit while she checked on Stan's location. He had not sent any updates, but he was moving. This time he was in the middle of nowhere, but moving toward a highway at a normal speed. "Must have got his flat fixed," she mumbled to Flib. She was still a bit edgy as she waited on late morning regulars.

"Good morning, I'm finally on the way to Brevard," Stan chirped when Siobhan answered his call.

"Sorry, but this has got to be kinda quick. Big group just came in for early lunch. How many flats did you have last night?" Siobhan replied, watching Mary signaling her to wait on customers.

"Too many. I must've rolled over some nails at the warehouse or a construction zone I drove through. I'll tell you more when I get back, but all's well for now."

"Okay. Mary is coming after me. When'll you be back?"

"Tomorrow afternoon. After the Classic Car Rally. It's on the way home."

"Siobhan, get off the phone and get to your customers!" Mary growled.

"I heard that. You better go. Love you," Stan chuckled.

"Yeah, me too you," Siobhan sighed as she ended the call. Dropping the phone in her apron she thought, *"All's well,"* that *has got to be a coverup for something's wrong!*

Dropping his phone in the console, Stan thought to himself, *She knows I'm lying. Not sure how, but she knows. I'll have to come clean when I get back to Oliver Springs.* Sighing, he took another bite of his sandwich and a swig of his drink.

Leaving Hendersonville, Stan encountered several small communities then a larger splash of shopping and business known as Etowah. Beyond that, the drive to Brevard was a two-lane road filled with twists and dips, large mature trees lining both sides. Auto repair shops, convenience stores, agricultural businesses, brick homes, and mobile homes dotted the scenery. Stan might have found the drive relaxing had he not been trying to simultaneously figure out answers for too many questions.

Who was that voice, that baritone? I know I've heard it before. How many girls are being sold through that warehouse? I can't call the police, Turner's notes say that the sheriff's office and local FBI may be on Cunningham's payroll. . . . Who was that baritone voice? Maybe I can work on it at home where I have better resources. I have my computer with me; I just need a good Internet connection. Feeling his belly hurt, he moaned, "I need better bandages!"

As he got close to Brevard, the scenery became more commercial; Stan even saw a Walmart. The cut on his stomach still stinging, he went in to purchase bandages and medical supplies.

Resuming his travel, the SmartPhone GPS brought him into Brevard around the south side, rather than through the center of town. Passing apartments and a middle to upper-class residential zone, he was directed around a city park. Passing a municipal swimming pool on the right, his digital companion announced, "You have arrived at your destination on left."

Trying to decide between two small brick homes, Stan rechecked the address on his driver's license. Looking at house numbers by the front doors, he realized the address he wanted was behind the two houses. Pulling into a long dirt driveway, he continued to a two-story brick home and parked. The number beside the front door was 127. Looking toward steps going up the outside of the building he saw a mailbox marked 127-B, which matched his license. Looking at his key ring, he selected the house key and climbed the steps. The key fit the door lock and Stan cautiously turned it, hearing his name called as he opened the door.

Looking down the driveway, toward the pool, Stan saw a young woman in a two-tone green swimsuit waving at him. She had a boy, about two years old, in tow. Stan went down to the driveway to meet her.

"Hello, Stranger," she chirped cheerily. She stood about five feet six inches tall and had shoulder length brown hair with auburn highlights. Her swimsuit displayed very female curves, however a bit of a baby bump caught Stan's eye. Seeing Stan's reaction, she was quick to respond. "It's not yours, though I guess it could be. No, it's not. You going to be here long this visit?"

"Not sure . . . no. I just needed to pick up some things and spend the night. Is there a problem?"

"When Billy sees your car, he's liable to come up and ask you to leave. You've been paying rent six months at a time and don't spend much time here but he thinks you an' me are foolin' around. We only had that one time, last summer after swimming. Something about a hot afternoon and wet swimsuits!" Pausing her run-on monolog, she looked hungrily at Stan. "Hmmm . . . no, I better get supper fixing. But I wanted to let you know, Billy's after you to leave." She continued looking Stan up and down and teasingly licked her lips. "Well, I better get Mickey down for his nap and figure out what I'm fixin' for supper. Watch out for Billy to come knocking as quick as he sees your car. Good to see you again."

Recalling he wanted to get on the Internet, Stan felt a faint memory and asked, "Did you ever get Internet?"

"Yeah, but you'll have to get the password from Billy. Good luck with that!"

She then disappeared into a door below the stairs. Stan

went back to his upstairs apartment. Closing the door, he took inventory. One big room with a kitchenette, small table with four chairs, a living area with a sofa, television, and coffee table. Two doors off the main room. Looking in the door to the right, he found a bathroom. The door to the left led to a small bedroom with a double bed, chest of drawers, and a closet on the wall next to the bath. All in all, not a bad apartment for a single person or young couple.

The closet had two pairs of khaki slacks, three long sleeve sport shirts, and a pair of shoes - cross-trainer style. A chest of drawers had a few shirts, underwear, socks and other meager belongings. Moving to the kitchen, Stan checked the refrigerator, an older model with the ice box inside. Half a dozen eggs, a carton of spoiled milk, one stick of butter, half a loaf of moldy bread, and one bottle of beer. One and a half trays of ice in the freezer section.

Opening the beer and taking a gulp, he continued to check kitchen cabinets and found a small assortment of pots, pans, plates, etc. Stepping back toward the door, Stan scanned the apartment looking for a hiding place. What might he have left here for safekeeping? *Heat vents are next to the floor, not a likely place.* Checking the bathroom, he found a heater in the wall, similar to Siobhan's, but there was nothing hidden there and it worked. Cliche as it seemed, he even checked the toilet tank, full of water. Returning to the bedroom he checked all the drawers in the chest before getting a chair from the dining table and checking the top of the closet. To his surprise, there was a removable panel in the ceiling, about two feet square.

Lifting the panel to the side, Stan used the flashlight on his phone to look into the hole. It was just that, a dark hole. Sliding the panel back into place he felt a string tickle his arm. Removing the panel again and setting it on the floor, the finder climbed back on the chair and carefully pulled on the string. After pulling about eighteen inches of string, a box appeared at the edge of the opening. Stan removed the box, which was an old shoe box, men's cross-trainers size nine. Looking inside, he found two bundles of cash, a pistol, a full box of ammunition, and a passport in his name.

Stan stored the box, and its contents, as well as the clip from his attacker's gun, in the chest of drawers, then replaced the hidden panel and cleaned up behind himself. Placing the chair back at the dining table, Stan felt a burning pain. All the stretching and twisting he had been doing caused his cut to cry out for immediate attention.

After removing his shirt, Stan spread the supplies from Walmart on the kitchen table. Gritting his teeth, he pulled off the bandage applied earlier at the service station. The slice bled only lightly. While cleaning the cut, he pondered going to an emergency clinic, but decided he really did not want to deal with questions that would come with dressing this type of wound. After mopping the area with alcohol, he applied a generous amount of antibiotic cream and multiple large bandages, enough to hold the cut closed and absorb any bleeding that might follow. All things of urgent nature taken care of, Stan laid down on the bed and quickly fell asleep.

Waking three hours later, Stan realized how hungry he was and made ready to go find supper. Halfway down the stairs, he was stopped by a muscular young man stomping deliberately up the stairs. This stern-faced man wore a mechanic's uniform bearing the dealer name "Egolf of Brevard" over the left pocket. Over the right pocket was his name, "Billy," and title, "Service Manager."

Jaws locked and eyes focused on Stan, Billy growled hostilely, "I want you gone. You can stay the night, but be gone with all your stuff TOMORROW!"

Stan smiled politely. "No problem. Should I just leave the key in the mailbox? I may be leaving rather early."

Backing down the stairs, the landlord relaxed a bit, becoming more professional. "Sure. Where do I send your rent refund?"

"Don't worry about it. . . . No, let somebody who needs a bed stay for the rest of my paid up time. Is that okay?"

"I'm not going to let some bum sleep in my house!"

"No, but there are a lot of folks down on their luck in need of a smile and an opportunity. You got several churches in this town, two at the top of the hill, as I recall. Ask them for a name. You'll be glad you did." Seeing Billy was stunned by his comment and still carrying a lot of anger, Stan abandoned thoughts of the Internet. "Now, if you don't mind, I was heading out to get something to eat."

"Yeah, sure." The man finished backing down the stairs and stepped out of the way. "Tomorrow!"

Stan waved as he walked toward his car. "No problem! Thanks for the hospitality."

Daylight was struggling to push the night away on Saturday as Stan redressed the cut on his stomach. There was no bleeding but the cut was a bit red and very tender. Satisfied the bandage would get him through the day, he stuffed his clothes and the shoe box into a sports bag he purchased at Wal-Mart the night before. Grabbing a breakfast biscuit and coffee at a local McDonalds, he turned into Pisgah Forest on highway 276. Fortunately he finished his biscuit before encountering the endless twists and turns that took him over the mountain. Highway 276 crosses the mountains through Pisgah National Forest and there is no commercial signage, no business, and very few homes for almost thirty miles. It is primarily pristine forest. Without traffic, this road was fun to drive and took his mind off the cries of the girl in the Hendersonville warehouse.

Arriving at the Smokey Mountain Event Center with the early birds, he searched for a fresh cup of coffee. The rally was set up in the Richland Creek Meadows section of the fairgrounds, where there were no permanent facilities. Port-a-johns had been lined up on one side and food trucks were still arriving. Stan walked up to the one food truck already open for business.

"You got coffee?"

"Just drew the first cup. Fresh and hot." The vendor replied as he took a sip from his own mug. "You want large or huge?"

"Large will be fine, thank you." Stan chuckled at the sizing of the cups. The large was actually only twelve ounces, which was plenty.

Having no recollection of ever attending a road rally, Stan marveled at how two distinct worlds quickly developed. Walking away from the food trucks, he saw part of the pasture filling with cars setup for display. The second world gathered around a rally tent, between the parking and display areas, and was already busy checking in drivers for the touring event. Drivers and navigators chatted with other teams as many tinkered with their engines or programed the route into rally apps on their phones. One older couple still used an old rally "computer," which actually just tracked mileage and time.

Stan watched as cars were inspected and certified for the event. They were then lined up according to check-in times. The first car started the course at 8:25 a.m., heading in the opposite direction of incoming traffic. After watching the first three teams leave, at three minute intervals, he returned to the show grounds area, which was rapidly filling with cars proudly put on display.

Sipping at his coffee, Stan strolled through rows of antique roadsters, celebrated touring models, even a few modern adaptations of old classics. Some were professionally restored, others obviously done by amateurs in home garages. Owners displayed pride and enthusiasm when talking about their vehicles. Surrounded by their energy and excitement, Stan felt himself falling headlong into this world, until he saw a group of young women touring the displays. They reminded him of the warehouse and then, why he was at this rally. With a heavy heart he resumed looking for the stolen Salmson.

Late in the morning, about 10:30, Stan bumped into Ferguson and his son, who were also browsing and drooling over classic autos. They talked as they wandered together around the show. Neither had any news about Ferguson's missing coupe. Ready to get home, Stan reluctantly agreed to keep looking and said his farewells.

Returning to his car, Stan noticed a man dressed as an old brit, standing next to a classic racing green MG roadster. Curious, he strolled over and asked about the car, which had a "For Sale" placard on the front windshield. Stan examined the car while talking with the "brit."

"You just had it painted," Stan observed.

"Yes, sir. The final touch on a long and expensive restoration. Far more costly than I had ever imagined or was prepared for. I fear this may not be the hobby it once was." The man spoke with a British accent, however Stan thought it was a put-on.

Continuing his examination, Stan found a brass ID plate in an obscure location. It identified the car as Ferguson's stolen Salmson.

"How much you asking?" Stan asked, hatching a plan to recover the vehicle.

"I must have twenty-five thousand American, just to cover my costs."

"Hmm, that's a bit rich. I could go twenty. I have five thousand on hand as a deposit."

"No. I could not dip below twenty-four."

"Twenty-two five?" Stan countered, realizing he was about to win.

"Twenty-three, including your five on deposit, balance on Monday and it is yours. If you have a check, I might be able to verify it here and now. You can drive this classic home today. I would have to hold the registration papers until funds were actually received."

Seeing Ferguson and his son heading for their car, Stan agreed to the deal. "Sure. Let's do that. Look, I see some friends of mine. Let me grab them to drive my car home and I'll get my checkbook."

Rather than scream out to Ferguson, Stan used his cell phone. When they arrived at the car, Stan gave Ferguson's son the keys to his Explorer, whispering, "I saw several policemen near the registration area; we need their help, but I don't want to alert this thief. Find them and tell them what's going on. Suggest they approach like you were caught breaking into my car." As the boy started to walk away, Stan called, "Checkbook's in the center console, not the glove box."

Seeing Ferguson recognize the car, Stan turned away from the brit and spoke softly. "Brad, I've never really worked on a car like this and I believe there are a few flaws in his restoration. Do you think you can help me bring it back to it to its true glory?"

"Sir," the brit interjected in his artificial accent, "we all like to put our personality into our cars, but there is nothing wrong with this one."

Brad rolled his eyes and examined the car in detail, becoming more sickened each time he found a detail painted over in green. Rising from the engine compartment, he turned to Stan and saw his son returning with two police officers, one on either side as though he had been caught doing something wrong. Brad immediately understood what was happening and sighed with relief. "That really is an atrocious paint job."

Stan stood close behind the brit as Brad Ferguson showed the police a copy of the flyer he had printed up and his registration and title for the stolen car. In less than ten minutes the police had the thief in handcuffs, who protested claiming, "I bought this vehicle at auction two years ago!" He continued blabbering as he was led away.

Depressed over the work facing him to restore the Salmson to its unspoiled condition, Ferguson was still delighted to have his car back. He wrote Stan a check, which Stan folded and put in his pocket without looking at it. He smiled as Brad's son examined every detail of the car.

Walking back to his Explorer, Stan gazed across the meadow, the cars on display, and rally cars still leaving to run the course. Thinking back on earlier conversations, he thought to himself, *This could be fun. The people are nice and driving these hills would be a treat with Siobhan as navigator. This is a world I've never experienced, at least I don't think I have. It could be fun . . . some day . . . right now, I have bigger problems.*

Chapter 15

Stan left Waynesville shortly after local police took the thief away. Driving to Oliver Springs, he thought about the girls in the warehouse and about Siobhan. He silently expressed thanks that she was not put in any danger as a partner on this excursion and was glad to be heading home to her. His mind was at a loss, however, as to what to do about the warehouse situation. *What would an Army Intelligence Officer do?* he asked himself repeatedly. His answer was always the same. *I don't have the resources of the Army or Marines to call on and somebody inside the FBI is part of this.* Frequent twists and turns of Interstate 40 helped refocus his anxiety as he wound his way through the mountains, from North Carolina back to Tennessee.

Arriving home, he was delighted to find Flib waiting outside the front door. Stopping to scratch his friend's neck, he felt good to be home. Stepping inside the apartment, his senses were aroused by a complex array of aromas. Siobhan had prepared a dinner of roast chicken, asparagus, fresh stuffing, tossed green salad, and dinner rolls. Smells of chicken and rolls set Stan's appetite dancing with anticipation. Flib slipped past him as he stood in the doorway.

Hearing Stan come inside, Siobhan emerged from her bedroom, dressed in a sheer lavender chiffon dress. Freshly styled hair bounced on her shoulders and her eyes had an intoxicating sparkle.

Blown away by her beauty, Stan forgot to breathe. Enjoying the vision before him, he finally drew a breath. "I'm going to have to go off more often if this is the way I'm greeted when I come home," he chuckled, a smile brightening his weary face.

"Oh? You see something you like?" Siobhan replied, her voice flowing with a cool smoothness that heightened Stan's desires.

In the next beat of his pounding heart, Stan forgot all his problems, all his reservations, and all his inhibitions melted. He took Siobhan into his arms and kissed her, releasing all his pent-up passions.

Their embrace carried them into Siobhan's bedroom where she proceeded to remove Stan's shirt, gasping when she saw the bandage across his stomach. Her manner immediately jumped from seductive to demanding. "Okay, what happened!?"

Stan took a deep breath and replied as calmly and reassuringly as possible. "Just a little run in with a mountaineer. It's okay. I'm okay. Wasn't there something else you were interested in?" He bent over and began kissing and nibbling on her neck; his fingers undoing her dress.

Seeing no blood or reason to pursue the conversation at that moment, Siobhan yielded to Stan's passionate advance. "I want the entire story, later!" she sighed, yielding to her own desires.

Supper was delayed two hours and a bit cold. To their surprise, Flib had snatched only one dinner roll and was not apologetic about it. The chicken was resting in the oven.

"We found Ferguson's car in Waynesville," Stan commented as they sat to their table. "He was none too happy watching the police load it onto a carrier. They said it'd be documented as evidence and he could probably pick it up toward the end of next week."

"Not to be out of line, but did you collect a reward?" Siobhan asked, briefly stroking Stan's hand.

"He wrote a check. I haven't looked at it. I'll do a mobile deposit tomorrow."

"What about your 'run in' with a mountaineer and spending the night in the woods?"

"I went to investigate a Cunningham warehouse, after dark. When I got back to the car, one of their goons was slashing my tires. He came at me with his knife before I could stop him."

"How bad is it? REALLY!"

"A slice. Not too deep or long. Doesn't need stitches, but after our 'exercise' it is a bit tender."

"I want to see it, after supper. Something tells me it's a bit worse than a simple 'slice'."

"That's fine. I need to change the bandage anyway."

"So, did you find out anything in your snooping?"

"Yes, however I want to review some camera footage before we talk about it."

"Camera footage?"

"Yeah. One of the cameras in the equipment case we found in the Explorer does video recording. I hope the audio is decent.

Something for me to explore tomorrow."

"What about Brevard? Any new revelations there?"

"I got kicked out of my apartment!" Stan laughed. "Seems I might have had a fling with the lady of the manor and her husband didn't want it to happen again. Not even sure it happened the first time."

"You'd forget something like that?" Siobhan's voice was filled with doubt.

"I couldn't even remember their names! His was 'Billy.' Said so on his shirt. And I found a hidden surprise."

Siobhan stopped eating and waited. "Yes?"

"I had apparently stashed a shoe box with a bit of cash and a gun in the ceiling. A pocket Glock. Small but effective. Designed for concealed carry. Not sure why I hid it there but sure glad I found it."

"Okay. Now you have a gun. Not real happy about that, but I suppose you might need it. How much money?"

"Two bundles of mixed twenties and hundreds. I haven't had time to count it. Again, something for tomorrow. Maybe you can count it while I check out the camera." Stan paused, took a couple bites of chicken, and stared at Siobhan, who again wore her lavender chiffon dress. "Have I told you how beautiful you are tonight?"

Siobhan blushed brilliantly.

While cleaning the kitchen, Stan bumped his injured stomach into the counter. Seeing him wince, Siobhan stopped and marched him into the bathroom. Stan gingerly grabbed the edge of the bandage, then pulled quickly but carefully. The slice was red and angry, showing early signs of an infection.

"You have more bandages?" Siobhan asked, without any sympathy.

"Yeah. I bought an entire box. And some antibiotic, which doesn't seem to be working."

"Go get it, while I finish cleaning up, but DON'T put a new bandage on yet! I want to see what you're using."

Stan dug the medicines from his overnight bag while Siobhan washed pans and dishes, leaving them to drip dry.

Meeting in the bathroom after fifteen minutes, Siobhan looked at his off-brand antibiotic and tossed it in the trash can. Handing him a hand towel, she advised, "You'll want to put this below the cut." As soon as Stan complied, she washed the wound with hydrogen peroxide. As the slice fizzled, she washed it again. After daubing it dry with a gauze pad, she handed Stan a tube of name brand antibiotic. "Use plenty of this. Don't know why but the cheap stuff never quite works." Giving him a bandage, she kissed him affectionately. "I need to dry the dishes and put them away."

Siobhan woke in a much improved mood Sunday morning. Slipping out of bed quietly so Stan could sleep, she climbed into the shower. While rinsing her hair, she felt his arms wrap around her. After a bit of play, she reached down and removed Stan's bandage, which was now falling off. The redness had faded.

"Make sure you rinse it with hydrogen peroxide and use the good stuff." After kissing him, she stepped out of the shower.

While Siobhan was at work, Stan fixed a light breakfast of sausage and eggs, which he shared with Flib before setting to work transferring recordings from his camera to his computer. Watching the video, he again became sickened by the girl's cries. Determined to do something to move this case forward, he began analyzing voices. While the video was excellent, the audio lacked a great deal in quality. He could make out multiple voices and their words were understandable, but that was about the extent of it.

Wanting to clean up the audio quality, Stan searched the web for utilities. Not of a mind to invest in an audio editor that promised everything yet delivered nothing, he focused his search on "free" and "free trial" utilities. After two hours of searching and testing, he downloaded a stripped down tool called "Clean Stream." While all other utilities could add effects, backgrounds, and fancy enhancements, this one did essentially one thing: it removed background noises, resulting in a cleaner audio stream. The trial version was limited to a sixty-second sample and would not save the result. Stan was impressed enough to pay the $59.95 for a full version, which also came with a second utility for split screen comparison of multiple streams. Forty-five minutes into cleaning the audio stream from his camera, Stan was interrupted by a phone call from Siobhan.

"You busy?"

"Not too busy to take a break. How are things at Pearl's?"

"Slow, today. I just wanted you to know that I enjoyed last night, but I don't like you running off alone. You come back injured."

"Sometimes it has to be done. I don't want to put you in harms way."

Siobhan paused, then asked, "Have you deposited that check?"

"No. Suppose I should do that before it gets lost. I need another cup of coffee, too. Do you deliver?"

Siobhan paused again, then chuckled. "Nope. Dine in only. We just got a group of customers. Love you."

"I love you, too. See you soon."

Stan then went in search of the check from Ferguson. He found it still in his shirt pocket on the floor in Siobhan's room. Unfolding it as he returned to the kitchen table, he smiled and showed it to Flib. "$5,000 - not bad for a half-day's work!"

Completing the steps to deposit the check, he recalled taking pictures of license plates. Using a site he found on the "dark web," Stan quickly identified a single owner for all three cars. JWX Enterprises. It took a little longer to track down the owner of the helicopter. Using images from web searches, he found it was privately owned by a pilot who flew corporate executives around the mountains, Terrence Bascomb.

Stan rocked back in his chair and pondered aloud. "No direct links to Cunningham. We know JWX is dirty and helicopters don't have to file flight plans. Easy pickup at Cunningham's house and back again. I wonder if the neighbors hear anything they'll talk about? Then . . . how do you get to the neighbors?"

Stan's pondering was interrupted when Flib pawed at his leg. "I suppose you want to go out for a stroll? At's okay, I never got a coffee refill. Thanks for reminding me." After letting the dog out the kitchen door, he fixed another cup of coffee.

Settling back to the table, Stan isolated the two recordings of the baritone voice. "Gently, Jimmy, don't damage the merchandise." "Careful, gentlemen. You can do what you want after you buy; till then, it's eyes only." After studying the clips for fifteen minutes, he selected "you can do what you want" and loaded it into the comparison tool. He then went to the recordings from phone calls intercepted by Turner and loaded them into the tool, one at a time. Two and a half hours later, Siobhan broke his concentration when she began rubbing his shoulders.

"What are you doing?" she asked.

"Comparing voices. Trying to identify a voice I heard in that warehouse." Stan was obviously frustrated.

"Any luck?"

"Not really. Nothing we could take to court, anyway. I see similarities but no positive matches. If I had better samples or a better utility that could run comparisons without my eyes and ears, I might find something. The one I bought online this morning can compare only two streams at a time. It looks for a match and doesn't pick up similarities. They have to be fairly close."

"Who do you think it is and where did you get the sample you're trying to match?"

"The sample is from the warehouse, Thursday night. Who? Don't know. I'd like it to be Cunningham, but can't say it is with any certainty."

"You going to tell me about this warehouse?"

"Yeah, in a little bit. I need lunch."

"Lunch was over a long time ago. I'll see what I can fix ya. Where's Flib?"

"I let him outside a couple hours ago, I guess."

Siobhan opened the kitchen door. Flib wasn't there. Stepping out into the yard, she looked around. Not seeing their four-legged companion, she called loudly, "FLIB!" There was no response and Flib did not appear. Looking back into the kitchen she told Stan, "I'm gonna go find Flib."

"Hold up, I'll go with you. I'll go out the front and meet you around the end." Stan then pushed away from the table and hustled out the front door. His cut failing to stretch as he moved, pain streaked across his stomach. He pressed it briefly with his hand.

Siobhan met Stan at the end of their building. Seeing heightened concern on her face, Stan tried to relieve her worry. "He can take care of himself." His voice was calm but his heart was racing.

Siobhan glared at Stan then took action on her own. "I'm going down to the highway. You can come if you want."

Fear mounting with each step, their eyes constantly scanned the area until they reached the road that connected the apartments to the highway, about thirty-five yards from their apartment. Before they could take another step, a car sped past them, leaving a cloud of dust and dirt. Stan started to yell at the driver for being reckless, but stopped when he saw the North Carolina license plate.

Looking back to where the car came from, Siobhan noticed a clump of golden fur beneath a bush. Her heart pounded as she raced across the yard. Squatting down next to a bush, she sighed with relief as Flib looked at her then quickly turned his head back to the road. "Found him!"

Stan immediately joined her. "What was he doing here?"

"I don't know. I found him just lying here like a sphinx looking off that way." Siobhan pointed through the bush. A bit of dust was still floating on the side of the road less than twenty feet away. Undaunted by Siobhan's petting, Flib continued to watch the car that had just sped away.

When the car was out of sight, Flib got up and led Stan to the Explorer, where he sat by the front left tire. Stan looked in the wheel well and saw nothing. Seeing Flib tapping his front feet and growing impatient, Stan felt the well with his hand and found something new. Looking again, he found a magnetic disk and popped it loose. About the size of a fifty-cent piece, the device was camouflaged to match the undercoating of the wheel well. Pondering the find for a moment, he dropped it on his seat and told Siobhan, "I'll drop it off somewhere, later."

Seeing a neighbor's utility truck, she suggested, "What about somebody who drives all over the region without going anywhere?" She then pointed to the van labeled Highland

Telephone Cooperative. "He'll definitely keep them guessing."

Laughing, Stan checked the device again to make sure it was not explosive, then put it in the rear left wheel well of the van. "You're devious!" he chuckled as they all went back inside.

"So, what aren't you telling me about this warehouse?" Siobhan asked before Stan got back to his computer.

Looking at his coffee cup and realizing its contents were cold, Stan asked, "What do we have to drink? Something cold?"

Siobhan sighed and went to the refrigerator. Looking inside she reported, "Not much. Two cans of beer, an old Diet Rite cola, a pitcher of ice tea - not sure how old, and an almost empty bottle of wine."

Stan walked over and looked over her shoulder. "Ice water." After retrieving a glass, he filled it with ice from the freezer and water from the tap. "You want one?"

"No, I'm good. What about the warehouse?" Siobhan insisted.

Taking a gulp of water, Stan relented. "Let's sit down, more for me than you." After settling on the sofa, he answered Siobhan's question. "Cunningham Corporation co-owns two warehouses in the woods outside of Hendersonville. JWX is the other co-owner. They are using one of the warehouses for sex trafficking. I watched as a young girl was hauled out of a locked cubicle and put on display. Two men examined and apparently fondled her quite a bit. I couldn't see that part. She was rather vocal about telling them to keep their hands to themselves, as was the proprietor, whom I never saw but heard. His is the voice I've been trying to match."

"How many girls?"

"Don't know. I only saw two, but there were a dozen or more cubicles. Doors with padlocks on a long hall between me and the 'viewing lounge.' As near as I could make out, there were three buyers, one host, one rather large and armed handler, and several drivers - whom I believed to be armed. And I didn't have a gun at that time. When they left, I could see girls in a bus and believe more were in two delivery trucks."

"Did you call the police?"

"Not on your life. I'm certain the local sherif's office is in on this business and we know someone in the FBI is too. Who do I call?"

"But you now have pictures. Evidence!"

"Yes, but evidence against who? We only have our suspicions and nothing to support them one way or the other."

"How old were these girls?" Siobhan's face was growing pale.

"I only saw the two. They couldn't have been more than sixteen. Possibly much younger."

Siobhan looked at Stan for a few seconds before running into the bathroom. Stan heard her vomiting and coughing. After washing her face, she returned. "What can I do to help you stop this?"

"Short of calling the US Marine Corps, I don't have a plan. We need rock-solid evidence and law enforcement we can trust. We have neither."

"So what are your plans?"

"Right now, find more voice recordings of Albert Cunningham and see if I can get a match, or at least some confirmation that it was him I heard. Then I guess I need to get some evidence on the guy or a pattern of activity around that warehouse. When are they 'open for business'?"

"Turner's notes don't have anything you can use?"

"Don't think so. Near as I can figure, I've caught up with him, reached the end of his investigation, so to speak. I'm now where he was when he disappeared."

"Well, don't just sit here drinking water, get to work. We have young girls to save!" Siobhan then stood and put her hand out to help Stan to his feet. Seeing Stan wince again, she suggested, "How about I fix you a sandwich while you change your bandage? Then you get back to work."

Chapter 16

Stan lost no time searching for voice recordings of Albert Cunningham. He found an abundance of samples through WLOS-TV, the Asheville ABC news station, covering the Cunningham campaign for city council and a few on YouTube. Realizing that the quality of his camera recording was not the best, he focused on finding a recording where Cunningham said the words "you can do what you want," or something similar. This was the phrase he had been using as his test model. He was delighted when he found a news clip where Cunningham said, "Tell me what you want the city to do for you and I'll see that it gets done!"

Loading the key words, "what you want," into his audio comparison utility, Stan held his breath while listening intently. His ear said they were the same, identical, however the computer result was a disappointing 65% probable match. Good, but not good enough. Accepting he was not going to get a voice match, Stan went in search of a link between Cunningham and JWX Enterprises. This search had been fruitless before and was again. The only thing he could prove at this point was that both JWX Enterprises and Cunningham co-owned a compound with two warehouses in the mountains outside Hendersonville, NC. Digging up the county records on this property again, his disappointment grew. The Cunningham on the Register of Deeds record was listed as "Cunningham, et al.", with the same postal address as JWX Enterprises. No direct link to A. D. Cunningham other than the names were spelled the same.

Frustrated by his lack of progress, Stan entered "Cunningham, et al." in the Google search bar. Enticed by an instant return, he was just as quickly disappointed when it was ninety-one million hits. Several men and women named Cunningham wrote articles for medical journals. They included associates who assisted in preparing the articles as "et al." Willing to try again, he added "asheville" to the search phrase and narrowed the return to 540,000. Most of these seemed to be delinquent tax notices for owners with "et al." in names of the registered owners. About to give up, he stumbled across a recent article about Albert Cunningham in the Asheville Citizen-Times gossip column.

Are there wedding bells on the horizon for Asheville's favorite councilman, Al Cunningham? While not in council chambers, Mister Cunningham has been keeping company with the elegant Gwendolyn Turner, owner of After Six Limited - attire for the discriminating lady. Discriminating indeed, for Mrs. Turner has recently filed for divorce at the Buncombe County Courthouse. But where is her husband? According to undisclosed sources, the elusive Mister Turner has been AWOL for more than two months. Mister Cunningham is one of Asheville's more delectable bachelors and you can bet we'll be watching this one!

"Siobhan, look at this," Stan called after reading the gossip.

Siobhan stood beside him and read the text on his computer screen. "So, we're not the only ones who can't find Mister Turner. I wonder if she really knows but won't say anything to the press. Could be bad for the image of a woman like that to actually 'misplace' a husband."

"Good point. I wonder if we've been going about this from the wrong angle. We need to see what she knows . . . or doesn't know."

"Ask her," Siobhan replied, turning toward the kitchen and thinking about supper.

"Sure. Just walk into her store and ask," Stan retorted.

"Why not?"

"Have you forgotten? She is a front for the Cunningham cartel and is laundering money for them. Turner absconded with half-a-million dollars floating through the After Six accounts and is now being hunted by gangsters who want their money back! They've got to be watching her store, not to mention her house and that run-in at the hotel and being thrown into a boxcar. I wouldn't get within two blocks of her shop before being grabbed by their henchmen."

Siobhan pulled the last can of Diet Rite soda from the refrigerator and popped it open. As the fizzle subsided, she replied, "No, but I could."

"What are you thinking?" Stan was intrigued and turned away from his computer to pursue this conversation.

"I could go in as a customer and nose around. Try to get her talking . . . I'm good at getting people to talk."

"Too dangerous, but a good idea. You can't go in alone. We need someone to go with you. Reckon Mary would like to play?"

"Not on your life! She wouldn't be caught dead in a place like that. I'll take Flib!"

"Flib can't protect you . . . exactly . . . but he could carry a camera so I could watch from the car. And he could make a fuss if needed, couldn't you boy?"

Having heard his name in the conversation, Flib sat up and sauntered over to Stan, who reached out with both hands to scratch his chin.

"This might work. I could wire you for sound and video and do the same with Flib. It would take me a few days to collect the equipment and we'd need to get Flib cleaned up, a bit. This might just work."

"Hear that Flib? You and I get to be real life spies!" Siobhan snickered as she crossed the kitchen and began loving on the dog.

Stan went to work Monday morning, searching online for tiny cameras that would broadcast a signal at least two blocks. Finding a store in nearby Oak Ridge that boasted spy cams as a specialty, he drove to their store that afternoon. The image painted on the internet was of a pristine, high-tech store with "all the latest gadgets and creative personnel who could solve your trickiest surveillance problem." What Stan found was a twelve foot by sixteen foot shed behind a lower-middle class house in a questionable neighborhood. Its proprietors were an old man, in his late sixties, and his grandson. The old man seemed to have considerable experience placing cameras where they didn't belong and his grandson knew exactly which equipment had what capabilities and advantages. After forty-five minutes and five hundred dollars, Stan had what he felt would work.

On the way home, Stan stopped by a pet store and purchased an elaborate collar for Flib. This leather strap was mounted with sparkle from one end to the other and included a "diamond encrusted" name tag. The "diamonds" were sparkly dust glued to a black tag, which Stan elected to not have engraved.

Tuesday morning, Stan went to work hiding microphones and cameras. The tag on Flib's new collar was shaped like a dog bone and measured 1 ½ inches by 5/8 inches. The camera lens with imbedded microphone was a black circle measuring 3/8 inch across. Stan drilled a hole through the center of the tag, just big enough to feed a thin black wire through it. He fed the wire along the s-hook holding the tag to the collar and fixed the camera in place with a spot of tacky glue. Satisfied the camera was not obvious amidst the sparkle of the tag, he went to work on the collar. The collar was two layers of thin leather, the inner layer protecting the animal's neck from all the spangly studs mounted on the outer layer. Using a razor blade, Stan sliced a small grove in the inner collar to hold the camera transmitter. To any casual eye, the camera apparatus would be invisible.

Siobhan had given him a floral broach, measuring 1 1/4 inches in diameter, to hide her camera. It had jeweled petals and stem coming off a golden center. The old man at the camera shop recommended a "jeweled" camera to match women's jewelry. Stan paid the extra ten dollars for a silver toned unit. After carefully removing the golden center of Siobhan's broach, he inserted the silver camera. It looked somewhat odd at first, but on second look the lens did disappear into the broach. Understanding that this camera would most likely be hidden in jewelry, the grandson had provided a smaller transmitter that fit neatly around the backside of the broach.

Stan's next task was to test his new spy cameras. Both units transmitted to a single relay unit which Siobhan could carry in her handbag. Initial tests around the apartment worked better than expected; providing clear images and excellent sound. When he took Flib outside for a "field test," he ran into trouble. Both cameras had to be within fifteen feet of the relay unit, which Siobhan would be carrying. If Flib wandered too far, his connection was lost.

Part of the observation package was a "home unit," a portable receiver and recorder which had to be within two blocks of the relay unit. When they took everything outside, they found Siobhan could go nearly a quarter mile before Stan's home unit lost reception. Everything was going according to design and looked great until Flib trotted across the parking lot. The tag jiggled and twisted, sending images that nearly made Stan seasick. Siobhan provided a piece of black floral wire, which Stan wrapped around the tag, s-hook, and collar. Once stabilized, Flib's camera provided excellent images with minimal distracting movement. The one potential drawback was the floral wire kept the tag from dangling. It hung somewhat loose, but when Flib sat and looked up, the camera tended to follow the angle of his head. If anyone were watching him, this might be conspicuous. Siobhan's camera never posed any problems during tests. Stan also added a miniature receiver Siobhan could hide in her ear, so he could talk to her privately.

Wednesday evening Siobhan and Stan worked out a cover story and picked out the best dress Siobhan had in her closet. Modeling the outfit, she looked positively elegant, except for the handbag. Stan didn't see any problem with what she had, however he did agree to purchase a new fashionable mini-bag on the way to Asheville. Flib didn't appreciate the collar but co-operated.

Before leaving Pearl's on Thursday, Siobhan told Mary she wouldn't be in on Friday and should be back Saturday morning.

"Where you going this time?" Mary growled, trying to not show concern.

"Stan and I want to go shopping."

"You can't go on your day off?"

"No, we want to take advantage of a special sale. He's going to buy me a new dress and accessories."

"New dress, huh. I'll get one of the other girls to cover for you. You better have your fanny in here Saturday! Bright and early!"

Stan rented an SUV - Crossover for the excursion and the threesome took off as soon as Siobhan got home. Their first stop was an upscale women's apparel shop in Knoxville for a handbag, then over the mountain to North Carolina. Unable to find a Motel-6 near Asheville, Siobhan used her smartphone to book them into a Holiday Inn west of the city for the evening. Feeling confident and anonymous with a rental car, Stan took Siobhan to a bistro in the River Arts District. She saved a considerable portion of her dinner for Flib, who was left to guard the car. After dinner, Stan drove them past the painted warehouses he had found on his previous visit. Siobhan was impressed by the local art.

Having reviewed their plan three times Friday morning, twice in the hotel and once while driving into town, Stan parked the car a little more than one block from After Six. Taking a deep breath, he got out and walked around to the back door on the passenger side. Dressed in a black suit and standing formally erect, he opened the door. Siobhan stepped out, followed by Flib. After winking at Stan, she walked away with Flib strutting at her side. Stan quickly returned to the driver's seat and watched on his monitoring station, which sat on the front passenger seat.

Siobhan walked through a small park, which included an ornate fountain, enjoying the shade of redbud trees lining the walkway. Reaching the street, she looked across at a museum, then crossed and turned left. Walking casually toward her destination, she lingered a few seconds to look into a business where "bean to bar luxurious chocolate" was being poured into molds and churns produced "frozen perfection" ice cream. Her mouth watering slightly, she continued, lingering again to look at books in the window of the next store. Flib looked up at her, sniffing the air several times as they strolled toward After Six Limited.

Seeing Siobhan browse display windows of After Six before approaching the door, which was inset about six feet from the front of the building, a doorman quickly granted her unobstructed access. Flib paused at the door and did a quick examination of this man who let them in. He was tall, large in his torso, well dressed, and needed a shave. When the man looked down, Flib moved on to catch up with Siobhan.

Ten feet inside the shop, Siobhan stopped, removed her dark glasses, and surveyed the sparsely populated racks of gowns. Polished chrome and mirrored displays lined the walls, each elegantly presenting only a sample. Eight carousels of less expensive apparel were scattered around the front of the store. The rear of the store was a seating area featuring plush sofas and chairs, where shoppers with appointments could comfortably view models showing off selected gowns. Flib stood attentively at Siobhan's side, studying each of the other six people in the store, one at a time.

"Dogs are not allowed! You'll have to leave it outside," a woman announced with an air of disdain.

"Oh?" Siobhan replied with surprise. "Franz is not only allowed but welcomed in Beverly's on Rodeo Drive." With her own air of heightened superiority, she turned and started to leave. "Come, Franz. They don't want our money here. No surprise."

Before they could reach the door, an elegantly dressed woman intercepted them. "My apologies, Martha was a bit out of line. I am Gwendolyn Turner, owner of After Six Limited. How might I help you today, Miss . . ."

Flib sat at Siobhan's feet and examined this new woman with interest. She was well dressed, wearing a lot of sparkle; her hair was neat, and she had only a hint of overly sweet perfume, unlike the old bat who wanted him to leave. She positively reeked of cheap cologne. His head cocked just a tad, he continued to watch this second woman as Siobhan played her part.

"Missus, actually. Missus Arthur Thomson of Beverly Hills. My friends call me Sharon."

"What brings you to our city in the clouds, Sharon?"

"My husband thought it would be a nice change for me to get out of The Hills and into some mountains."

"Oh, very nice. What does your husband do?"

"He's a financial advisor. Meeting with a client and his banking friends. I like traveling with him when I can. Get to see lots of different cities."

Something about Siobhan's demeanor relaxed Gwendolyn. Knowing a personal touch would encourage greater spending, she volunteered, "You are lucky to be able to travel with your husband. Mine spends most of his time away on corporate business. Unfortunately, he has little time for me, even when he is home."

"Maybe you should put him to work in your shop."

"No, that would be disaster. He has no fashion sense whatsoever! How did you find our shop? Did your hotel concierge recommend us? I like to reward those who help us."

"No, I was just wandering and saw your wonderful window. It looks delightful; do you mind if we just stroll around?"

"Certainly, make yourself at home. We do have some selections made just for us, if you would like to take something *unique* back to 'The Hills'."

Flib stood and looked around, again. Seeing a young woman flipping through dresses on a nearby carousel, he sauntered over and sat, looking over his shoulder at Siobhan.

"Oh, look. My fashion advisor has found something he likes."

"Your fashion advisor?" Stan chuckled in her earpiece. *"Don't overplay your hand. I'd like Flib to be less noticed; he is your guardian. Don't compromise him. I'm getting great video of the room from his collar tag. Stand back from the woman if you can, all I can see on your camera is her abundant cleavage."*

Gwendolyn walked beside Siobhan to the rack where Flib sat. "He has excellent taste. This shipment just arrived from our private designer. Let me see, you would be a size six?"

As she reached onto the rack and removed a dress for Siobhan, a man entered the shop. He was well-dressed, in his late thirties, and moved with confidence and carried an aire of power. His companion, another man built much like the doorman, stopped at the front of the store, clasped his hands in front of him and surveyed the room. He and the doorman looked like a pair of matching bookends.

"Excuse me, please, Sharon. I'll be right back." Touching Siobhan lightly on her shoulder, Gwendolyn stepped over to a small desk where this new arrival waited.

Having watched the man's entrance, Flib brushed against Siobhan's leg and led her over to another rack, which stood only six feet from Gwendolyn and her visitor. When Flib sat and looked around, the camera hidden in his collar tag fixed upon a rack of nightgowns. Flimsy things in pastel colors. Siobhan casually lifted one out. Both cameras revealed a sheer modesty panel in the shape of a "V" on the front. Flib's camera included a yellow lily embroidered at the left hem. When Flib stood and turned, his camera focused on Gwendolyn and her guest who were talking in whispered tones. Siobhan recognized the man from pictures she had seen on Stan's computer. Mister Albert David Cunningham. Seeing Flib facing the couple, She also turned slightly so her microphone might pick up their whispers.

"So, you know the papers are talking about us getting married?" Cunningham teased. His voice was full of mirth and his eyebrows danced playfully.

"Yes, but not until we can get rid of my husband. Can't serve divorce papers until we locate him." She reached over and smoothed a wrinkle on the front of his coat.

Cunningham stared into Gwendolyn's eyes, his manner growing somewhat intense, his voice slightly strained. "That's why I'm here. We've managed to do just that. His body was found in Georgia. A bit burned and unrecognizable, but DNA results confirm it's him." Seeing she accepted his news, he relaxed and continued. "You have time for lunch?"

"In a moment, I have a customer I need to close." Gwendolyn looked toward the carousel of gowns where she had left Siobhan, but she wasn't there. Looking around, she saw the door closing. Siobhan was outside the shop, turning to the left.

Having sensed a nervous tension growing in both of the whispering people, Flib had brushed against Siobhan and quickly led her out the door. Seeing nothing in her hands, the doorman held the door open as they left.

Chapter 17

Siobhan strode quickly to the car, wanting only to disappear. Stan jumped from the front seat, dutifully positioning himself and opening the rear door for his passengers. Flib casually jumped in, without a care in the world. Siobhan slid in and moaned, "We need to get out of here! NOW!"

Stan closed the door and looked back at the front of After Six, Ltd., as he walked around the car. Seeing no activity that concerned him, he slipped into the driver's seat. Closing the door, he glanced in the rear view mirror and saw Siobhan near tears. Forcing himself to focus on their escape, he started the engine and pulled into traffic without saying a word. Moments later he turned into the Ingles parking lot on the other side of Beaucatcher Mountain. Parking to the side, near some trees, he jumped out and ran around to Siobhan's door.

"Are you okay?" Stan asked Siobhan, placing a hand on her arm. She nodded, allowing Stan to look over at Flib. Calling the dog out of the car, he grabbed his head with both hands and began rubbing him affectionately. "YOU were fantastic! I can see there is nothing to worry about when you are on alert! Fantastic job little man!" He then reached into his pocket and produced a wrapper containing a bit of bacon from breakfast. "You deserve this and a lot more!"

Turning back to Siobhan, he again placed a hand on her arm. "You feel cold, are you sure you're okay? You did a great job and the two of you found more information than I dared hope for."

Siobhan stared at Stan as though looking through him. Her eyes tearing up, she confessed, "I have never been so scared in my life as when that man showed up! My heart began racing and I fought every impulse to just run out of there."

"Siobhan, you weren't in any danger. Had there been trouble, I was only seconds away," Stan assured her as he rubbed her arm for comfort.

"I don't know. It might have been his manner or that body guard standing at the door. Just something about the whole experience terrified me."

"Well, I couldn't tell it. You did a great job. You held it

together and got what we needed!"

"What? What did you see that I didn't?"

"First, that man *was* Cunningham. A stroke of dumb luck, being at the right place at the right time! As you looked around, I considered bugging the place, now I don't have to. He told us Turner is dead, though I'm not sure I believe him. A charred body in another state is too convenient. Then, those nightgowns! If I'm not mistaken, the girls at the warehouse were wearing gowns just like them."

"Did you see the sign that said they were exclusive to After Six, Ltd.?" Siobhan lit up a little as she contributed to discovery.

"Yep and that ties Cunningham to the warehouse through After Six. I'll bet a good prosecutor could make it stick."

"Can we go?" Siobhan sighed, placing her hand on Stan's. "I'm ready to put After Six behind me."

Without another word, Stan moved his monitoring station to the trunk and helped Siobhan to the front. Seeing they were about to go, Flib jumped into the back seat. Stan rubbed his furry assistant's head once more before closing the door and returning to the driver's seat.

Leaving Ingles, Stan piloted out to the 240 bypass, exiting onto north bound Merrimon Avenue. Siobhan began to relax and enjoyed the scenery.

Turning into Lakeview Park, Stan continued to the area where Cunningham lived, stopping near his gated driveway. Looking around, he drove south down a nearby street. Winding down the mountain, about seventy-five yards from Cunningham's gate, he noticed an older couple working in a flower garden in their front yard. Stopping the car, he got out and approached them.

"Excuse me, do you have a moment to answer a couple questions about some noise complaints?"

"I don't hear any noise," the old man replied.

"Not now, however my office has received a number of complaints about helicopters flying too low over this neighborhood. Have you heard any helicopters?"

"Every Thursday night, nine o'clock sharp!" the woman replied. "Been going on now for months. Who did you say you were with?"

"You said 'nine o'clock sharp,' how so precise about the time?" Stan continued, ignoring her question about his identity.

"That's when *Law & Order, SUV* starts. Noise of that helicopter always interrupts the opening scene! That Cunningham should use a car like the rest of us." She was now becoming quite agitated.

"How do you know it was . . . who, Cunningham?"

"When reruns started, we went outside about quarter to nine. I wanted to see who was doing what," the man replied. "Took off from the Cunningham estate and zipped off toward the airport. Bloody nuisance. Didn't vote for him the first time and won't next time neither!"

Stan smiled inwardly at their irritation. "Do you have any idea if, or when, he returns?"

"Sometimes, just past midnight," the man continued.

"How do you know that is when it's returning?" Stan prodded.

"Nature calls, young man. My bladder wakes me up right about midnight and I'm in the loo as that noisy beast flies overhead."

Chuckling slightly, Stan closed the interview. "Thank you very much. You have both been a great help. May I check back with you if we need any more information?"

"Sure, why not," the man replied with a nod.

"Who did you say you were with?" the woman asked again, challenging Stan's credentials.

"You do have a beautiful flower garden," Stan responded, once more dodging her question. "I may have to visit you for some advice about my own yard. Thank you, again, for your help." He then returned to the car.

"What was that all about?" Siobhan asked as they drove away.

"Confirming another piece of the puzzle. Cunningham uses a private helicopter service to get to his warehouse in Hendersonville. I'd like to get the pilot to confirm it."

"They didn't say the helicopter flew to Hendersonville," she objected.

"They said 'the airport,' which happens to be in a direct line from Cunningham's estate to the Hendersonville warehouse."

Stan smiled as he pulled back on Merrimon Avenue, heading north to Interstate 26, then home to Oliver Springs.

Arriving home mid-afternoon, Stan lost no time booting up his computer and retrieving pictures he had taken of young women in the warehouse. He then pulled up the video from that morning in After Six, Ltd. Satisfied that the lingerie the girls wore was the same as those sold at After Six, even down to the icon stitched onto the hem, he went to the After Six, Ltd. website. He found the same lingerie listed as "Made exclusively for the discriminating clientele of After Six, Ltd."

"Gotcha! Twice!" Stan declared jubilantly.

"Not quite," Siobhan retorted. "Anybody could have purchased, or stolen, a bunch of those night gowns."

"Okay, Miss Smarty. Ruin my happy party, but with the helicopter traffic and the gowns, that noose is getting closer to being a custom fit for Mister Albert Cunningham. I just need some kind of power to grab him with, a reliable authority. Where are the marines when you really need them?"

Siobhan went through her morning duties getting Pearl's Diner ready for Saturday breakfast customers. Seeing that her manner was slow and methodical, absent of her normal conscious intent, Mary realized that her mind was not on her work. "So, I don't see you wearing a fancy new dress."

"No. No new dress, but I did get a new purse," Siobhan snickered.

"A new purse? What was this trip all about, really?" Mary pushed.

Siobhan sighed and took a deep breath. Looking at her friend, emotions welled up and she nearly broke down in tears. "If I tell you, you've got to *promise* to keep it just between the two of us."

"Sit down." Looking across the kitchen, Mary bellowed, "Horace, finish preppin the grill!" Settling into a chair next to Siobhan, she continued, "Now, we've got some time."

Siobhan looked at Mary, wondering if she should trust her with Stan's latest discoveries. Knowing she was about to burst inside from the pressure of keeping these secrets, she drew a deep breath and began to unload her burden. "Okay. When Stan went to Asheville last week, he discovered an operation where they are selling young girls in a warehouse . . . but he couldn't do anything about it. Seems the local sheriff and possibly the FBI are in on this." Siobhan paused to draw another deep breath. "Yesterday, we learned Turner, the man Stan was working for, has been found dead in Georgia and there are really strong circumstantial links between Cunningham and the girls at that warehouse." Siobhan paused again. Biting her lip, she continued while choking back tears. "Mary, he was cut in a knife fight after investigating the warehouse and I have no idea who is after him." A tear rolled from her right eye as she continued. ". . . He also confessed to blowing that car up on the Knoxville highway! . . . I'm scared I'm going to lose him again!"

"Hmpf," Mary responded, unhappy with the situation. Watching Siobhan wipe her eyes with a napkin, she asked, "Do these bad guys know about you?"

"They know where I live!"

"But do they know YOU?" Mary persisted. Her face and manner tightened with concern.

"No, not that I know of. I've only gone with him twice . . . to Georgia and this weekend to After Six in Asheville."

"Probably not smart enough to link the two," Mary mused. "Tell me about your visit to After Six."

"It's a very posh store. Lots of exclusive gowns and Missus Turner, Gwendolyn, is a gorgeous woman! But to be honest, the hero of the day was Flib. He guided me around the store and then got me out of there before things went bad. If it hadn't been for my furry protector, I would have panicked when Cunningham's bodyguard started checking me out."

"Checking you out?" Mary challenged, clearly growing more concerned.

"Well, not me exactly. He just kept watching everything and everyone in the store while Cunningham was there. Sent chills down my back."

Mary spent nearly a minute pondering what Siobhan revealed. "Change of subject. Where is your super sleuth this morning?"

"Home. He said he wanted to review everything he had and

try to make a plan for the next step."

"Good. Call him and tell him to be here about ten. A woman came in yesterday looking for 'im. Could be she has a job that might be a gentle distraction. He might not be able to help her right now, but since she came looking for him, he should at least talk with her."

"What's it about?" Siobhan asked, perking up from her self-imposed gloom.

"I'm not his receptionist and I have no idea why folks come to my diner looking for your boyfriend; seems odd to me. Just call him and tell him to get his behind over here by ten." Standing to resume her morning duties, Mary considered contacting Jack, her friend in Washington.

Chapter 18

Flib jumped from Stan's Explorer and raced up to Siobhan, who was sitting outside the kitchen door at Pearl's. Enjoying a break between breakfast and lunch, Siobhan welcomed her golden friend with both hands. Looking up as Stan approached, she confessed her indiscretion. "I told Mary what's going on. I'm sorry, but I was about to burst with panic this morning."

Kissing her lightly, Stan set her worries to rest. "That's okay. It's a lot to take in and I think we can trust Mary. I bet she knows lots of secrets. Now, why am I here?"

Seeing Stan with Siobhan, Mary poked her head out the door. "Mister Investigator, you have a new client in my diner. She just arrived."

Touching Siobhan lightly on her shoulder, Stan followed Mary through the kitchen into the dining room. Mary pointed to his special guest and he stepped over to her table. She was early-fifties, conservative in appearance with short brown hair, curled close to her head. She wore a light blue pants suit, made from summer-weight wool, with a white blouse.

"Good morning, I'm Stan Winthrop. You are looking for me?"

Mary interrupted the conversation before it got started. "Can I get you anything? Coffee?"

Startled by Mary's question, the woman replied, "Coffee would be nice. Thank you."

"Me, too," Stan added as Mary walked back to the kitchen.

Barely smiling, the woman looked at Stan and continued calmly. "Mister Winthrop, I was given your name by Oliver Winston. I understand you recently did some security work for him."

"Yes. What can I do for you, Miss . . ."

"Missus . . . Brenda Buchanan. I recently discovered a personal treasure is missing. A rare book signed by the author. It has a personal inscription that makes it quite valuable to me."

"Your coffee, ma'am. Would you care for anything else?" Sylvia asked as she delivered two cups of steaming coffee, with a small pitcher of half-and-half.

Blushing just slightly, Missus Buchanan replied, "No. Thank

you."

"When did you notice the book was missing?" Stan asked, resuming their conversation.

"Two days ago, Thursday, I guess."

"Have you notified the police? That will be required if you have to file an insurance claim."

"Yes. They took a report and said they'd post it on their network. Whatever that means."

"Okay, do you have any idea who might have taken the book?" Stan asked, sipping from his coffee mug.

"My niece visited last week, but she denies taking it."

"Did she have any friends over while she was visiting?"

"She and her mother visited for three days. My sister-in-law and I were gone part of that time, so I don't know . . . not for sure."

"But you do think she has something to do with this disappearance."

"I asked her but she denies ever seeing the book."

"What do you think? Could she have an accomplice?" Stan cocked his head slightly and looked steadily in Missus Buchanan's eyes.

The woman became visibly uneasy, shifting in her seat and stirring her coffee, without adding anything to it.

Stan broke the silence. "Okay, I'll need full particulars on this book, everything you can tell me about it, and the names and addresses of your sister and niece."

"The name of the book is 'Yesterday's Treasure' by Gerard Johanson. Why do you need information on my sister-in-law and niece? I told you they didn't take it."

"Missus Buchanan, do you want me to try to find your book?"

Sighing, the woman looked down at the table for several seconds. "Okay. My sister-in-law is Martha August. She lives on Vista Drive in Clinton. I don't know the house number. Her daughter, Suzanna, is currently living in an apartment somewhere in Clinton. 'Suzanna' is spelled with a 'z'."

Stan wrote the information on a napkin. "Okay, how do I get back in touch with you and what is your limit on recovery costs? That is, my out of pocket expenses that you will cover."

"My phone number is 865-265-0113. As for what it costs to get this book back . . . I want my book back."

"Okay, Missus Buchanan, I'll look into your book, however, I must tell you that I'm already heavily involved in a rather intense investigation. If I get new information on that case, I may have to put you on hold for a spell, so I don't know how long this will take. Is this agreeable?"

Her eyes pleading for help, she agreed. "Yes, I understand. But, please, I really do want my book back."

Stan pondered silently for a few seconds before continuing. "I understand. Tell you what, I have some time this afternoon. Let's start with where the book is supposed to be. Can we meet at your home about three-thirty? I'll need your address."

Missus Buchanan wrote her address on another napkin and handed it to Stan. "That will be fine. Thank you." Getting up to leave, she reached into her purse to retrieve her wallet.

"I'll take care of your coffee," Stan offered. "I have a special account here."

She smiled and walked toward the door, appearing somewhat more hopeful than when she arrived.

Siobhan asked Mary if she could leave early, at 2:00, when the dining room closed. Knowing it had been a light lunch shift and seeing that her tables were clean, Mary agreed. Siobhan then rushed home to shower and change so she could keep the three-thirty appointment with Stan.

Arriving at the Buchanan house, Stan was impressed with how well groomed the yard was. In fact, the ranch style brick and stone home presented itself as a very desirable property. Seeing her guests arrive, Brenda opened the front door, greeting them warmly.

Stan began his investigation by examining the display case where the book should have been. It was a vertical oak case standing six feet tall, two feet wide and about a foot deep, with glass filling three sides and polished brass handles and hinges. Five glass shelves held various knickknacks including miniature glass sculptures, multiple Hummel figurines, some carved ivory, and glass stands for two books. One of the books was missing.

Using a pen to lift one of the brass pendant handles, he could see they had been wiped clean. Checking the oak frame, it too appeared to have been recently wiped clean.

"Did the police fingerprint this cabinet?" Stan asked, stepping back and scanning the furniture once again.

"Yes. They didn't find anything and left an awful mess. I did clean up after they left." Brenda exhibited some disgust.

"You do have quite a collection," Siobhan commented as she surveyed other collectibles placed around the living room.

"Thank you," Brenda replied. "Each one means something to me, personally, but none are as dear to me as that book."

"I need to look outside, check your windows. Do you normally leave any unlocked?" Stan asked as he walked toward the door.

"Only my bedroom window. I keep it open for fresh air at night."

"Is it open now?"

"I suppose so; should I check?"

"No. I'll find out when I walk around the outside of the house. Siobhan, why don't you check . . . no, second thought, come with me."

Stan checked the door frame before going through. Finding nothing of interest, he circled the house, examining the ground below each window. Three windows on the front were all locked and showed no signs of forced entry. When he got to the bedroom window, on the end opposite the living room, he saw scratches on the screen's frame. The ground was covered in mulch and provided no useful information. Continuing around the house, he found no other evidence of break-in. Returning inside, he asked Missus Buchanan to show him to the bedroom, where he went straight to the window that had scratches on its screen. The window was covered with a sheer curtain and framed by heavier drapes that could be closed in winter. He did find a piece of mulch on the floor, an inch or so from the wall. Examining the window sill, Stan found it, too, had been wiped clean, apparently with some kind of polish.

"This is where the thief came in," Stan announced confidently. "He knew what he wanted and most likely walked out one of the doors. Now, who is he and how did he know when to visit? Misses Buchanan, would you please call your sister-in-law and see if she is available?"

Ten minutes later, Siobhan and Stan were heading for Clinton, thirty miles away.

"What are you thinking?" Siobhan asked as they traveled.

"My gut tells me this is an experienced thief who sells his, or her, stuff on eBay. Didn't touch any of the other collectibles, which could bring a quick buck at any pawn shop. They took only one thing. A book. An original printing, signed by the author. I checked this book out on Amazon and it didn't get great reviews. The author is popular and a signed copy might fetch a good price in some circles, but I'm not sure those folk shop for books on eBay or Amazon. They live in those little shops around the corner that are musty smelling and have rooms in the back for really valuable editions."

"You don't think the thief might sell the book in one of those musty shops?"

"Might, but really valuable volumes usually get to these shops through estate liquidations, not break-ins. Somebody definitely wanted this book. Who?"

"It wasn't listed on eBay?"

"Not yet. A smart thief won't list right away. They'll wait a month or so, let the heat die down."

"Would a smart thief be stealing stuff to sell on eBay?" Siobhan asked with a chuckle.

"Good point."

Arriving at the address in Clinton, Stan and Siobhan found a comfortable forest green and white craftsman style home, considerably smaller than Missus Buchanan's residence. The neighborhood was very clean and welcoming. A hefty man opened the door after Stan knocked a second time.

"Yes?"

"Mister August?" Stan inquired politely.

"Yes?"

"My name is Stan Winthrop and this is Siobhan Thomas, my associate. Is Missus Martha August available? We did call to say we were on the way."

"Sure. Come in," the man stepped aside, holding the door so Stan and Siobhan could enter. "This is about some missing book?"

"Yes, sir. We have been asked to look into the disappearance of a collectible."

A petite woman in her late-forties entered the room. She wore a simple cotton house dress and had graying hair bouncing about her shoulders. "Yes? What is this about a missing book?"

Stan completed his scan of the room and looked squarely at Martha August. "Your sister-in-law has employed us to look into the disappearance of a book. I understand you visited with her for a few days last week. Do you recall seeing this book in her curio cabinet?"

"Look. Brenda has a lot of nice things on display. She usually makes a point of showing them to me when she gets them, but to be honest none of them interest me. As you can see, we're not collectors." Seeing Stan was still waiting for an answer to his question, she continued. "But no, I do not recall seeing the book. I wouldn't even know the book existed had she not told me about it."

"When was that?" Siobhan asked, politely.

"I guess about a week or two back. She doesn't like to visit here, so we go to Hamack's over on the boulevard. I love her, but she can be a bit of a snob."

"What did she say about the book?"

"Oh, she had just got a letter from the author. He's going to be in town soon and wants to 'drop by' for a visit. They were an item, years ago. Or so she says."

"Did she make you think the book was valuable?" Siobhan asked, her curiosity growing.

"Oh, the way she talked, it's the most valuable book ever published."

Stan puzzled for a few seconds before continuing. "Did anything unusual happen at the coffee shop that day?"

"No, not really. Weren't but a few folks there, never are 'cept at lunch." Martha stopped and thought for a moment. "No, there was something different. When she paid, the hostess said her card failed to scan and asked for either a check or cash to cover the tab."

"And she paid by check?" Stan assumed out loud.

"Yes. She was in a fit, too. Kept saying, 'There is nothing

wrong with my card! I use it everywhere!'"

Just then Stan's phone beeped an alarm. Taking it from its holster, he glanced at the screen. "Please excuse me, I need to check this." Stan then flipped through screens on his phone. After a couple minutes, he resumed the conversation. "The book has just been listed on eBay. Current location is listed as Marlow, Tennessee."

"That's between here and Oliver Springs. Small community north of Oak Ridge," Mister August interjected.

"I don't mean to be too suggestive, but do either of you or your daughter have any friends or acquaintances in Marlow?" Siobhan asked, as delicately as possible.

"I don't know a soul from Marlow and I doubt my daughter does either. At present, she likes to associate with a darker, more gothic crowd. Gothic would not do well in Marlow."

Stan moved to close the interview. "One more question and we'll be out of your way. Do you happen to know the name of the hostess at Hamack's?"

"Not a clue, sorry," Missus August admitted.

"Well, thank you for your help. Have a good evening." Stan then turned toward the door, which he held open for Siobhan.

As they pulled away and began their journey homeward, Siobhan asked, "So, do you have an idea what happened?"

"That's easy. Buchanan bragged about having an incredibly valuable book in an open restaurant. The hostess faked running her card, hoping to get a check, which she did. The check had the home address of this valuable book. Knowing the address, she arranges, possibly with a partner, to steal the book. Unable to get the money she wants from a book store, she lists it on eBay."

"How much?"

"She evidently did her homework. Not a very expensive book to be a 'collectible.' I found out-of-print copies on Amazon for eighty dollars and she has listed it as an 'author personalized copy' with a starting price of one-twenty."

Smiling with delight, Siobhan asked an obvious question. "And how much did you bid?"

"Eight hundred, but I hope to have the book in hand before the bid closes in five days. There are other, more important, problems at hand."

Driving through Marlow on the way home, Siobhan suggested they stop at a diner for supper. "And we can take something home for Flib. I'll bet he's lonely."

They found Flib waiting at the front door where he danced jubilantly, greeting his people, until he caught the smell of a fresh pork chop Siobhan had saved for him. Stan shook his head, commenting, "He could have gone with us if he hadn't taken off while you cleaned up."

"Yes, well, I'm sure he has his own haunts he needs to visit," Siobhan replied stroking Flib's back.

When Flib finished the chop, Stan squatted down and asked, "Mister Flib, did anyone come visiting while we were gone?"

Flib looked to the side, as though pondering the question. After a few seconds, he laid down and looked up at Stan.

"I guess the home front is secure, which allows me to see if I can find out who's listing that book for sale." Stan then opened his notebook computer and began searching the dark web. Thirty minutes later, he closed his computer and joined Siobhan on the sofa. "Got a name and address in Marlow. Now, I just need a trustworthy officer to help me bust 'em."

The next morning found Stan sitting in their apartment studying images from the warehouse and Siobhan's visit to After Six, Ltd. Siobhan busied herself waiting on Sunday morning regulars at Pearl's, many who did not come in during the week. Seeing two men who were "occasional regulars" enter, she grabbed a coffee pot and two mugs and headed to one of her two open tables. The men saw her waving them over. As they sat, Siobhan poured their coffee and began a conversation.

"So, you got the weekend shift again . . . anything happening?"

"Ah, the life of a detective . . . never a dull moment," one man replied.

"Except in the thriving metropolis of Oak Ridge, Tennessee. Just enough crime to keep a seasoned policeman interested," the other chimed in.

"What'll it be for breakfast?" Siobhan asked, doing her real job.

"Two eggs, fried, with country ham and biscuits," the first detective replied.

"I'll do the same," the second agreed. "Second thought, add some orange juice."

After taking their orders, Siobhan asked, "Have you guys seen anything about a collectible book stolen from a house here in Oliver Springs?"

"Rare book?" the first officer asked.

"Don't know that it's rare, just collectible," Siobhan replied.

"Yeah. As a matter of fact I was cruising reports yesterday afternoon and saw a hit on a stolen book in Chattanooga. Rare book dealer had seen a notice and reported someone trying to sell a book by the same title. Local detective is going to follow up. Hasn't yet. Not that I saw anyway."

"Breakfast will be right out, boys." Siobhan smiled and returned to the kitchen where she hung the order and put in a call to Stan. The detectives were just finishing up when Stan arrived. Siobhan took him out to meet them.

Seeing that Siobhan had some trust in these two men, Stan asked for their help. "That book, Siobhan asked about, I have a line on where it is. For sale on eBay by someone in Marlowe. Could you come with me to see about it? I'll pick up your breakfast and maybe add lunch."

"You wouldn't be trying to bribe an officer of the law, would you?" the older detective jabbed.

"No, sir! Just acknowledging a favor, if there is one."

"You can go, Mark, if you want to. I need to follow up on that stolen bicycle," the younger officer replied, picking up his ticket.

"Sure, I'll go . . . but keep in mind I can't go inside unless invited and I can't rummage around. Book will have to be in plain sight. But, I'll do it for Siobhan. Name's Mark Hendricks, and you are?" the older detective extended his hand in introduction.

"Stan Winthrop. Thank you for your help." After shaking the detective's hand, Stan picked up his breakfast ticket. "Shall we go?"

= = = = = = =

Arriving at the address in Marlowe, a small row house in need of attention, Stan took the lead by knocking firmly on the door. He was just raising his hand to knock a second time when the door opened. A young man, in his late twenties, wearing pajama pants and t-shirt rubbed sleep from his eyes as he looked out. Seeing two casually dressed men, one in a sport coat, and only an older Ford Explorer parked on the street, his barely discernable voice yawned, "Yeah, what?"

"My eBay name is snobber45 and I bid on your rare book. My attorney has advised me to examine the volume before the close of the auction. May I see it?" Stan asked, his voice calm and unpretentious.

"Yeah, come on in, I'll get it for ya." The sleepy man then turned back into the house leaving the front door wide open.

Looking over his shoulder at Mark, Stan smiled when the detective shrugged his shoulders and put his hand forward, indicating it was okay to continue.

"Your attorney?" Mark smirked as he followed Stan.

"Whatever it takes to get the book back," Stan replied.

Both men stood in the center of a small living room filled with furniture covered in dirty laundry and food wrappers. The young man returned a moment later, holding out two books.

"Here, you didn't say which one you bought."

Stan accepted the leather-bound volume of *Yesterday's Treasure*. Mark accepted a second leather-bound volume, *The Complete Gulliver's Travels*. After reading the inscription on the title page, Stan flipped through the book. Seeing no damage, he nodded to the detective.

The young man stretched a bit while his two guests examined the books. When he put his hands down, the Oak Ridge detective displayed his badge and addressed him, "Son, you are under arrest for breaking and entering, and possession of stolen goods with intent to sell. You have the right to remain silent. Anything you say can and will be used against you in a court of law. You have the right to an attorney. If you cannot afford an attorney, one will be provided for you. Do you understand the rights I have just explained to you? With these rights in mind, do you wish to speak to me?"

"What? I thought you guys just wanted to look at the books

. . . am I under arrest?"

Shaking his head, the detective used his cell phone to put a call into the local police station. When they arrived, and the suspect was properly handcuffed, officers of the Marlowe Police and the Oak Ridge detective executed a search of the entire premises. They left with a trove of stolen treasures, most of which had already been repeatedly listed on eBay.

As Stan started his Explorer, Mark removed a book from his coat pocket. "Here's the book you were after. I don't think they'll need it, though a good defense attorney might ask why we were there. I don't think he'll be getting a 'good' attorney, but keep the book handy."

"Thanks. You just made a lady very happy." Stan smiled as he pulled away from the curb. While driving to Mark's office in Oak Ridge, Stan asked, "Mark, you seem to be a real-life honest cop. What makes a person sworn to upload the law either ignore it or take advantage of it for personal gain?"

"Except for greed, it's not always for 'personal gain,' as you put it. More often, in small departments like Oak Ridge, we have officers and detectives who grew up here. You might call them 'country boys.' Thing is, they know everyone from when they were young and that tends to cause officers to apply the law differently. They might write a damaging ticket to a tourist who floats a stop sign, then look the other way when a childhood friend commits a felony. Are they bad cops? Not sure I can answer that, but it's a problem everywhere, just more prevalent in small departments. Why do you ask?"

"I need some trustworthy law enforcement in Hendersonville, North Carolina. Notes I have from a friend tell me to not trust the local sheriff's department nor the local FBI."

"Do you trust your friend?"

"Yes, pretty much."

"Then don't trust the local law enforcement. You need to bring in somebody from outside the region."

"You went outside your jurisdiction today; care to go to North Carolina?"

"Not really. Oak Ridge helps out a lot of surrounding communities, like Oliver Springs. I hope you noticed how quickly I got local authorities involved. While I help out around the county, when needed, going to another state is a whole different ball game. Sorry."

"Can't blame a guy for trying."

Missus Brenda Buchanan came by Pearl's Diner Monday morning, as instructed when Stan called her Sunday evening. Finding the front door locked, she recalled that she was told to go around to the kitchen door. Seeing her walk around the corner, Stan got out of his Explorer and greeted her. After examining her book, she wrote Stan a check for $1,000.

Not looking at the check, but folding it and putting it in his pocket, Stan warned his client, "Missus Buchanan, the detective who helped get your book back warned me that they may need to borrow it if it becomes an issue in court."

She smiled, said "Thank You," and returned to her car.

Chapter 19

Lunch was winding down at Pearl's on Tuesday, when a stranger arrived. Stepping inside the door, this intriguing gentleman stood quietly and surveyed the nearly vacant dining room. Framed by light from outside, his appearance caught the eyes of two waitresses who were cleaning tables. Neatly trimmed dark hair, with not a strand out of place, clean shaven, standing six feet four inches tall with an active athletic physique, and dressed in conservative slacks and sport shirt, he was an eye full.

Sylvia abandoned cleanup and wiping her hands on her apron, approached the gentleman. "Grill's still hot if you're interested in lunch." Her voice could not have been more inviting.

"Yes, I could use something to eat. However, before that I need to see Mary." His powerful bass voice resounded with confidence.

Sylvia quickly showed the guest to a table she had just cleaned, then turned toward the kitchen, saying, "I'll get Mary and a menu."

Entering the kitchen, Sylvia grabbed a menu, handed it to Mary, and cooed. "There is one hunk of a man out there who wants to see you!"

A welcoming smile slowly softening her face, the guest stood as Mary approached his table. "Jack, what are you doing in my diner?" After exchanging a friendly embrace, they both sat. Seeing Sylvia and Theresa hovering close by, Mary turned to them and ordered a lunch. "Sylvia, bring our guest a Tennessee Classic Burger, fries, and . . . Jack, what will you have to drink?"

"Soda will be fine. No, make it tea."

"You heard the gentleman." Mary nodded at Sylvia to get moving, then turned back to Jack. "Okay, lunch will be a couple minutes. Why are you here?"

"After you called Saturday night, I got to thinking and spent Sunday doing a bit of research. Turns out Justice has several teams investigating a number of little anomalies around the Asheville area, across the southeast, actually. Individually, they don't add up to much, but collectively . . . well, I got to wondering if one man, or family, might be behind all of them. There are too many similarities to be merely coincidence; so I sent out some queries. Once again, when the answers started coming in, they didn't seem like much individually but when packaged together, they painted quite a different picture. Your man, Stan?"

"Yes, Stan Winthrop," Mary affirmed.

"He may have stumbled into something far bigger than he realizes. When can I talk with him?"

Mary looked toward the kitchen and called, "Siobhan!"

Siobhan came out within a few seconds. "Yes, ma'am?"

"What's Stan up to today?"

Trusting that Mary had confidence in her guest, Siobhan replied calmly. "He said he was going lookin' for an honest cop, but I think he's still reviewing everything he collected last week." She watched the guest as she spoke.

"I'm sorry," Mary apologized. "Siobhan, this is Jack. We worked together y-e-a-r-s ago. Jack, Siobhan is one of my best waitresses and Stan's girl friend."

Jack stood and offered his hand to Siobhan. As they shook hands, he continued. "I'd like to meet Stan. Would you please call him and ask him to come by?"

Seeing Mary nod assurance, Siobhan returned to the kitchen to call Stan. Sylvia stepped past her, delivering a platter overflowing with the best food in Eastern Tennessee, which featured a half-pound lean beef burger topped with a generous slice of ham and a fried egg. Fries surrounded a whole wheat bun, with tomato slices, lettuce, pickle, and peppers on the side.

Watching Jack's eyes double in size, Mary figured he would need time to eat his lunch and excused herself. "Looks like you have a job in front of you and I have chores in the kitchen. I'll be back when Stan arrives. Enjoy lunch."

Jack nodded silently and smiled with delight as he lifted the hefty burger.

Stan stepped through the back door of Pearl's kitchen about twenty minutes later. Mary nodded her head toward the dining room, then dried her hands and followed him. Jack mopped up the last of drizzle from the fried egg yolk with his last fry as they approached. Pushing the empty plate away, Jack smiled at Mary.

"Excellent burger. Possibly the best I have had in years." Looking to Stan, he stood and extended his hand. "I am going to assume you are Stan Winthrop."

Mary made introductions before Stan could speak. "Stan this is John Barnes; his friends call him 'Jack.' We worked together before I bought Pearl's. He is now with the U.S. Department of Justice as a . . ."

"Investigations supervisor," Jack interrupted. "I'm one of those faceless people who decide which crimes are investigated and which are put on hold."

"Stan Winthrop," Stan responded, offering his hand across the table. "What brings you here and why do you want to speak with me?"

Jack motioned toward a chair at his table. "Sit, please join us." Jack resumed his seat as Mary and Stan joined him around the table. "As Mary said, we used to work together. When your girlfriend confided in her about the troubles in North Carolina, Mary violated that confidence out of concern for your girlfriend's safety and for you. Can she join us?"

"Right here," Siobhan replied from a table behind Jack, which she was supposedly cleaning. Moving a chair next to Stan, she introduced herself. "Siobhan Thomas."

"Jack Barnes," Jack responded, again standing and welcoming Siobhan to the table. Looking around the empty dining room, he asked, "Are there any other ears around us I should be aware of?"

"No, everyone else is in the kitchen, CLEANING UP," Mary replied, raising her voice so all knew they were to work and not eavesdrop. Sylvia and Theresa scurried away from the door and resumed helping Horace clean the kitchen.

"Okay, now that everyone is here, I am also going to violate a confidence. Mary called me several weeks ago, concerned about Michael Turner's investigation into Cunningham. I did discover Turner used to work for Justice as an investigator, until he quit, presumably over an assignment. He wanted to investigate an up and coming politician named Albert David Cunningham, but there were no grounds. Mister Winthrop, your discovery of human trafficking hit a nerve, so I expanded my search, not just Cunningham but also related crimes in this region. One revelation led to another, including prostitution, human trafficking, and even a couple murders . . . anyway, what I found was a bunch of puzzle pieces that, by themselves, were meaningless. Local crimes that should be handled by local authorities. However, adding what Mary told me about your discoveries, they began to come together into what looked like a very serious network of organized criminal activities. After assembling a team to continue investigating these bits and pieces, I invited myself to meet with you to see what cards you really hold. Will they give us enough to indict Cunningham?"

Jack looked straight as Stan, who sat square shouldered, hands folded on the table, lips together but not tight, eyes fixed and showing no emotion at all. Had they been playing poker, Jack would have been concerned about what Stan held in his hand. Experienced in reading faces and body language, Jack read Stan as engaged, but not yet ready to share what cards he held. Knowing he had to get Stan's cooperation, Jack shifted in his seat, making himself more open and approachable. Raising one eyebrow slightly, he continued.

"What I would like to do, at this time, is to share with you what I've found and try to match it up with what you have. See if we can build a more complete picture."

Stan continued to stare at Jack, sizing him up and analyzing everything he had said. Everyone around the table grew uneasy in the silence, shifting in their chairs and looking from Jack to Stan, until Stan finally spoke. "Okay. But first, how much will you be relying on local resources, that is around Asheville?"

"None at all. I'll bring in my own team, whom I trust completely." Jack let a hint of an understanding smile crease the corner of his mouth. "And I have the entire U.S. Marshall's Office, should we need them."

"Okay, where? We can't use my place 'cause they're watching me and I don't want Siobhan put in any more danger than she's in now."

"You can use my place," Mary volunteered.

"How strong is your internet?" Jack asked. "We'll be burning up the net."

"Not so good. I use my phone for email," Mary replied, her face losing all excitement. "What about your hotel?"

"Hotel clerks tend to talk too freely," Jack answered with disdain. "I once had a team get burned by a talkative hotel clerk."

Everyone seemed to be thinking through a silent pause, then Stan offered a suggestion. "What about the Oak Ridge Police Department? Siobhan introduced me to one of their detectives who recently helped me with a job. He seemed okay."

"Not sure about their headquarters, but maybe they have an offsite office we can use. Siobhan, will you please call this detective friend?"

Stunned to be suddenly included, Siobhan agreed. "I don't have his number."

Stan stood and reached into his back pocket, removing his wallet. Taking a card from inside, he offered it to Siobhan. "He gave me his card."

"Why don't you call him?" she asked. "You're the one who spent the day with him."

"He'll ask me too many questions. Just ask him to join us here for a moment. No partners, just him." Seeing Siobhan was not convinced, Stan volunteered, "Come on, I'll make the call with you." He then followed Siobhan into the kitchen.

By the time Detective Hendricks arrived, the kitchen had been cleaned and all staff were gone for the day. Mary and Siobhan were doing pre-prep for the next day and met him at the back door. They showed him to the table where Stan and Jack were discussing Michael Geoffrey Turner.

Seeing the detective walking toward the table, Stan stood and greeted him. "Mark, thanks for joining us. This is Jack Barnes, with the U.S. Department of Justice. You recall I asked you about going to North Carolina with me?" Marc nodded, Stan continued. "I know you turned me down, but here is an opportunity to help without going to Carolina."

"We need a safe house with lots of privacy and a strong internet service," Jack interjected, his expression friendly and ready to do business. "Doesn't have to be a 'house;' a private office apart from curious eyes will do just fine."

Mark thought for a moment. "I have a weekend cottage up

on Norris Lake. Wife just had me install full internet services. It has one big living area and two bedrooms."

"What about neighbors?" Jack asked.

"None to speak of, mostly just weekenders."

"Will your wife let us rent it for a few days, possibly a couple weeks?" Jack continued.

"Sure, I suppose so." As the words left Marc's lips, he wondered if he should be offering the use of his cottage. However, knowing they could use some extra money to spruce the place up, he swallowed his worries.

Seeing the project taking shape, Jack clapped his hands together and smiled. "Great, that's one problem solved. Now, there is one more favor we need in your official capacity. It seems Mister Winthrop has an unwanted shadow. If we identify him, before we go to your cottage, can you arrange an arrest and keep him incommunicado for at least forty-eight hours?"

Marc started to wonder again, but quickly thought about what Stan had told him previously and added what this U.S. Justice guy told him. Realizing the scope of the problem and trusting that all would be okay in the end, he agreed with a slight nod of his head.

Chapter 20

Marc called his wife and told her of the arrangements he had made. She was not happy but agreed to the deal, providing she got to spend this unexpected income any way she wanted. He stipulated that at least half of it go into their cottage, then gave Jack and Stan the address, directions, and the key code for the front door.

Siobhan grudgingly agreed to spend the afternoon with Mary, as a precaution. Stan returned home to collect his computer, notes, and a change of clothes. Marc followed him, like a distant shadow, but parked in a retail area where he could watch traffic coming and going from the apartment. Two cars caught his attention, a white Lexus and a blue Toyota. Both cars sat in the parking lot he had chosen, each with a driver sitting behind the wheel. Both had a clear view of Stan and Siobhan's apartment. The Lexus had Georgia plates. The Toyota was from North Carolina.

Seeing Stan loading bags and equipment into the Explorer, Flib jumped into the front seat. Stan looked at him and pondered. "I'd love to have you with me, but I'm afraid of what might happen around here. Siobhan will be back later this evening and I need you to keep an eye on her. Keep her calm and out of trouble. Do you mind?"

Flib moaned and slowly exited the vehicle. Stan tried to pet him, scratch his neck with appreciation, but Flib refused to stop until he sat in front of the apartment door. He stared coldly as his human talked on a cell phone.

"Siobhan, I'm leaving a disgruntled companion at the front door."

"Flib wants to go, too." It wasn't a question.

"Yes, but I'd feel better if he was here with you. See you in a couple days . . . love you."

"Me too, you."

Stan tossed his phone on the passenger seat and looked to his golden friend. "Take care of her for me. And you, too." He then slipped behind the wheel and left, looking in the rear-view with regret as he pulled away.

Turning left onto the Knoxville highway, Stan looked

around for Marc's car. Not seeing him, he hesitated briefly before following Marc's directions.

Marc watched Stan's Explorer journey toward Knoxville and waited. Seconds later an old black and yellow pickup truck followed in the same direction. Noticing the North Carolina tags, Marc joined the parade, radioing a description of the truck to a patrolman who was waiting for the call.

Marc had advised Stan to take a rather roundabout route from Oliver Springs toward Norris Lake, which is northwest of Knoxville. When the black and yellow pickup raced through a "pink" light to keep up with the Explorer, he was pulled by an Oak Ridge policeman. A second Oak Ridge police vehicle pulled in front of the truck seconds later, blocking any avenue of escape. Marc arrived as the first officer wrote the driver a ticket. When the traffic officer handed the citation to the driver, the second officer took the driver into custody. Before the driver was put into the patrol car, Marc searched him for weapons, contraband, and phones. Finding nothing, he checked the truck and found a mobile phone and pistol. Seeing that the serial number had been scratched off the gun, he bagged it as evidence before attempting to remove the battery from the phone. Finding the telephone sealed, he slipped it into his pocket. Finished with the truck, he had the arresting officer radio for a tow to relocate it.

"Sir, you can't do that," the traffic officer objected.

"Normally, I would agree," Marc explained. "However, this man's wanted on federal racketeering charges." Thinking to himself for several seconds, he then extended his hand. "Officer, may I please have your copy of the traffic citation."

Realizing this was not a request, the traffic officer ripped out the ticket and handed it to Detective Hendricks. "I don't know that I like this, Sir."

"Don't worry, he'll be treated fairly."

The traffic officer pondered a few seconds silently, then returned to his patrol car. As soon as he left, Marc gave some last minute instructions to the arresting officer and went in pursuit of Stan's Explorer. Catching up with Stan on the outskirts of Knoxville, he resumed following him. Satisfied there were no more shadows, he stopped at a convenient strip mall where he smashed the phone he had taken, disposing of the pieces, and any hidden trackers, in a dumpster. Heaving a sigh, he returned to his office in Oak Ridge.

Marc arranged to take the rest of the week off and drove to his lake cottage early Wednesday morning. Aromatic remnants of bacon and coffee greeted the detective as he walked into the main living area. Furniture had been moved aside and folding tables filled the space. Scanning the kitchen, he found it had been cleaned up and two coffee pots sat steaming on a pair of hot plates. Jack, Stan, and two other men puzzled over pictures, official Justice Department reports, and personal notes. Stepping over to a table in the middle of it all, Marc found a collection of highway maps pieced together to form a map of the southeastern United States, from Maryland to Florida, west to Kentucky. Brightly colored circles called his attention to Westminster, Maryland, a town northwest of Baltimore; Irmo, South Carolina, just north of Columbia; White, Georgia; Hendersonville, North Carolina; and Macclenny, Florida, west of Jacksonville. All were communities near larger metropolitan centers. A large white board in front of a fireplace had state names across the top and crimes down the left side, including auto theft, prostitution, human trafficking, cigarettes, extortion, and murder. Check marks and notes below state names indicated which crimes had been found in which states.

"Impressive picture, don't you think?" Jack asked as he joined Marc.

"Very. What does it all mean?" Marc responded, not fully understanding what he saw.

"Well, in short, the U. S. Department of Justice had leads on crimes in these areas. Mister Winthrop's notes, or those from Michael Turner, are helping us tie them all together. He had threads of a network, we had centers of crime. Their notes have put names and faces to ghosts we were searching for. Now, we almost have a picture of a very well organized network."

"Almost?" Marc challenged.

"Not quite there, but Turner and Winthrop have a tremendous compilation of information. We're still going through it."

Marc began to get excited about what he was seeing. "What can I do to help?"

"To begin with, join us and listen. As you get a handle on what we have, start going through Winthrop's treasure trove. Look through old stuff, new stuff, doesn't matter. We need at least three sets of eyes on each piece. Anything you find of interest, bring to me or Steve."

"Steve?"

"My apologies." Turning toward the other men, Jack interrupted them. "Gentlemen, this is Detective Marc Hendricks, our host and new team member. Marc, that scruff on the end is my second, Deputy Steve Malcolm. Next to him is Deputy Mike Durant and you know Stan. These men have worked with me for years and can be trusted with anything you have to say. Mike is also a pretty good chef. Okay, break's over, back to work."

Each of the men came over to welcome Marc to their team before returning to their separate and often joint investigations. All five men spent the entire day examining and comparing documents, notes, and pictures from Turner, Winthrop, and Justice. Three computers were used to search law enforcement databases and public sites on the internet for links and related information. As the day wore on, an increasing number of discoveries were discussed by the team before notes were added to the white board.

With the arrival of dusk, everyone dropped their pens, markers, and folders and flopped into chairs. Only Jack remained standing, studying the white board.

"What gives, boss?" Steve asked, popping open a bottle of beer.

"Florida. I really wanted to tie this Cunningham clan to that Florida murder. Everything else is clean; we have a network. I can almost admire how discrete and clean it is, but I really wanted to close that one in Florida. It's a perfect match."

Grunting as he stood, Stan went to his notebook computer and sat down. Without a word, he ran a broad search on his Turner folder, using one word. Florida. Realizing what he might be doing, the other men watched from where they sat. No one said a word. Each waited for what seemed an eternity.

"Three hits on 'Florida'," Stan announced after a moment

of silence. "It seems we have one newspaper article and two personal notes."

Jack strolled over and looked at Stan's screen. "Let's see what you have."

The newspaper article offered nothing new, however the first note linked to the date of the murder. The second tied the same date to an event at Cunningham Tractor and Farm Supply in White, Georgia.

"Possibly," Jack said. "Mike, why don't you work on supper while Stan and I see if we can beef up this Florida link."

An hour later, Mike had supper ready and everyone else had to pause their searching. About to push away from his work, Jack spotted a familiar name in Turner's notes. "Mike, keep it warm for a few more minutes!" He then sent Steve and Marc back to Justice records to try to tie the name to Florida. Thirty minutes later, hunger drove searchers to yield their current effort as Marc declared, "Gotcha!"

Everyone scrambled to Marc's yellow notepad where he had mapped out a series of diverse links. "We have Abercrombie, a known hit man, in Florida at the time and date of the murder. Traffic camera got him two blocks from the victim's house. His 'day job' is working the warehouse for Cunningham Tractors in White, Georgia. Now . . . Turner knew this guy was associated with Cunningham in Asheville and has a picture of him in Hendersonville, North Carolina three days later. Coincidentally, that was a Thursday afternoon, the same day they do the 'girl sales' at the JWX Enterprises warehouse. DOJ documents place him at a Maryland human trafficking site on Friday, the next day. Maybe moving merchandise?"

"That sure is roundabout," Steve complimented.

"Yes, but it's solid!" Jack added. "Let's eat."

Conversation during supper was light and hopeful, especially when Jack asked Marc about the car following Stan.

"We got him," Marc chuckled. "Turns out he ran a light trying to keep up with Stan. Yellow going red. A traffic cop pulled him, then a friend of mine took him into custody. I confiscated his phone and a pistol."

"Where is he now?" Stan asked, a bit concerned.

"If all is going according to plan, he should be in process of being moved to the second precinct holding facility."

"Did you think to grab the traffic citation?" Steve queried.

"Yes. It's in my pocket," Marc replied, appreciative that someone thought to ask. "I didn't think you would want it entered into the public record, where someone might find it."

Jack nodded slightly, grinning appreciatively between bites of meaty lasagna. "What are you doing with him?"

"First he went to my precinct, the third. Then, rather than feed him, he was to be moved to the second for the evening. After breakfast he should be moved to county lockup for twenty-four hours. Then, we can either cut him loose or put 'im somewhere else."

"Where is he from?" Steve asked.

"North Carolina. No, his driver's license is Georgia, but his tags were Carolina."

"What happened to his phone?"

"I was worried about tracking bugs so I destroyed it and discarded the pieces in a trash can at a strip mall."

"Hmmm . . . and he had a pistol? Was he carrying a license?" Jack asked.

"No. I did ask my friend and he said there was no license. Serial number has been scratched out, too."

"Where is the gun?"

"In an evidence bag in my desk."

"Okay, you said he is being moved to county?"

Marc nodded.

"This can work. Have your friend take the gun to county and I'll have a US Marshall pick both up. Charge him with Interstate Weapons violation. They can take him to a small Federal facility in Butner, North Carolina. You can count him as lost until we need him." Jack smiled contentedly and took another bite of cheese-laden pasta. "Good dinner, Mike. Thanks."

After supper was cleaned up, the men relaxed in chairs pushed back around the edge of the living room. "What now?" Stan asked.

Jack heaved a sigh before responding. "Tomorrow, we do it all again. Verify every link to every crime. Get them ready to put before a judge."

=======

Thursday went quickly as the five men retraced every thread and link. Satisfied they had a solid case, Jack called them together at three thirty. "Gentlemen, you have done an excellent job. Steve, Mike, the two of you pack everything back into the van and put Mister Hendrick's cottage back the way we found it. Marc, I need you to write me a short note about how much we owe you for the use of your cottage. I'll write you a check before I leave and I'd love to have you on my team for the next phase of this operation, if you're interested."

"What's the next phase?" Marc asked, a touch of excitement filling his face.

"We go arrest these scum. I'll deputize you as a U.S. Marshall."

"Yes. I'd like that."

"Good. Give all your contact information to Steve. It'll take several days to set this up then it will happen fast. Stan, I need to speak with you in private." The team commander led Stan into one of the two bedrooms and closed the door. "Before I left Washington, I did some investigation into Michael Geoffrey Turner. He left an address and a key with his handler, which I checked out on the way to Pearl's Diner. Turns out he had another lock box in Knoxville, which you hadn't discovered yet. Inside was a transaction log, at least I think it's a log book. Some of it was straight forward but most of it is written in code. From what I could gather, he had been siphoning funds from the Cunningham operation, through the wife's store. I don't know where he stored this money, or if it even actually exists. You'd need to know his code to figure that out. As his only representative, I am going to transfer all responsibility for the contents of this box to you. Here's the address and the only key Justice has. We no longer have any knowledge of its existence."

Shaking Stan's hand firmly, with respect and gratitude, Jack handed Stan a small brown envelope. "You have done Justice a great service and I'm counting on you helping us close this operation down."

Accepting the envelope without looking at it, Stan smiled, "You can count on it. I want to take Albert David Cunningham down so everyone can see."

"You could be exposed as an investigator and might not be able to effectively do undercover work in the future."

Stan pondered a few seconds. "Okay, but I want to be a part of it."

"Trust me, you will be." Jack shook Stan's hand once more then turned toward the door. "I need to pay our landlord."

Chapter 21

Concerned about Siobhan's safety, Stan had asked her to spend the afternoon after their meeting with Jack, at Mary's. Siobhan didn't like the idea of needing a baby-sitter, nor did she like the idea of Stan running off with a U.S. Deputy Marshall, even if he was a trusted friend of Mary. She did, however, agree to Stan's request.

Sitting in Mary's apartment, above Pearl's diner, Mary and Siobhan chatted over cups of coffee, mostly about the men going to Marc's lake house. Siobhan was feeling uneasy and a bit jealous when her phone rang. Seeing it was Stan, she answered right away. Still annoyed that he had left her, she always welcomed the opportunity to talk with him . . . affirm that he still needed her.

"Siobhan, I'm leaving a disgruntled companion at the front door," Stan announced, without giving Siobhan a chance to say "Hello."

"Flib wants to go with you." Siobhan was not surprised; she wanted to go as well.

"Yes, but I'd feel better if he was here with you. See you in a couple days . . . love you."

"Me too, you."

The line went dead. Siobhan drew a deep breath and let it out slowly.

"What gives?" Mary's face crinkled with concern.

"Nothing. Absolutely nothing . . ." Siobhan paused in mid thought, sighing as she continued. ". . . except that Stan is going off to work with the Justice Department and wants me to get Flib."

"That wired-hair heartbreak is welcome to stay here as long as you want. Why the heavy sigh?" Mary responded cheerfully, drawing another gulp of hot coffee.

"We've gotten comfortable. Stan and me. We barely know one another . . . not really . . . but we have gotten comfortable with each other. Is that bad?"

"Not in my book. How many couples have you seen sitting across the table from each other and they do nothing but bicker and fight about nothing. Those that last through the ages are the ones who are comfortable with one another. Sure, there are those who argue about nonsense for decades and say they're happy, but those who really enjoy one another's company are comfortable." Mary paused as she thought about dangers Stan might present. Considering what she had personally witnessed of his behavior, she put her concerns aside. "Count your blessings and enjoy your good fortune."

Siobhan pondered Mary's words for several minutes before asking that question Mary did not want to hear. "Mary, what did you do with the Department of Justice?"

"Nothing. Never worked for them."

"Then how did you work with Jack?"

Mary drew in a deep breath and let out a heavy sigh. "We both worked for an investigative unit loosely attached to the US Marshal's office. We handled agents who lived under cover, investigating crimes for Justice, the military, FBI . . . whoever needed our special services. Our guys were trained to get into places others couldn't, to see things that others looked past, and to collect evidence that would guarantee conviction. And every one of them had a lot of proven experience."

"And Turner worked for you?"

"Not me. We had about a dozen handlers across the country and each had a stable of four to six agents. It was our job to get the right man into the wrong job and then run interference when things went sour."

"Wait . . . you said 'right man in the *wrong* job'?" Siobhan interrupted.

"Yes, none of these jobs should have existed, they were all wrong to start with. These men, and two women that I know of, were tough, ruthless, and one hundred percent business. We had to try and match talents to needs. Whatever it took to get the job done, which is why I was worried about you being with Stan. If he is cut from this stone, he can be unpredictable at best and at worst, deadly to anyone around him."

Shaken by Mary's disclosure, Siobhan shuddered. "Why do we have men like this?"

"Darlin', most of these guys were elite among Special Forces, trained to do the unthinkable. We need them because organized crime does not honor court orders nor demands to cease operations. We need to match our opponents, at home or abroad, with the same tactics and methods they use . . . and before you ask, what they do has to be legal, strictly speaking, officially. Some of these guys walk a real thin line, but they get the goods so the law can be enforced or the military can act with competent intelligence." Mary looked at Siobhan, who looked like reality had just slapped her with a cold, wet, week-old dish rag. "Shouldn't we be getting Flib?"

Flib sat outside the door to the apartment, staring down the parking lot and didn't flinch a muscle when Siobhan parked her Subaru Forester in her usual spot, just twenty feet away.

"What's he looking at?" Mary asked, then quietly got out of the car and looked across the parking lot.

Siobhan got out and joined the gaze of the other two. Not seeing anything strange, but knowing her apartment had been watched in the past, she retrieved her cell phone. Not knowing the number for local police, she called 911. Siobhan and Mary were still trying to figure out what Flib was staring at when they saw a police cruiser cross the highway from the shopping area at the bottom of the hill, continuing until it parked next to Siobhan's car. Before the officer could get out of his car, a blue Toyota screeched out of the parking lot.

"Do you know that car?" the officer asked Siobhan.

"No," Siobhan replied calmly, bending over to scratch Flib who had just joined her next to the car.

"It was parked down on the end," Mary interjected. "Next to the white Lexus." She took a second to notice his name tag. Allred.

Removing a note pad and pen from his shirt pocket, the officer turned and looked at a white Lexus parked at the end apartment on the other side of the parking area. Turning back to the women, he gestured over his shoulder with his pen, "Who lives in that apartment? Where the Toyota was parked." He began recording notes in his pocket notebook.

"I don't know. I thought it was empty," Siobhan responded. "At least it was last week. Has been for a couple months."

Pointing to the apartment in front of their cars, the officer inquired, "You live here?"

"Yes, sir."

"Okay, you two go inside. I'm going to check that apartment and I'll be back in a few minutes." He then got back into his vehicle and drove to the end of the lot, parking behind the Lexus. After recording the Georgia license plate and using his radio to acquire available information, he walked to the apartment door.

A man in his mid-thirties, dressed in khaki slacks and plaid sport shirt, answered the officer's insistent knock. "Yes?"

"Sir, did you have someone visiting you a few moments ago, who drives a blue Toyota?"

"Yeah, what of it?"

"Sir, I am asking you to warn him to slow down. There are a number of children and pedestrians in this area. I would hate for someone to get hurt because your friend was in a hurry."

"Yeah, okay. I'll tell him. Anything else?"

"No, that's about it. By the way, I saw your car has Georgia plates. Will you be staying here long?"

"Does it matter?"

"Yes, sir. If you are moving here permanently you need to register your vehicle with Tennessee DMV within thirty days."

"No. My home is in Atlanta. I'm only here for a short-term job."

"That's fine, sir. Welcome to Oliver Springs and please do ask your friend to slow down."

The man closed the door without responding.

Feeling a shiver of distrust go down the back of his neck, the officer got back into his car and left the apartment area. Reaching the highway, he turned toward Oliver Springs and drove a big loop, returning to Siobhan's apartment fifteen minutes later. Once inside, he attempted to put her concerns to rest.

"I asked the gentleman to tell his friend to not speed around the neighborhood. They are apparently here for a short term job and I have no reason to suspect otherwise. His plates came back clean. Is there a reason you think we should keep an eye on them?"

"My . . .," Siobhan stopped as she began to speak and

looked to Mary. Mary shook her head slightly, warning her to not say anything. Drawing a deep breath, Siobhan continued. "No, officer, I guess not. Thank you for checking for us."

Looking at the two women, the officer realized there was a lot not being said. "Yes, Ma'am. May I have your name and information for my report?" After recording address and pertinent contact information, the officer concluded his visit. "Okay, I'll spread the word to keep an eye on that Toyota and if anything comes up, don't hesitate to call. That's what we're here for." He then returned to his car and left.

"He knows you're worried about something," Mary commented as Siobhan closed the door. "Smart cop! Almost as smart as Flib there." Mary squatted down and scratched the golden protector.

"I need to let Stan know we're being watched. He was afraid of this," Siobhan sighed apprehensively.

Mary responded without hesitation, "I wouldn't do that ... not just yet, anyway."

Puzzled and concerned, Siobhan asked, "Why?"

"He will be worried about you and drop what he's doing to be back here with you. According to Jack, Stan's now an important part of tying up this investigation. Let them work together, you can fill Stan in when he returns. Besides, probably nothing, anyway."

Siobhan looked at Mary, wondering about what she had just said, then started toward her bedroom. "I'll get a few things and we can go back to your place."

"Tell you what. You got a good TV, why don't we just hunker down here for a few hours. Kinda make sure that guy with the Lexus doesn't come calling."

Siobhan smiled, nodded, and turned toward the refrigerator. "We have two diet cokes, three beer, and I can fix some popcorn if we don't have chips."

"Sounds good."

The next two days were busy at Pearl's, which was good for Siobhan because Stan's calls were few and far between. As they cleaned up the kitchen Thursday afternoon, Mary tried to appease the distraught waitress. "He'll be back when he's back. Could be tonight or next week. Did he say how much longer he might be gone?"

"No. Last report, this morning, was they had a map, or something, and were going over everything again to make sure they had it right."

"Well, that's a good sign. Be patient and get your tables clean." Mary then popped Siobhan with a towel, which made her smile, just a bit.

Returning to the dining room with pan and wash cloths, Siobhan was interrupted by the arrival of two men. She recognized one, in uniform, as the policeman who had been by her apartment Tuesday evening.

"Excuse me, Ms. Thomas," the officer called respectfully as they approached. "May we speak with you for a few minutes?"

Setting her pan and cloths down, Siobhan led them to a clean table asking, "What do you need?" Her voice was laden with curiosity and suspicion.

"Ms. Thomas, this is Detective Roger Simpson, with the Oliver Springs Major Crimes Division. He has some questions for you."

"Miss Thomas, first I need to tell you that you are not under investigation. Officer Allred, here, told me about the cars in your parking lot. Normally, I wouldn't have given it a second thought, but it turns out that Lexus license plate is from the same county as the Buick that blew up a couple weeks back. Bartow County, Georgia. I'm not a man who believes in coincidences. Do you have any personal knowledge of the car that blew up?"

Siobhan drew a deep breath, but before she could respond, Mary came up behind her. "Siobhan, is there a problem? Officer Allred, nice to see you again."

"No, ma'am," Siobhan replied. Relieved to have Mary beside her, she drew a deep breath before continuing. "This detective was asking about the car that blew up on the Knoxville Highway,"

"My word, that was the talk of the diner for days," Mary chuckled. "Every one of our regulars had a different theory about the who and why of that thing. What did you fellas need to know?"

"I was asking Miss Thomas if she had any personal knowledge about the incident," the detective repeated. "You are . . .?"

"I'm the owner of this diner, Mary Mooney."

The detective looked toward his officer, who nodded affirmation. Satisfied it was okay to proceed, he repeated his question to Siobhan. "Miss Thomas, you were telling me about the car that exploded on the Knoxville highway."

Siobhan looked at Mary, who responded with an oddly expectant expression; eyes open wide and eyebrows raised. Reading her expression, Siobhan responded confidently. "As Mary said, it was the talk of the diner for days. I don't know anything more than all the speculation spread over breakfast by gossipy patrons."

Not taking his eyes off Siobhan, the detective continued. "That's fine. Now, what about that Lexus at your apartment, has it done anything to cause further concern?"

"Not really. It never goes anywhere, but I could swear somebody is behind the curtain watching me come and go . . . probably just nerves."

"Probably. I'll have Officer Allred and his crew keep an eye on it, just the same. Do you live alone?"

"No. My boyfriend lives with me."

"Would you mind if we stopped by to talk with him?" the detective pushed.

"Fine with me, but he's out of town at present and I don't know when he'll be back."

The detective drew a pondering breath and let it out slowly. Removing a card from his shirt pocket, he handed it to Siobhan. "Would you please ask him to call me. What's his name so I'll know why he's calling?"

"Stan Winthrop."

"Well, thank you for your time." The detective stood. The officer followed his lead. "I apologize for interrupting your work. Please ask Mister Winthrop to call me as soon as he returns." Looking toward Mary, he nodded slightly. "Ma'am."

As the two men left the diner, Mary turned toward Siobhan. "That guy has a nose for trouble. You better tell Stan, but DO NOT let him call him! Not yet, anyway."

Chapter 22

Jack's team quickly restored Marc's cottage to its pristine condition. All of their gear loaded into their van, they departed at four o'clock, heading back to Washington, D.C. Smiling, Marc folded Jack's unexpectedly generous check, slipped it into his pocket, then waited for Stan at the front door. Everyone out, Marc locked the door and said farewell to Stan. Marc followed Stan's Explorer as far as the highway, then sped past him.

Continuing down Highway 61, toward Oak Ridge, Stan began thinking about the brown envelope Jack had given him. Lifting it from his shirt pocket, he read the address written on the outside - Walker Springs Lane #264. "How did Jack get Knoxville from this address?" he thought out loud. Passing under Interstate 75, his curiosity got the best of him, so he pulled into a 76 Travel Center and parked.

Using his phone, he Googled "Walker Springs Lane." A cluster of addresses showed up in Knoxville. No other city was listed. "This has got to be a first! A street name that exists in only one city in America?" Chuckling, he clicked on a link for the Fifth Third Bank at 8331 East Walker Springs Lane, Knoxville, TN. Clicking on "Get Directions" he found this bank was located off I-75 / I-40, not far from the turnoff to Oliver Springs. "Why not?" he asked softly, then went into the travel center to get a cold drink.

Using the GPS in his phone, Stan arrived at the Fifth Third Bank on Walker Springs Lane just over half an hour after opening his cold Coca-Cola. Reading the box number on the envelope once more, he pocketed the key and went inside.

"I would like access to box number 264," he told an assistant manager.

The manager, a young man, professionally dressed and groomed and acting with a high degree of confidence, looked at the clock. "We close in ten minutes."

"I just need to retrieve some papers."

"Yes, sir. I will need your identification, please," he replied, exasperated by the inconvenience so close to closing. After rapping the keys of his computer and double-checking Stan's identification, he looked up without expression. "I am sorry,

Mister Winthrop, you are not on the approved access list."

"Yes, I understand how that might be. The box belongs to my employer who is believed to be deceased. I need papers in the box for a provisional estate settlement."

"You will need to provide a death certificate and order from probate court before I can provide access. Will there be anything else?"

Stan looked at the cold expressionless face staring back at him. Seeing that this man was strictly by-the-book and could not care less about the customer in front of him, Stan retrieved his driver's license and left.

Pressing #1 on his speed dial as he got into the car, Stan also put his phone on speaker and started the engine of his Explorer. Siobhan picked up on the second ring, as he backed out of the parking space.

Not in the mood for the same news of another delay, she answered curtly, "Yes?"

"Hello, gorgeous! Do we have plans for supper?"

"I take it you are finally coming home?" Siobhan replied, relieved to hear good news, but now in a mood to play.

"Yeah. Party broke up at the lake and I don't have anywhere else to go."

"I guess I could find something. What do you think about grilling a slab of beef?"

"Sounds good. You want me to pick it up on the way home?"

"Sure. Stop at the market. Oh, get some fresh veggies, too."

"Will do. See you in about an hour. Love you."

Siobhan hesitated before answering. "You said that a couple days ago then disappeared. You may have to give me some physical proof of that statement."

"Hmmm, maybe I should skip the market and just come home?"

"I want STEAK! . . . Love you, too."

Eager to get home, Stan ignored the white Lexus and blue Toyota parked at the end apartment. Grabbing a bag of groceries from the front seat and his computer bag from the back, he stepped lightly toward the door. Finding the door locked, he put the groceries down and pulled out his keys. Gaining entry, he was greeted by Flib, who while overjoyed at his friend's return, quickly shifted attention to the aromas escaping from the grocery bag.

"HELLO! Anyone home?" Stan called out, wondering what waited for him.

Siobhan closed the refrigerator door, a beer in one hand. "You want a beer while we fix supper?"

Stan looked at her and smiled with delight. She had not dressed to seduce, as when he went to Asheville, rather she wore jeans, sandals, and an old t-shirt. She had brushed her hair.

"Sure, I'd like a beer, but there's something else I want first!" Crossing the living room, Stan dropped his computer on the sofa, and the groceries on the kitchen table. Leaning over, for Siobhan was a head shorter than he, Stan wrapped both arms around her and planted his lips across hers.

When they finally came up for air, Siobhan drew a deep breath. Exhaling slowly, she remarked, "Yes, that will do . . . for now."

"For now," Stan agreed.

While Stan grilled steaks, Siobhan prepared a fresh salad and home fries. He told her about events at the cottage, ending with, "Now we wait for a call from Jack."

"Speaking of calls, a Detective Simpson wants you to call him as soon as you get back into town. Mary said you might not want to."

"What does he want?" Stan removed their steaks from the grill and the conversation moved to the kitchen table, where no time was lost cutting into the meat and digging into fresh vegetables. Siobhan continued their conversation between bites.

"Somebody from Bartow County, Georgia, has moved into the apartment on the end. Seems the car you blew up was also from Bartow County. Simpson doesn't believe in coincidence."

"Okay, and what does Mary have to do with all this?" Stan paused eating and stared at Siobhan, who proceeded to tell him about Mary's past. When she finished, Stan swallowed a mouthful of potatoes before responding. "I knew there was more to her than Pearl's. I wish I had asked Jack about her."

Jack walked into his Washington office early Friday morning and dropped his briefcase and computer on his work bench. Turning back into his secretary's reception office, he immediately started a pot of coffee. This office was small, room enough for the secretary's desk, two guest chairs, and a coffee station. Lifting a half empty bottle of spring water from the cabinet below the coffee station, he noticed that a case of six gallon bottles of spring water had been delivered while he was gone. He didn't really care that this water made better coffee, it was simply more convenient than traipsing down the hall every time he wanted some.

Coffee started, he turned back to his office. Eyes passing over his secretary's desk, he sighed with regret. Thinking he would be gone longer, he had given his secretary the week off and didn't want to deal with her complaining about being called back early. Not today.

Returning to his office, he saw that his team had already delivered research they had developed at Marc's cottage. Familiar boxes sat on top of an eight-foot table which filled most of the wall just inside the door to his office, with ample room between the side of his desk and the table for easy movement. Being 'old school,' Jack preferred paper to digital and his manager's desk was covered with well-organized folders containing information about investigations he needed to consider. Three guest chairs sat in front of his desk and an empty coat rack sat in the corner behind the door. Windows took half the wall behind his desk, with filled bookshelves covering the remainder.

After docking his notebook computer and turning it on, he returned to the gurgling coffee pot. Moving the half-full pot out of the way, he put his ceramic mug in its place. Once filled, he returned the pot and sipped his coffee en route to his desk. After sitting, adjusting himself for long term comfort, and taking a large gulp of hot coffee, he opened a template he had developed for requesting judicial warrants. At 12:30 p.m., he ordered a sandwich and soda from a deli down the block and continued working. At 4:38, he picked up his phone and punched in a number from personal memory.

"Eleanor, this is Jack Barnes. Is Judge Driscoll available to sign a few warrants?"

The voice on the other end was very female and friendly. "Sorry, handsome, the judge left at noon and won't be back for two weeks. Taking the family for a spell of sand and surf. Can I do anything for you?"

"Two weeks?"

"That's what his calendar shows. Two weeks personal leave. Not to be disturbed."

"Yeah, okay. . . . I'll try Carpentar. Thank you."

"Hey, Jack. When do I get to collect on that drink and dinner you promised?"

"Soon. Let me wrap up this project that has me in its grip. I promise."

"I'm going to collect!"

"Yes, ma'am. It will be my pleasure. Talk with you later."

After hanging up the phone, Jack pulled the writing shelf from his desk and ran his finger down the list of names taped to it. Finding "Carpentar," he read the number and names next to it and placed the call.

An older female voice answered on the third ring. "Judge Carpentar's office."

"Missus Edwards, this is John Barnes in Justice Investigations. Is Judge Carpentar available to review arrest warrants for approval?"

"I'm sorry Mister Barnes, but Judge Carpentar is on indefinite leave of absence."

"Nothing serious I hope," Jack responded with honest concern.

"You must have been out of town. The judge suffered a heart attack two days ago. He's resting comfortably, but we do not know when, or if, he'll be allowed to return."

"Yes, I have been out of town collecting evidence and building a case. Please give his honor my best wishes for a speedy recovery. He's one of our good ones."

"I'll pass the message on. Anything else?"

"No, thank you. Good bye."

Jack hung up the phone and pushed back into his chair.

Neither of his reliable go-to judges was available. He had strong professional relationships with both men. He didn't have that same bond of trust and cooperation with any other federal judges. Knowing he was on a tight schedule and needed warrants to schedule twelve teams of U.S. Marshals from three offices for raids in five cities, he punched in the phone number for the "justice on call."

This office maintained contact with a federal justice twenty-four hours a day, 365 days a year. Jack met both of his preferred justices through this service but knew these men and women were not always the most cooperative. He was given two appointment opportunities, five forty-five that evening or eleven-thirty tomorrow morning, Saturday. Knowing he would be pushed to make the appointment, he did accept five forty-five.

Walking into the Warrant Justice's office at five forty-six, Jack approached the clerk's desk and announced himself. "John Barnes, U.S. Department of Justice Investigations Division, here for warrant approval."

The young woman looked at Jack and pressed the intercom button as she lifted the phone on her desk. "Your five forty-five is here, sir." After a few seconds she hung up and looked back at Jack. "You may go in. Judge Lassiter is waiting for you, sir."

Jack's heart sank in his chest as he turned toward the door. He had heard Lassiter was tough on warrants, wouldn't approve anything the least bit questionable, but this was their first meeting. He would have to be sharp and on his best behavior if he was to succeed in this part of his mission. Closing the door behind him, Jack stepped confidently toward the desk in this small, barren office shared by judges who rotated through this duty.

"Judge Lassiter, thank you for meeting with me so quickly."

"What do you have?" the man behind the desk asked without any further cordiality. He appeared to be of average build for a man in his early fifties. His voice was a bit tenor, however it was firm and his stern face confirmed that he meant business.

"Twenty-seven warrants that will involve U.S. Marshals from three separate offices and will be executed on twelve separate sites in five cities." Jack opened his brief case and removed the stack of warrants.

"Okay, what's the big picture?"

"We have discovered a crime syndicate involved in human trafficking, prostitution, illegal cigarette and alcohol sales, fire arms sales, extortion, and murder."

"Where is their center of operations?"

"Outside of Atlanta, Georgia."

"How did you find them?"

Jack could tell this was going to be a lengthy cross-examination. The judge was asking questions without looking at the first warrant. "I received an inquiry from a private citizen about one of our operatives who was acting independently. Researching that inquiry led me to three separate justice investigations already in process. Information from the agent tied them all together."

"How reliable is this agent's information?"

Not wanting to add another layer of complexity, Jack elected to treat Turner and Winthrop as a single source. "I rate it as extremely reliable, sir. Much of what he provided corresponded directly with what we already had. Interviewing the agent himself, I found him to be highly credible."

"You said you want to use U.S. Marshals, any local law enforcement?"

"No sir. Our information leads us to believe local law enforcement is complicit in at least three of the locations."

"Do your warrants include law enforcement individuals?"

"Yes, sir. Six."

"Remove them and set them aside for now. Then we can review what you have."

Justice Lassiter challenged each of the remaining twenty-one warrants, approving nineteen of them. He excluded the single warrant for records in White, Georgia based on lack of indisputable evidence, which was what they were after.

"Your honor, Cunningham Tractor is the center of this entire operation," Jack objected. "You are asking us to cut the legs off and leave the body intact."

"Mister Barnes, you have shown me nothing that could not be explained by regular business of the tractor enterprise. You show me one indisputable link between Cunningham Tractor and any one of these other operations and I'll let you shut them down."

Jack thought he had presented this evidence but knew better than to argue. He sat quietly as the justice also excluded the warrant for Taylor Abercrombie, the hit man linked to the Florida murder, citing, "You have nothing concrete on this man, everything is circumstantial. I reject this warrant and further direct that you may not pursue him. If I learn that he is arrested singularly or not at one of the approved locations, I'll have your badge." He then approved five of the six warrants for law enforcement officers.

Finishing the review, he looked at Jack sternly and concluded. "You seem to be ready to execute these warrants, however I'll not sign them open ended. You have four days, ninety-six hours."

"Your honor, I need time to coordinate with offices beyond my own and they need to be executed on Thursday evening for maximum effectiveness."

"Why Thursday?"

"That is when they hold sales at the human trafficking locations. 'Merchandise' is collected during the week and moved out immediately following the sale."

"Very well, I'll give you until 11:59 p.m. Thursday. Not one minute longer."

"Yes, sir. I understand. Thank you for your assistance and cooperation."

After collecting the signed warrants, Jack left, exhausted and in need of a very stiff beverage.

Chapter 23

Jack called Steve and Mike to his office early Saturday morning. These two men had been on this project from the beginning, even researching and assembling data in Tennessee; Jack needed their help scheduling execution of the warrants. All three men stumbled over the same problem, timing.

They had warrants for three warehouses where human trafficking took place Thursday evenings. Based on reports from Stan and U. S. Department of Justice agents, they knew merchandise, i.e. girls, were collected each week through Thursday afternoon and sales began at nine o'clock. If the agents wanted to wrangle sellers and buyers, they would have to wait until nine o'clock. A second group of warrants included auto shops, which were also best served "after hours." Warrants for individuals and law enforcement officers could be executed at any time.

Picking up Cunningham and securing records at Cunningham Tractor, which Jack did not have a warrant for but was still pursuing, became both key and problematic. All three agents agreed that the most important warrants had to be executed simultaneously or they would risk losing key evidence. Losing Councilman Cunningham was not an option.

While Jack reviewed his abundance of notes, Mike and Steve trolled the internet for current information about Albert David Cunningham. Mike found an Asheville gossip column which revealed an invitation to the North Carolina Governor's Office early Friday morning. Cunningham's public calendar confirmed that he would be "out of town" and showed appointments through four o'clock on Thursday, which was not uncommon. Steve uncovered reservations for three rooms at a hotel in Raleigh, the capital city of North Carolina, in Cunningham's name for Thursday night. Special requests included two adjoining rooms and late arrival was indicated. Mike checked Asheville area airports, but could find no record of a reservation or private flight plans.

"It's still early," Jack mused aloud to the others. "If he's flying private, he could file flight plans a couple hours before leaving. Still, if he has a hotel waiting, he's going Thursday evening. We need to grab him before he leaves for Raleigh. The adjoining rooms tells me he's taking Missus Turner with him. My gut tells me he'll pick her up at her shop and drive from there to the airport. That would put them in Raleigh after nine, which would be 'late arrival'. What do you think?"

"Works for me," Steve agreed.

Mike nodded agreement as well.

"What time does her shop close?" Jack asked.

Looking in a folder labeled "Gwendolyn Turner," Mike replied, "Six o'clock."

"Okay. All teams will have to be in place by quarter past five and we strike as soon as Cunningham arrives. We'll miss the buyers at the warehouses, but I have a feeling we'll be able to track them down without difficulty." Jack looked at the faces of his teammates and sighed, not with relief but with apprehension. "You guys go home, be with your families. I'll let you know tomorrow which teams you'll lead."

Jack sent e-mails to senior officers, whom he knew personally and trusted, with the U.S. Marshall Service in Atlanta, Georgia; Baltimore, Maryland; and Columbia, South Carolina. These messages outlined the project and request for manpower, but did not include specifics on targets or locations. He also sent a message to another friend, Lewis Anthony, with the Georgia Attorney General's Office, asking for his help. He barely had time to shut down his computer before his phone rang.

"Jack Barnes, why in the world would you need help from the State of Georgia?"

Chuckling, Jack explained his situation, including the abduction of Stan Winthrop and suspected murder of Michael Geoffrey Turner. When he finished, the voice on the other end laughed.

"You dog. That outfit has been on our radar for a couple years. If you can substantiate the abduction or murder, I can help you."

"The abduction, yes. We have the victim on our team."

"Good 'nuff for me, sir. When do we shut 'em down?"

Jack replied, "Thursday, end of day." After a bit more discussion about timing, Jack ended the phone call at 2:30 p.m. After making important notes, Jack wanted to call it a day, however he knew he had to make two more phone calls.

Both calls were brief and to the point. He asked Detective Marc Hendricks to join his team Thursday afternoon for a party in Hendersonville, North Carolina and Stan Winthrop to join him in Asheville, North Carolina. Meeting time and location had not yet been established, but he needed to know if they could join him. Both men agreed without hesitation and said they would be ready.

"Thursday . . . good. I'll wait for the details. . . . Bye." Stan finished his phone call, put the phone down, and looked at Siobhan. "We've got 'em; now just need to pick 'em up."

"Thursday . . . THIS Thursday?" she replied with surprise. "He doesn't waste any time, does he? Do I get to tag along?"

Stan looked at this young lady who not only had his heart but had come to his rescue more than once. "I don't know that you're on the invite list and it could get a bit dicey. You've seen these thugs up close." Seeing Siobhan's expression drop, Stan shifted his thoughts. "Hey, YOU are MY 'team,' and I say you go, too. After all, you've already been to After Six and know your way around, sort of."

Squatting down to pet their furry teammate, Siobhan asked, "What about Flib? He was with me last time."

"Sure. If it gets too dicey, he can distract the bad guys. I'll let Jack know when he calls with the details. Meanwhile, you need to tell Mary that you're taking Thursday off, and probably Friday as well."

Siobhan ruffled Flib's neck exclaiming, "You hear that Mister Flib? We get to nab the bad guys!"

Torrents of rain swept across the southeastern United States on Sunday, continuing from Mobile, Alabama across to Newark, New Jersey into Monday evening. Siobhan and Stan took advantage of the weather and relaxed in front of their television Sunday afternoon, until Mary knocked at their door.

"I'm sorry to barge in like this, but I have to know," Mary exploded as she entered the apartment. "What is going on? Why do you need Thursday AND Friday off? You drop a bombshell like this and walk out the door?! You CAN'T be going shopping again!"

"Actually, we are," Stan chuckled. "We've placed an order and need to pick it up."

"Let me guess. You placed the order with Jack Barnes and pickup is in Asheville." Mary's expression was now nervous, tense with concern. Seeing affirmation on Stan's face, she continued. "How many men on the team?"

"Don't know yet. We've just been told to be in Asheville on Thursday. Details coming when he gets them developed," Stan confessed readily, believing Mary had ways to get any information she wanted from him.

Turning to Siobhan, she resumed her challenge. "So, why are YOU going? Have you been deputized as well?"

Siobhan smiled and replied with a bit of laughter, "Oh, no. I'm simply going to see about a dress before After Six, Limited is closed for good. Flib has offered to pick out something elegant."

"THIS IS NO SPRING PICNIC!" Mary exploded. "Those guys I told you about who don't play by the rules, this is them! This is NOT amateur hour. Both of you need to step aside and let the U.S. Marshals do their job."

Stan turned Mary toward him, a hand on each shoulder, and spoke calmly. "Mary, we will be part of a team. A team made up of trusted U.S. Marshals, and yes, I believe they do know what they are doing. I would NEVER allow Siobhan to go into any situation where I thought she was in any real danger. . . . Now, would you care to grab a beer and share our popcorn and movie?"

Jack Barnes spent Monday morning confirming that teams of Deputy U. S. Marshals in three regional offices were being made ready. Each team would be led by a captain in whom he had personal confidence and trusted without question. Warrants were then sent to each captain by Federal Express. Monday afternoon he secured permission to use Schenk Job Corps Center to launch North Carolina operations and completed his lineup of required deputies.

Jack called Stan midmorning Tuesday. "Stan, you go to After Six with me on Thursday."

"Wouldn't have it any other way. Siobhan is coming with me. She's been to After Six before. You've seen her recorded visit."

"Yeah, her and a dog . . . yeah, I think I like that idea. She can go in first and maybe get customers out of the way. Do you still have the recording equipment?"

"Yes."

"How far does it reach?"

"We parked about a block away."

"That's good. You can bring it along. Have her record what happens. . . . Yeah, I do like that idea. Our guys will be wearing body cams, but this will give us another view that the government won't know about or grab, in case we need to see something off the record. What about the dog?"

"Flib's part of my team."

"Okay, this will work. I need you to meet up with the team near Brevard at the Schenk Job Corps Center. Take Highway 276 into the forest, follow signs to Davidson River Campground. Schenk is right next door. Follow the road around, there is a big parking lot on the right just before you get to the buildings. Be there at two o'clock, Thursday."

"No problem. What about Marc? Where's he going?"

"He'll be with the team at the Hendersonville warehouse. We'll all be meeting at Schenk. Anything else?"

"Yes, one more thing. How do I get Mary off my case? She's scared stiff."

"Mary sent a lot of men into impossible situations. I think that's why she retired. One of her best didn't return. Tell her you'll be beside me; that might help."

"Okay. See you in a couple days."

Wednesday morning Siobhan went to work, as usual. Mary had been very cold to her on Tuesday and Siobhan had hopes that all would be normal again. Receiving the message that they would be with Jack had done little to warm her heart.

Stan pulled his surveillance equipment out of the closet and checked all components and batteries. Everything was spread out on the table when he was interrupted by an insistent knock on the door.

Opening the door, Stan found two men in suits. Before he could say a word, the man in the front asked, "Stan Winthrop?"

"Yes, what can I do for you?"

The man then produced a gold shield and introduced himself. "Sir, I am Detective Roger Simpson, with the Oliver Springs Major Crimes Division. My associate is Detective Lawrence White. May we come in?"

"I'm rather busy at the moment. What is this about?"

"I appreciate that, sir, but it would be better if we talked inside." He then began to push his way past Stan.

Not wanting to be bullied nor expose his equipment on the kitchen table, Stan put his hand on the detective's chest to stop him. "I said I am busy. What is it you need to talk about?"

Seeing Stan tense up, as though a tiger ready to launch, Detective Simpson backed up. "Sir, what can you tell us about the car that blew up on the Knoxville highway a couple weeks back? Did you have anything to do with it?"

Still tense, Stan assumed a professional calm before replying. "What makes you think I had anything to do with it?"

"Miss Thomas, your girlfriend, filed a complaint against the residents on the end, with the white Lexus. She claims they have been watching you come and go. Turns out that Lexus and the car on the highway are from the same county in Georgia. I don't believe in coincidences, so we are following up every possible link to that car burned up on the highway."

Stan grinned a bit as he replied, "I can't tell you a thing. I was out of town. I did, however, see the fire engine and several men poking around in the wreckage as I came into town."

"Out of town? Where?"

Stan thought quickly, knowing he did not want to admit to being in Bartow County, Georgia. "Spartanburg, South Carolina. Then returned by way of Hendersonville and Asheville, North Carolina. Before you ask, no, I cannot prove it. My gas tank was empty when I got back here and neither of the jobs I was pursuing panned out. A dry run."

"What type of work do you do?" Detective White asked.

"I help people find things. Jewelry, cars, books, whatever is important to them and they can't seem to locate."

"Are you currently working on a case?" White continued.

"I am, but I'm not at liberty to discuss it. Client confidentiality."

"I understand," Simpson relented. "Can you think of any reason the tenants of the apartment on the end, with the Lexus and Toyota, might be watching you or your girlfriend?"

"None whatsoever. When I have the time, I'll go ask 'em." Stan was now becoming agitated with the questions. "If there is nothing else, I do have work to do and I'm on a deadline."

Simpson looked at Stan carefully, attempting to read his face. "No. Thank you for your help and I apologize for taking so much of your time."

Stan watched as the two detectives turned to leave. When they reached their car, he closed and locked the front door. Hearing a scratching at the kitchen door, he crossed the apartment and let Flib inside.

"He's hiding something," Detective White said as he closed his car door.

"Yep . . . and I want to know what it is," Simpson agreed.

Chapter 24

After placing calls to Stan Winthrop and Detective Marc Hendricks on Tuesday morning, Jack called Lewis Anthony, with the Georgia Attorney General's Office. Stan and Marc were onboard and ready to go. Lewis Anthony was not yet ready to move.

"My boss, our Attorney General for the State of Georgia, doesn't think we have enough evidence to move on," Anthony explained. "He reviewed our records, two years of tracking what appears to be illegal activities, but he won't budge."

"Do you need his approval? Don't you have the authority to issue a warrant for records?" Jack pushed.

"Yes I do, but that would mean going against the current powers that be."

"How did he find out?"

"The judge who signed my warrants told him. That 'good ole boy' sort of thing." Anthony's voice had now become tense with the situation.

Jack thought for a moment, then asked, "Do you have a U. S. Judge you can trust with a volatile warrant?"

"Yes, I believe so. What are you thinking?"

"I recall seeing a document that cast doubt on a bid Cunningham Tractors made for a state contract. If I can find that, I'll send the warrant to your judge and you can exercise it, along with all your other warrants."

"Jack, ole boy, that warrant is already in my list and was signed by the judge. He laughed about it."

"Did you tell the judge when the warrants were to be executed?"

"Nope. I didn't know."

"Are you willing to rock the boat? It could cost you or make you a hero." Jack was now in sales mode.

"I like being a hero. You want me to assemble a select team of SBI officers and execute the warrants against the directive of our AG. Right?"

"Yep."

"Hell, I've been thinking it's about time for a long vacation anyway. Why not. . . . When do we strike?"

After personally speaking with each of the North Carolina team members Tuesday afternoon, Jack confirmed that all warrants had arrived at each of the other three U.S. Marshals' offices. Captains in Atlanta, Georgia and Columbia, South Carolina had theirs and now armed with specific locations were organizing men into secondary teams for their execution. The captain in Baltimore, Maryland had not yet received his package.

"I'll send a notarized set of copies with Deputy Steve Malcolm, who will be your second-in-command. He knows all the details on this case and what we need to grab for conviction," Jack groaned. His stomach rolled as he swallowed his feelings about the courier service.

The Baltimore captain called twenty minutes later, informing Jack his package had arrived. Jack responded, "Deputy Malcolm is still bringing a set of copies. You have an important list and will need all the help you can muster."

Wednesday afternoon Jack and his team moved into a motel in Brevard, North Carolina. Jack and Deputy Mike Durant took a drive around Hendersonville as the sun set. Finding two places Stan had used to hide himself on his trip to the warehouse, Jack used the one closest to the warehouse to park for a brief reconnaissance. Mike flew a silent drone over their target verifying its layout and approach. Before returning to Brevard, they stopped by the home of newly elected Sheriff Donald Whitsett, who had campaigned on cleaning up the Henderson County Sheriff's Department.

"I have never trusted those guys. How can I help?" Whitsett asked when presented with warrants on three of his deputies.

"I will have two Deputy U.S. Marshals in your office at five-thirty tomorrow afternoon," Jack explained. "Simply call these three in for an opportunity to join a special investigation. My men will make the arrest. If they don't come in, we'll pick them up later."

=======

Jack and Deputy Bert Long, his second in command for the "After Six" visit, drove through Asheville again Thursday morning, just to get a fresh feel for where they were going.

Bert noticed a narrow alley behind the building that housed After Six, commenting, "We need at least one man in that alley. Possibly two."

"I don't expect much resistence inside, so you should be able to get two," Jack agreed as they left downtown.

Stan, Siobhan, and Flib locked their apartment and climbed into Stan's Explorer at 11:30 a.m. Thursday morning. The white Lexus followed them until they turned in at Hardee's, then resumed following them when they pulled out of the drive-thru and turned toward Knoxville. Proceeding through Oak Ridge on Hwy 62, the Lexus was pulled over by local police. Breathing a sigh of relief, Stan looked at the car now immediately behind and recognizing the driver, waved. Marc Hendricks waved back.

Stan thanked Marc for his assistance with the Lexus when they stopped briefly at the North Carolina Welcome Center. "Jack's idea," Marc confessed.

After stopping in Mills River, between Asheville and Brevard, for cold drinks, the Tennessee Contingent of Jack's team arrived at the entrance to Davidson River Campground at 1:42 p.m., eighteen minutes before their scheduled rendevous. Turning left off Highway 276 they admired the Davidson River laughing over rocks below the bridge. Continuing another fifty yards, they saw an older woman hanging a "No Vacancy" plaque at a roadside information station. Thirty yards farther, the road split. Davidson River Campground, to the right and now at capacity, had a line of campers and RVs waiting to check in. Just beyond the split in the road, a sign for Schenk Job Corps Center pointed to the left. As the road curved into Schenk, they passed a stone wall commemorating the Civilian Conservation Corps. Leaving the cooling shade of overhanging trees, they continued past an open grass field to the left, then another to the right, a baseball field, then a parking lot on the right. Pulling into the parking lot they saw four cars on the far side, next to a pair of tennis courts, and a row of oak trees shading spaces along the road. Marc moved toward the shade before Stan did.

Stan, Siobhan, and Marc were sipping their drinks beneath a large oak tree at the edge of the parking lot, when four black SUVs and two black sedans pulled in and parked beside their cars. Stepping from the lead SUV, Jack called, "Good, you're here. Let's get started."

Mike quickly pulled a tripod from his SUV and set it up in the shade, near where Marc, Stan, and Siobhan sat. Flib, who had been exploring the baseball field, sat between Stan and Siobhan and intently watched proceedings. Jack placed two white twenty-four inch by thirty inch cards at the base of the tripod. Nineteen men in black gathered around the tripod and Jack. Recognizing only Mike, Stan asked, "Where's Steve?"

"Baltimore," Jack replied, "which is a good place to start this briefing. We are one of four operations in a coordinated campaign being conducted today by the U. S. Department of Justice, plus one more by the State of Georgia. Our expected trigger time is five thirty this afternoon. I will be watching for target number one to arrive at After Six in downtown Asheville. As soon as he walks through the door, I will release a signal for all teams to proceed. You guys as well as teams in Maryland, South Carolina, Florida, and Georgia. Taylor and Jerry, the Sheriff of Henderson County is expecting the two of you to be in his office at 5:30. You don't wait. Make your arrests when your three subjects arrive. The rest of us have to wait."

Jack then selected one of the cards from the base of the tripod and set it up where everyone could see it, a diagram of the warehouse area outside Hendersonville. "Mike, your team should be parked and ready by four thirty. Hendricks, you ride with Mike. Leave your car at the service station at the bottom of the hill. Stan gave us two great locations, which we saw last night. Make sure you cannot be seen by vehicles we expect to arrive shortly after five.

"Stan, what can you tell us about the area near Cunningham's residence?"

Not expecting a question, Stan took a deep breath and pictured the area in his mind. "It is upper class residential. Cunningham's estate is at the top of a hill, overlooking the valley. Lots of trees shading streets. Streets are kind of narrow."

"What about that couple?" Siobhan interrupted.

"Great idea! There is an older couple who live down the hill from Cunningham. Street across from his gate, then down on the right. They might let you park in their drive. They don't like him."

"Carter, do you have that? We have six men in the local U.S. Marshal's Office on standby, if you need them for search and seizure."

"Why aren't they with us now?" Carter asked.

"We know Cunningham has bought at least one agent in the local FBI office. I don't want any leaks on this move and as Stan said, no place to park. They'll come in as soon as you call them. You'll have the gates to the estate open by then and they can park inside.

"Now for the man himself." Jack changed diagrams on his tripod. "This is downtown Asheville. We need to arrive separately, between 4:45 and 5:00." Looking at members on the downtown team, he identified two men who were larger in size. "Terry will be on the alley, watching for escapees out the back. Tommy, you are his second, if we don't need you inside. We won't know until we move. The plan is for Siobhan and the dog to go in first, around quarter past five. She'll have audio and video so we'll know what we are dealing with. Stan and I will go in as soon as Cunningham arrives, that's when we'll know which door Tommy goes to. I'm expecting one driver and two bodyguards, but these guys are big and mean. George, I want you to block departure. As soon as we go in the door, use your vehicle to pen his car in. Bob, you drive mine and block his rear.

"Mike, your warehouse team should move in as soon as Cunningham arrives downtown. You'll have to get his gate open; you won't be able to crash through it. Get in as fast as you can to save records."

"Jack, do you mind if we deactivate the gate ahead of time?" Mike asked, concerned about the delay.

"Stan, can they get to that gate without being seen?" Jack asked.

"I doubt it; hundred feet or less from the building . . ." Stan paused as he pictured the gate in his mind, suddenly recalling a memory from his distant past about a weak point in the gate control. "If they haven't discovered it, the mechanism that controls the gate has a flaw. Break the cover off; use a pry from the bottom, it'll pop up. On the upper right side is a switch; push it from standby to service, then push the red button. Should take about fifteen seconds to gain access and another twenty or so for the gate to be open enough for you to get in."

Jack stared at Stan with wonder. Mike, however, asked, "And if they've fixed this flaw?"

"You'll need a screw driver for security screws to remove the cover, then the code to put it in service mode. Try '936752'." Stan replied confidently.

"'936752', right. And if that doesn't work?" Mike continued, not sure if he believed what Stan said.

"Scale the fence," Jack replied. "You can then open the gate from inside. Remember, there will be young women inside, as well as records. We don't want to lose any of them. At five thirty, expect at least four heavy weights inside. Also, there should be a bus, passenger van, and two cargo vans. Four vehicles. If one of them isn't there, watch your backside, they could be coming in late."

"If we don't have all four vehicles, I'll send someone out to watch the road," Mike thought out loud.

"Good call," Jack agreed. "Okay, any questions? We need to hit hard and fast and get this over with. Mike, if you need more personnel to care for the women or search and seizure, call Sheriff Whitsett. Any questions?" Jack looked at all the faces in front of him, then looked at his watch. "We have about an hour before we go catch bad guys, so relax and check your equipment. Get your vests on! Hendricks, Winthrop, Siobhan, I need you three over here. Mike, you too."

Looking at his three non-deputies, he continued. "Raise your right hand. Do you solemnly swear to uphold the constitution of the United States of America, to uphold and enforce its laws and protect its citizens without regard to race, sex, or age, and to obey orders and directives of duly appointed Sheriff and Deputies of the United States Marshall's Service? Say 'I do'."

"I do," the three responded in unison.

"By the power vested in me as an officer of the United

States Department of Justice, I appoint you Special Deputies of the United States Marshals Service, with all powers and protections afforded thereby. Witnessed officially by Deputy Marshal Mike Durant."

Siobhan looked a bit glassy-eyed and shivered slightly as a chill ran down her back. Stan and Marc took the oath in stride and never shifted a muscle, except to lower their hands.

"Marc, do you have black?" Mike asked.

"Yes, just didn't want to drive in all black. I'll go change at my car." He then turned to leave.

"Remind me to give you a U.S. Marshall Vest before we leave," Mike called after him.

"Stan, you'll need a vest as well, but don't need to be in black," Jack suggested. He then studied Stan and pondered. "Tell you what . . . no, wear the vest over what you have on. Siobhan, I don't have a vest to fit your figure and I need you to be inconspicuous."

"If there's any shooting, I'll grab her and put her on the floor," Stan volunteered.

"There won't be any shooting, this is a dress shop," Siobhan replied.

Jack smiled. "I hope you're right, but don't be too sure. Let Stan protect you! Let's get ready. Stan, I need to see your surveillance equipment."

Deputy Attorney General Lewis Anthony walked into the Waffle House Restaurant on Hwy 411 in White, Georgia at 5:04 Thursday afternoon. He was accompanied by three agents of the Georgia State Bureau of Investigation. All were in good spirits and enjoying a joke as they sat in a booth near the middle of the front wall.

A waitress in her mid-fifties, with a friendly face and dressed in a Waffle House uniform, placed four glasses of ice water on the table and prepared to take orders.

"Hey Gloria! Where's my waffle? Did you have to go squeeze the eggs from a chicken or something? Come on, I gotta get goin!" a man in the back corner bellowed.

The waitress looked over her shoulder and yelled back at

her customer sitting at one of only two other tables occupied at the time. "Be patient, Gary. I got others to wait on. Your order'll be up in a sec." She then turned her attention back to the four men in front of her, speaking politely. "I'm sorry about that. What can I get you gentlemen?"

"Just coffee all around," Anthony responded with a smile. He then put his phone on the table where he could see when the screen came to life.

"Order up!" a chef called and slid a plate of waffles and fried eggs to the ready shelf.

"I'll have your coffee in just a sec," the waitress told her customers, smiling as brightly as she could. She then retrieved the order and delivered it to Gary. "See, that didn't take so long, now did it?"

Seeing a crack in Anthony's phone, one of his companions chuckled, spinning the device toward himself. "How long have you had that old thing?"

"A few years." Anthony turned the phone back so he could read it. "Screen got cracked a couple days ago. I'll get it fixed when I have time. It's a good phone."

While Gloria was setting coffee cups on the table for Anthony and his companions, Gary's phone rang, playing "Dixie." His mouth full of waffle, he answered. "Yeah?" . . . "What, now? I just got my dinner!" . . . "Yeah, okay, but you owe me for dinner." He then pulled out a well-worn wallet, removed a ten-dollar bill, and dropped it on the table. Pushing past Gloria, he knocked her into the table causing the coffee pot she was holding to crash into a glass in front of Lewis Anthony. Water and ice spilled across the table, soaking Anthony's phone.

"GA-ARY!" the waitress screamed.

Lewis Anthony grabbed his phone and a handful of napkins, but he was too late. The screen had already flashed and gone black. Looking out the window he saw four Georgia State Troopers sail down the highway, his armed force for raiding the Cunningham complex.

Heading into the parking lot, Gary saw the State Troopers, too, and stopped in his tracks. Two patrol cars traveling together was common, but never four. Looking at the black SUV beside him, he noticed the state owned license plates. Turning around, he glared at the men still moping up their table. Whipping out his cell phone, Gary jumped into a black and yellow pickup truck and screeched out of the parking lot.

"We've been made!" Deputy Attorney General Lewis Anthony exclaimed. "Dirk, call the patrol and tell them to be ready to follow us into Cunningham's." All four men scrambled from their table, out the door, and jumped into their state-owned black SUV. They screeched out of the parking lot seventy-five seconds behind Gary; blue lights flashing in their grill. The time was 5:12 p.m.

Chapter 25

Jack parked his Explorer a block away from After Six, Ltd.; as luck would have it, in the same spot he had used during their previous visit. Opening the tailgate, he reached under the privacy cover and switched all his surveillance equipment on. Methodically, he checked the reception from Siobhan's pendant camera and microphone, and Flib's collar camera. Satisfied all was working, he pushed the record button and closed the tailgate. Siobhan stepped nervously from the front seat after Stan opened her door. Flib hopped over the seat, out the door, and sat on the sidewalk, waiting.

"I'll be right behind you," Stan assured her and squeezed her hand.

"You better be," she said as she walked away. A black SUV caught her attention as two men got out of the back seat with the vehicle still in the traffic lane. Both men were dressed in black and wore plain black nylon jackets. They walked toward Stan as Siobhan walked toward After Six, Ltd. The time was 5:12 p.m. and the sidewalk was filling with people heading home.

"Missus Thomson, you came back!" Gwendolyn Turner exclaimed as Siobhan strolled nervously past the bodyguard at the door. "The way you left last time I was concerned I had done something to offend you."

"No, I'm sorry. My husband finished his meeting early and had sent me a text telling me to meet him across the square, right away. I could see you were busy, so I just slipped out," Siobhan explained. "I have more time today and I can see you only have one other customer; what do you have that might entice me into leaving some of my husband's hard earned money in your hands?"

"*Thanks for the intel, but don't overplay this,*" Stan whispered in her ear.

"I tell you what, Sharon, why don't we see what your fashion advisor picks out," Gwendolyn suggested, schmoozing her client. "What is his name?"

Siobhan froze for a second before responding, "Franz. Franz of Beverly Hills."

"How sweet." Gwendolyn bent over to talk with Flib.

"Franz of Beverly Hills, what should your mistress try on today?"

Flib looked around the shop, briefly, then sashayed around several floor racks before going toward the more exclusive section in the rear of the store. He sat in front of an elegant display of two gowns, one gold, the other shimmering green. Gwendolyn and Siobhan joined him.

"I think the green would suit you better," Gwendolyn suggested, looking closely at her customer. "You are a six? I believe we might have this in your size, let me check." She then went through a curtain in the back of the store. While she was gone, the one other customer left without purchasing anything. Martha, the attendant who disapproved of Flib, strode to a desk across the shop, scowling with every step.

"Just me, the owner, and one attendant," Siobhan whispered.

"*We saw her come out. Looks like Cunningham is arriving early*," Stan replied.

Georgia Deputy Attorney General Lewis Anthony, his team of three State Bureau of Investigation Agents, and six Georgia State Troopers barged through the front doors of Cunningham Tractor Sales and Service in White, Georgia, at 5:16 p.m. One agent and two troopers secured the administration offices and all computers, detaining two employees still working. Other agents and troopers continued to the service bay at the rear of the building.

Measuring about one hundred feet deep and fifty feet across, the service bay was large enough to handle four commercial tractors at one time. The black and gold pickup truck they had seen leave the Waffle House minutes before was in the door to bay one, engine still running. Four men were gathered outside the service office, adjacent to bay one. One man raced back into the office while pressing a speed dial on his phone. Two men ran toward the pickup, but stopped when a trooper fired a warning shot. The fourth man, Taylor Abercrombie, ran for a nearby door.

Bursting through the door, Abercrombie turned left and

found an armed Georgia State Trooper. A large man, Abercrobie wasted no time and plowed his fist toward the trooper's face. Dodging the worst impact of the blow, the officer took only a glancing hit. The near miss caused Abercrombie to stumble and the Trooper responded by ramming his own elbow, with all of his one hundred ninety pounds, into Abercrobie's back, forcing the fugitive face-first against the wall. A second trooper quickly came to his aid, effectively subduing the "Florida Hit Man," who was arrested for assaulting an officer and promptly read his rights.

Only one Cunningham family member was on site at the time of the raid, and AG Anthony did not have a warrant with his name on it. Searching the administrative offices revealed nothing of value to their case of organized crime, however they did find a room hidden between the service area and sales offices. This secret office contained a treasure trove of records, books and ledgers dealing with businesses other than tractor sales, and a computer. They now had enough evidence to satisfy the State of Georgia and keep the U. S. Department of Justice busy for many months.

At 5:18 p.m., Cunningham's driver pulled into a space not marked for parking, located across the narrow street from After Six. As he put the limousine into park, the car in front of him pulled away, so the driver eased down into a proper space. His car now sitting in parking gear, with the engine idling, Cunningham and his bodyguard climbed out and crossed the street.

Gwendolyn emerged from the back room of After Six, Ltd. with a gown across her arm as Cunningham and his bodyguard stepped through the front door. Seeing their arrival, she walked to the desk. "Martha, will you please assist Missus Thomson."

Martha accepted the dress and started toward Siobhan as Cunningham stopped to answer an unusual ring from his phone. It sounded like a European siren, which caused everyone to stop where they were. "Yes?" . . . "When?" . . . "Okay. Thanks."

Cunningham turned to leave the store. Seeing three men storming toward the door and two black SUVs trapping his car, he ordered his two guards, "OUT THE BACK!"

Without hesitation, Cunningham raced across the shop, grabbed Gwendolyn by the arm, and disappeared through the door to the back room, where she had just been. Both guards were immediately behind them. Jack, Stan, and one other man burst through the front door, "U. S. Marshall" emblazoned across their chests.

Deputy Marshall Terrance Oliver pulled his Glock pistol from its holster and lowered it toward the two men who exploded into the alley from the rear of After Six, Ltd. Both men stopped immediately, however the front man, Cunningham's bodyguard, picked up a pipe that was near his feet.

"I suggest you put that down if you want to continue breathing," Tommy announced from behind the door, his pistol pointed at their backs. The man dropped the pipe and both raised their hands. "Smart move, now on your knees, stretch out, and place your hands flat on the wall where we can see them."

"Siobhan, would you please keep this lady out of my way," Jack forcefully requested, as he advanced to the rear of the store. Siobhan waited for the three men to pass before crossing the store and herded Martha safely behind the desk. Jack, Stan, and one of the deputies followed Cunningham and his men through the door to the back. All had guns pulled and ready. Looking out the front, Siobhan saw two Deputy Marshals putting handcuffs on Cunningham's chauffeur, and two more heading around the outside of the store. Drivers eager to get home and trapped behind the blockage on the one lane street were now sounding their car horns.

Arriving in the back room, Jack found it empty. There were racks of clothes, boxes of merchandise, and normal inventory, but no people. Looking to the right he saw a door closing and signaled his deputy to follow. Opening the door, the deputy stopped and surveyed the situation. Turning back inside, he reported. "Both are in custody."

"Okay, where are Cunningham and the woman?" Jack asked. Stan and the deputy began searching the main room and all smaller adjacent rooms. Jack did find a loading or freight door, but it was padlocked on the inside. He checked it to see if it might open, groaning when it refused his efforts.

Outside, one of the deputies on the street cleared the traffic blockage by moving their SUV to the sidewalk; he then joined the search inside. The second outside deputy waved traffic past the arrest scene, while keeping an eye on the chauffeur and all vehicles.

Still in the showroom, Flib kept close to Siobhan throughout the raid, carefully watching people rushing to the back. Now that all was quiet in the store, he casually trotted to the back to see what was so interesting. He found men moving boxes, opening and closing doors, and pounding on walls. Jack kept looking toward the ceiling and curling his lips. Stan stood in the middle of the room, turning slowly, apparently searching for something.

Cocking his head to one side, the curious dog walked through several z-racks of dresses, sniffing as he went. Coming to built-in shelving, extending floor to ceiling and eight feet wide, near the back wall, the golden investigator stopped. After sniffing the lower shelves, he sat quietly facing the shelves, and listened and stared.

Looking more up than down, Jack stumbled over Flib, who moved out of the way then returned to his spot. "Hey, Stan. Can you do something with your partner, here?" Jack complained.

Stan walked over and squatted down next to Flib, who looked up briefly before returning to his staring. Following Flib's lead, Stan began looking at the floor and area around the shelves. Jack joined the examination, but neither could identify what continued to hold Flib's attention.

Having been relieved of her guard duties in the shop, Siobhan joined the men in the back. Winding between racks of dresses, she squatted next to Flib and rubbed his chest, laughing, "Mister Flib, why don't you show these silly men what they can't see."

Flib looked up at Siobhan, stood, and walked over to the shelves. After sniffing the bottom right cubicle, he bumped the box in it with his nose. Three feet of the shelf on the right side smoothly pivoted open, revealing a metal door. Jack tried to open the door, but found it securely bolted.

========

Operations in Westminster, Maryland and Irmo, South Carolina proceeded as planned. Teams moved on Jack's command at 5:19 p.m. Warehouse employees put up minimal resistance at both locations, surrendering when they realized they were outgunned by U.S. Marshals. Medical personnel were called in to assist young women found locked in wooden cubes, essentially shipping crates, eight feet on each side. A total of seventeen young women were released, ranging in age from fifteen to nineteen years, all showing signs of malnourishment, many with multiple bruises.

Sixty-two crates of untaxed cigarettes and alcohol were confiscated in Maryland, and an automotive "chop-shop" was discovered in South Carolina. All warrants were executed successfully.

The raid in Macclenny, Florida was a bust. The team found a warehouse that had been cleaned out. A newspaper found on the floor was dated two days prior.

While waiting outside the warehouse in Hendersonville, North Carolina, Deputy Marshal Mike Yoblanski and Detective Marc Hendricks reevaluated their approach. As soon as the signal came from Jack, 5:19 p.m., one SUV rushed to the gate outside the building. A deputy jumped from the back seat of the vehicle, carrying a pry bar. When he attempted to pop the cover from the control panel, nothing happened. Remembering the code Stan had given them, Marc quickly joined him and punched the numbers 9-3-6-7-5-2. Nothing happened. Looking around the box, he discovered a small red button on the bottom. Pressing the button activated the gate, which slid open. Mike drove their SUV through, however before deputies could reach the warehouse door, a black service van arrived. Deputies assumed an offensive posture, pistols drawn and ready. The van tried to back up but was blocked by a second U. S. Marshal SUV.

Still holding the pry bar, a deputy popped the front door of the warehouse open. Two shots ricocheted off the door frame over the deputies' heads when the door opened. Dropping to the floor in the doorway, U.S. Deputy Marshal Mike Yoblanski fired a single shot, hitting the inside shooter in the shoulder and disabling his shooting hand. Seeing his partner shot, another man laid his weapon on the floor and raised his hands in surrender. A third man escaped out the back door, but was apprehended by deputies going around the outside of the building.

Eight young women were released from cells, four more from the late arriving van. All were malnourished, some dehydrated, and many bore bruises on their legs and arms. Mike called on Sheriff Whitsett to provide medical support for the young women and injured shooter. While investigating the site, Deputy U. S. Marshals discovered a storage room filled with untaxed cigarettes, cases of assorted alcohol, and old records of the Cunningham organization.

Carter and two other Deputies entered the Cunningham residence without resistance. After an hour of searching they had only the business card of a private helicopter service.

Looking at the steel door found behind the wall of shelves, Jack turned to his deputies and commanded, "Mickey, go get the laser."

Mickey hustled out to their SUV, still parked on the street outside After Six, and retrieved a large metal case.

"How much longer?" an Asheville police officer directing traffic asked.

Mickey shrugged his shoulders and lugged the case inside. Once back at the metal door, he opened the box and removed a device that looked like a large space gun. Hanging it on his shoulder, Mickey pointed toward the edge of the door and flipped a switch. A bright red beam hit the door frame. Mickey then guided it down the edge, between the door and the frame. Five minutes later, Jack reached out and pulled the door open.

"Mister Albert David Cunningham, you are under arrest for multiple accounts of human trafficking, conspiracy to commit murder, and complicity in other crimes. Do you need to hear the list now?" Jack announced.

Stepping outside of the eight by eight foot room behind the steel door, Cunningham replied, "I want my attorney present before I make any comment."

Jack continued, "That's fine, sir. You have the right to an attorney. If you cannot afford an attorney, one will be provided for you. Do you understand the rights I have just explained to you?" Jack waited until Cunningham nodded. "Okay, you have already said you want an attorney, somebody cuff him and put him with the others."

"YOU SAID HE WAS DEAD!" Gwendolyn Turner exclaimed when she exited the room and saw the men waiting for her.

The instant Gwendolyn Turner came into sight, Stan was overcome by dizziness. Her unique perfume flooding his senses, he collapsed to one knee and held his head. Siobhan grabbed him as he fell, preventing him from falling against the shelving. Struggling to breathe, he lifted his head, looking first at Siobhan then at Gwendolyn.

"YOU EVEN GAVE ME A CERTIFIED DEATH CERTIFICATE!" Gwendolyn screeched. Now looking at Stan, her face was pale as death itself.

Jack responded by placing a hand on Stan's shoulder. "Stan, you okay? What happened?"

"Stan? His name isn't 'Stan'! He's my husband, Michael Geoffrey Turner!" Gwendolyn continued, now in a more civil tone. "Went to Atlanta almost a year ago and never came back."

"Stan, what is she saying?" Siobhan pleaded. "Are you Turner?"

Drawing a deep breath, Stan replied, "It appears so. Lost memories just came back, like a raging river . . . flooding my brain."

Chapter 26

Everyone in the store room at the back of After Six, Ltd. stared at Stan in amazement and disbelief. Stan was still kneeling on the floor, holding his head and wincing with pain. Jack broke the silence after a couple seconds, "Stan? Are you saying that you are Turner?"

"Apparently so," Stan chuckled slightly, rubbing the sides of his head with both hands. "We knew I suffered some amnesia, apparently from when they clobbered me and threw me in the train car in Georgia. I found Siobhan because I had a pocket menu from Pearl's Diner in my boot. . . . Wow! This is a trip!" He shook his head from side to side as though this might help organize the memories that had just flooded his mind. "I've had a few memories trickle back, but . . . wow, nothing like this." He looked at Gwendolyn with resolute defiance. Turning toward Siobhan, his expression changed to one of peace and contentment.

Siobhan looked at Stan with a mixture of devotion and terror. Her eyes welled up, her lips trembled. Her fists clinched so tightly her fingers turned white, and her heart swelled with apprehension. She had come to love this man, but now had no idea who, or what, he was. Tears rolled down her cheek as Stan reached out for her hand. She immediately helped him back to his feet.

Craning his neck, as though trying to repair a damaged attachment, Stan moaned, "I need some air. Do you mind if we continue this later?"

Jack pondered the situation for nearly a minute before responding. "Go ahead. We have official business that needs to be taken care of here. It'll take an hour or more, so why don't you two . . . three, don't forget that dog, go outside. I'll see you when we finish here." Jack then turned to Gwendolyn Turner. "Gwendolyn Turner, I place you under arrest for money laundering and aiding the efforts of criminal activities. You have the right to an attorney. If you cannot afford an attorney, one will be provided for you. Do you understand the rights I have just explained to you?"

"Yes," she replied. Gwendolyn watched Siobhan support

Stan as they left with Flib trotting casually beside them. Eyes open wide, she fought to hold their tears back. Her lips trembled and her forehead was furrowed with wrinkles. Her entire face was a mixture of disbelief and a sense of betrayal.

"Cuff her and put her with the others," Jack directed. "Now, let's do our search for evidence. Terry, call Carter and see how things are going at Cunningham's residence."

Reaching outside, Stan drew a breath of fresh air and relaxed. Taking Siobhan's hand, he began pulling her across the street through the congested traffic toward their Explorer. "We need to get to the Turner residence right away!"

Siobhan balked and looked at Stan, still not sure who he was or why she was helping him. Stan squeezed her hand gently, explaining, "This is important for *us*. I'll explain later but we need to get there and gone as fast as possible."

Holding on to "*us*," Siobhan took a deep breath and settled herself, as best she could. She still loved this man and hoped . . . no prayed, that he was not going to become Turner, again.

Reaching their vehicle, Stan took a minute to turn his surveillance recording off as Siobhan and Flib got into the car. Slipping behind the wheel, Stan drove away from the square, turning north on Broadway to avoid the traffic outside After Six. Turning left on College, he then turned south on Lexington, continuing two blocks to a luxury condominium building. Pulling up to a security gate, he effortlessly entered a security code allowing them to park in a deck below the building.

Opening the door for Siobhan, he looked at their companion. "Mister Flib, you wait here and guard the car. We won't be but just a few minutes." Walking up to a security door, he again punched in a code and the lock clicked open.

"I hope you have a key," Siobhan chortled.

"Won't need one, digital lock. Gwen hates to carry keys."

Reaching the door to a penthouse apartment, Stan again let his fingers dance across a keypad and opened the door. Siobhan gasped at the openness of the room, the high end chrome and glass furniture, and absolute elegance of everything. She had just begun to look across the Asheville skyline through a glass wall when Stan called, "This way."

Siobhan followed Stan into a decadent master suite, gasping when she entered. The room was dark green with pristine white trim. The outside wall was essentially glass, looking out across the City of Asheville as it began its transition from daytime work to nighttime play. Centered along the largest wall was a king bed draped in an ivory bedspread with green stitching, matching the walls. Night stands on either side had small lamps which shimmered like gold. The ceiling was handmade lattice work, which continued uninterrupted across a false wall to the right. Behind this wall was the dressing area, which contained a long feminine dressing table, a gentleman's bureau, and two walk-in closets - his and hers - and an elegant bathroom that might make royalty jealous.

Stan wasted no time in pulling a chair from the dressing table into his walk-in closet. Reaching over a shelf just inside the door, he smashed the heel of his palm into the ceiling. A hidden panel popped loose. Feeling inside the now-exposed ceiling, Stan found a string which he carefully pulled until a brief case appeared over his head. After removing the case, he put the panel back in place, making sure the lattice pattern matched so that the panel was once again invisible. When he returned the chair to the dressing table, he quickly searched through two drawers, pulling out an envelope which he carried into the bedroom with his brief case.

"That looks just like the case from the bus station," Siobhan remarked as Stan placed it on the bed, spun numbers on the two locks, and opened the case.

"It is, an exact match," Stan replied with a smile. He then inventoried the contents: a passport and driver's license in the name of Michael Geoffrey Turner, a small pistol and box of ammunition, two bundles of bills, each labeled $10,000, and two ledger books. Flipping through the first book, he raised his eyebrows and dropped the book back into the briefcase. Flipping through the second book, he smiled broadly and returned it to the case. He then added the envelope from the dressing table, locked the case, picked it up and looked to his companion.

"Miss Thomas, don't you think it's about time we made our way home?" He offered her his arm, which she took, smiling with relief.

Once on the highway back toward Oliver Springs, Siobhan asked a question that had been bothering her. "How many guns do you need or have?"

"Need? Probably none now that Cunningham can't come after me, though some goons might still try. They don't really make you safer in general investigations, but can be necessary when dealing with hardened criminals . . . that is if you want to stay alive."

"So how many do you have?" Siobhan repeated.

"Two, plus the one Jack loaned me for today. I'll return it to him when he visits in a couple days." Stan looked across at Siobhan and seeing the concern on her face, made a bold statement. "I'd like to teach you how to shoot . . . how to handle a gun. Then you won't mind so much when I have to carry one, which I hope will be rarely. . . . Why don't you use your phone to find us someplace to eat, something Flib will like."

Flib barked once in agreement and licked his chops. Siobhan directed Stan to a Burger King at the next turnoff.

It was close to midnight when Stan, Siobhan, and Flib returned to their apartment in Oliver Springs. Stan noticed that the Lexus and Toyota were gone and the end apartment was dark, but did not say anything to his companions. Flib jumped out as soon as Siobhan opened her door. Stan stood beside his open door and stretched.

Looking across the car to the woman who had stood by him throughout this odd day, he asked, "Siobhan, why don't you open the door while I get the equipment." He then retrieved the brief case from the back seat and handed it to her before opening the back end of the Explorer. Once all equipment was safely inside and stored in the front bedroom, everyone went to bed.

"How would you like to go to Knoxville with me?" Stan asked as he fried bacon for breakfast.

"Today?" Siobhan asked, somewhat alarmed. "I should get to work."

"No, you have the day off, remember . . . Thursday *and* Friday."

Siobhan pondered a few seconds. "Why not. I want to bring Mary up to speed, but that can wait until after lunch. We are going this morning, right?"

"Right after breakfast. I need to visit a Fifth Third Bank. You can drive."

Dressed in clean slacks and sport shirt and carrying a brief case, Stan walked up to the manager's desk at the Fifth Third Bank on Walker Springs Lane in Knoxville, Tennessee, at nine-thirty. Dressed in a conservative spring dress, Siobhan stood beside him. She had no idea why they were there.

"I would like access to box number 264," he politely told the manager, an attractive woman in her mid-forties, dressed in a professional business suit.

"Two sixty four . . ." she repeated, recalling a memory. "We've had a lot of interest in that box lately. I recall a U.S. Marshall needed access a couple weeks ago. Do you have your ID card, Mister . . .?"

"Turner. Yes, I do." Stan reached into his pocket and pulled out his wallet.

The manager looked over to the assistant manager, calling, "Dwight, will you please help Mister Turner with his security box." Turning back to Stan and Siobhan, she instructed, "Mister Height will be glad to help you."

"Your identification please," the assistant manager requested as Stan approached his desk. His expression was cold, even to the point of being hostile. He put his hand out, for Stan's identification, without extending his arm, forcing Stan to reach across the desk. Heaving a heavy sigh, Height rapped keys on his computer, then looked up at Stan. Cocking his head to one side, he sneered, "Didn't you present yourself as . . . Winthrop, last week? I believe you said Turner was deceased. I'll need something more than an out-of-state driver's license."

"Will my passport suffice?" Stan replied, opening the brief case and removing said document.

The assistant manager examined the passport, then studied

Stan. After flipping through the pages and seeing multiple stamps, he returned the passport and driver's license. "I assume you do have your key."

"I do. May we proceed?" Stan responded, putting the documents in his brief case and getting a bit irritated with the assistant manager.

Height rapped the keys on his computer again, then pushed an electronic signature pad toward Stan. "Please sign the pad." As soon as Stan completed signing and returned the pen to its holder, Height removed a key from his desk and stood. Pausing briefly to look at Siobhan, he continued with a less than pleasant demeanor. "Follow me."

Once in the vault, the assistant manager scanned the boxes and stepped over to box 264, which was a medium size flat box. "Your key please."

Stan handed his key to the assistant manager who put both keys into the appropriate locks and opened the door. After removing the box and setting it on a table in the center of the vault, the banker removed both keys. "Will you need a room?" he asked, returning Stan's key to him.

"No, we won't be but a minute. Thank you."

As soon as Height left the vault, Siobhan choked back a laugh. "What is with that guy? I've never seen a bank person with that kind of attitude. Bank managers are supposed to be friendly. This guy definitely got out of bed on the wrong side!"

Shaking his head, Stan opened the metal box. It contained a single ledger book, similar to those found in his briefcase the night before. Flipping to the last page with entries, he chuckled with amusement. "Oh my. I had forgotten how much."

"How much what?" Siobhan asked as Stan dropped the ledger into his brief case.

"I'll explain in the car." He then returned the empty metal box to its cubicle and closed the door.

Passing the assistant manager's desk, Stan smiled and said, "Thank you. We're finished."

Height squinted his eyes and scrunched his face just a bit as he watched Stan and Siobhan leave.

"You'll never make manager with an attitude like that," his manager commented from her desk.

=======

"Okay, Mister Turner, how much what?" Siobhan asked as she piloted her Forester onto I-40.

"First, please don't ever use that name again, unless we need it to hide who we are. I am Stan Winthrop, not Geoff Turner. Turner is dead and I have the death certificate to prove it, took it from Gwen's dressing table. Now. How much? How does two point six million dollars sound? And that's only one account."

"One account?" Siobhan repeated, suddenly swerving across the lane beside hers.

"Yes, please keep your eyes on the road. Those ledgers we found last night . . . Jack needs one of them. The second is to be kept our secret."

"How much?" Siobhan asked, a smile brightening her face and her eyes twinkling.

"Only nine hundred seventy five thousand in that one . . . and change."

"Where is all this money and where did it come from? Is someone going to kill us in our sleep to get it back?"

"It came from the Cunningham syndicate. Shortly after I married Gwen, that is Turner married Gwen, he found out that she was laundering money for some two-bit criminals. Or so I thought at the time. I looked into their activities and realized they weren't so small. Actually part of a big crime family, the Cunninghams. Hundreds of thousands of dollars every month or so. They dropped off deposits on a regular basis, which Gwen ran through her dress shop. Whenever I could, I would check the drop and if there were two for the same amount, I'd liberate one. The larger ledger is a record of what I, as Turner, took from the crooks over four or five years. The smaller ledger is a record of similar activity from two other drop points over fifteen to eighteen months."

"Didn't anybody notice?" Siobhan asked, not quite believing everything Stan was telling her.

"Oh, I'm sure they did and I imagine somebody suffered for it, but they were all lifelong criminals and this money was from criminal activity. I did manage to talk a few kids into leaving the family, got them to look at the life they were in for. They'd give me evidence of an ongoing crime and I made sure they had enough money to get reestablished in another part of the country. Like the money, if you do it right nobody notices."

"What about the third ledger?"

"That is a record of family transactions and operations. My observations over two years. I tried to get this job as a formal assignment, but my superiors weren't interested. The Cunninghams weren't big enough at the time. I resigned and went to work gathering information on my own. The rest you know."

"And you're sure nobody is going to come looking for this money?"

"Look, it took several years, so I'm not sure if they even know it's gone. Besides, we just gutted their organization. You, me, Flib, and the United States Department of Justice. Feels good to be on the winning side, doesn't it?"

"Okay, where is it?"

"Offshore accounts. Down in the Carribean. I'll need to change details on several accounts so we can access them when we want to. Move some of it to local banks; make it easier to spend."

"How will you explain having all this wealth all of a sudden?"

"You sure are asking a lot of questions. First, we won't be wealthy, just spend what we need. Nothing flagrant. Besides, Turner died and left us an inheritance."

Siobhan grew quiet. Driving past Oak Ridge, she blurted out, "THAT'S THREE AND A HALF MILLION DOLLARS!" . . . "We could buy a house!"

"Yeah, I suppose so, but not until we get married."

Siobhan slammed on the brakes, then quickly pulled off the highway. "WHAT?"

"I said sure, as soon as we get married. You will marry me, won't you?"

Siobhan tried to dive across the car and grab Stan, but her seat belt snatched her back. Without thinking beyond that second, she unhooked her seatbelt, jumped out of the car and ran around to where Stan now waited with open arms. "Yes! Yes I will, as long as Turner is really dead."

"Like I said, I have a certified death certificate and, anyway, I like Stan Winthrop better."

They kissed one another like there was no tomorrow. Several passing cars beeped their horns. Coming up for air, Stan suggested, "How about I drive the rest of the way?"

Pulling up to their apartment, they found Flib sitting at the front door, staring down the parking lot once again. A black sedan, police cruiser, and police van were parked at the end apartment. Uniformed and plain clothes officers stood around the front door. Before Stan and Siobhan could reach their door, the black sedan parked next to their car. Two men climbed out, Detectives Simpson and White.

"Mister Winthrop, we need a word with you, sir," Detective Simpson called out.

"What's on your mind?" Stan asked as Siobhan unlocked the apartment door.

"We have some more questions about the residents of that end apartment," White continued. "May we come inside?"

"Sure," Stan agreed.

Simpson signaled for two uniformed officers to join them and told White, "Have them wait at the door. Just in case." White nodded. Simpson followed Stan, Siobhan, and Flib, who maintained a position between his people and the detective.

"Make yourself comfortable," Stan offered. He went to the kitchen and retrieved two Diet Rites from the refrigerator. Handing one to Siobhan, he asked, "Detective, would you like something to drink?"

"No, thank you. Can we sit around the table?"

"Only two chairs," Siobhan replied. "If you will bring a chair from the table, we can sit on the sofa."

Looking around the apartment, Simpson agreed. "That'll be fine. This shouldn't take too long." He set a chair between the table and the sofa and sat as White joined him. White stood beside the coat closet, just inside the living room and blocking the front door as Simpson began the conversation. "We got notice this morning to be on lookout for vehicles from Bartow County, Georgia. We got this notice because we had run queries on the two cars that had been parked at that apartment down on the end and that car that blew up a couple weeks back. White, here, also ran background checks on the two of you. Both came up clean. Miss Thomas, your record shows only an old speeding ticket, which has now expired. Mister Winthrop, you don't seem to exist. Why is that?"

Stan chuckled just a bit then looked Simpson squarely in his eyes. "I'm afraid you'll have to speak with the U. S. Department of Justice about that. I expect Investigations Supervisor Jack Barnes to be here tomorrow; you should be able to talk with him at Pearl's, probably around lunch time." Stan paused and looked at both men, who were obviously waiting for him to continue. "But, in the interest of being a good neighbor, I'll tell you what I can. I have been working undercover as part of a team investigating a crime syndicate operating out of Bartow County, Georgia. We raided their operations yesterday, throughout the southeast, and I believe we have successfully ended their criminal activities. Now, what more do you want to know?"

Simpson uneasily drummed his fingers in the air as he thought. "You say you were undercover; what is your real name?"

"Doesn't matter. I am Stan Winthrop."

"Now that your investigation is finished, will you be staying in Oliver Springs?" White asked.

"As a matter of fact, Miss Thomas has just agreed to marry me and we plan to purchase a house here."

White pondered a few seconds. "What work will you be doing?"

"I am an investigator, of sorts, as I told you before. I help people find things they lost."

"You'll need a license to work as a P.I.," Simpson quickly added.

"Won't be working as a private investigator, just a finder of lost valuables. Now, if you don't mind, I think I would like some lunch." Stan then stood and lifted Siobhan's hand, indicating she should as well. Winking at Siobhan, he added, "Maybe a homemade BLT?"

Simpson stood and returned his chair to the kitchen table. Stopping on his way to the door, he turned to Stan. "I don't trust you Mister Winthrop. I don't trust you because you are not telling us the whole truth. I'm not saying you're lying to us, but you aren't coming clean with what you know and might help us with other cases. I'm going to keep an eye on you and the first time you step across that magical line, I'll arrest you and forget where you're stored."

"I feel better knowing we have Oliver Spring's best detectives watching over our safety," Stan retorted. "And should you ever need to find some lost evidence, feel free to come by Pearl's and talk with me." He then herded the two detectives out the door and closed it politely behind them.

Siobhan struggled to not laugh at Stan's replies.

Siobhan arrived at Pearl's bright and early Saturday morning, just as Mary was unlocking the kitchen door. Mary saw her arrive but continued inside to fire up the grill. Siobhan wasted no time in starting the coffee service.

"Glad to see you made it back in one piece; what happened?" Mary asked coldly. Not having had any coffee to lubricate her throat, her question sounded like a snarl.

"We got them, and a bit more," Siobhan replied with a light cheery voice, her eyes dancing with delight.

"Explain."

At that moment, Sylvia and Theresa arrived. Horace caught the door as they closed it behind them. All staff now present, Siobhan whispered to Mary, "Cunningham and Gwendolyn Turner were arrested . . . and their two goons."

Placing her hands on her hips, Mary stared at Siobhan for several seconds before blurting out so all could hear, "And what is this 'bit more'?"

"I *was* Geoff Turner, but he is now officially deceased," Stan announced from the doorway.

Mary stared at Stan, unable to utter a word. Everyone else looked at Siobhan, then back to Stan, wondering what was going on. Then Stan felt a firm hand on his shoulder and a powerful bass voice commanded, "Get out of the door and show me the coffee pot!"

"Jack?" Mary blurted out. "When did my diner become a meeting place for the Justice Department?"

"We could find a Howard Johnsons if it would suit you better," Jack responded, smiling confidently.

"Get in the dining room . . . the three of you. I need an explanation," Mary directed, her voice leaving no room for challenge. "Sylvia, bring the coffee out as soon as it's ready. Horace, the grill should be hot; do up some ham, eggs, and toast . . . service for four. Bring it out ASAP."

When all had settled to a table in the dining room, Jack began the conversation. "Stan, you and Siobhan disappeared before I was finished with you. Where did you go?"

"You said I could go, so we left. Came home," Stan replied, feigning innocence.

"No, I said you could get some air. Where did you go?"

"We came home."

"You didn't go by the Turner apartment?" Jack pressed, his voice becoming more official than friendly.

"Why would we do that? I'm still sorting out all that's happened over the past year."

Jack stared at Stan, then at Siobhan. Mary broke the awkward silence, "Okay, somebody please tell me what happened."

Jack waited while Sylvia delivered coffee service around the table. She hung close to the table until Mary signaled her to return to the kitchen. "Well, thanks to the Turner / Winthrop contribution, we shut down the Cunningham crime syndicate. It'll take months to lay out all the pieces, but we rescued twenty-nine young women from slavery and uncovered a chop-shop. I don't know the total of untaxed booze and cigarettes, several cases of illegal firearms, and took four crooked cops off the street. Florida was a bust and Georgia started out as a comedy act but they got our Florida assassin on assault charges . . . tried to take out a Georgia State Trooper."

"Enough with all that, what is this about Turner?" Mary interrupted.

When nobody was forthcoming, Siobhan replied, "Stan was once Geoff Turner. When he lost his memory, from a clunk on the head in Georgia, he became Stan Winthrop, one of his cover names . . ."

"Alias," Stan corrected.

"Okay, aliases," Siobhan resumed. "When Gwendolyn Turner came out of a hidden room, which Flib uncovered . . ." She paused until Jack nodded his acknowledgment, "something about her triggered all Stan's lost memories . . . but he's still Stan Winthrop."

"I think it was her perfume," Stan agreed.

"How can Turner be dead if you are Turner?" Mary asked.

"Well . . . Cunningham provided a fully certified death certificate for a corpse in White, Georgia. It clearly identifies Michael Geoffrey Turner as having died in an automobile fire. So, as I really like Stan Winthrop better, I think I'll let Turner lie in his grave."

"What about legal papers?" Mary asked. "Won't you need a Social Security number and maybe a passport?"

"YES! He will need a passport, because I want to honeymoon in Scotland!" Siobhan responded, smiling from ear to ear.

"Honeymoon? So the two of you are going to tie the knot?" Jack asked.

"Yes, we are," Stan asserted. "And a honeymoon in Scotland sounds nice. . . . I guess I will need a passport."

Mary and Siobhan looked at Jack, waiting for a response.

Jack looked at the faces around the table and was bailed out of answering when Sylvia delivered empty plates and silverware for all. Theresa quickly followed, bringing platters filled high with scrambled eggs, country ham, and toast. As everyone scooped from the serving platters to their own plates, Jack changed the subject.

"So, did you ever visit that lock box in Knoxville?"

"What lock box? The one Justice doesn't know or care about?" Stan replied, cutting his ham and combining it with eggs for a hearty bite. When Jack just glared at him, he continued. "Twice. How did you get into it? Assistant Manager wouldn't let me in."

"U. S. Department of Justice identification works wonders. I dealt with the manager . . . delightful woman."

A smile crept across Stan's face as he offered Jack a deal he couldn't refuse. "Tell you what, Mister Barnes. You arrange new identities all the time, for witnesses in protection, right?" Stan waited for Jack to nod. "Okay, I found a ledger that might make tying all the Cunningham activity into a tidy little package. I'll give it to you in exchange for a Social Security Number with a history - you can use Turner's if you wish - and a valid U. S. Passport. All in the name of Stan Winthrop." Stan then pulled his wallet from his back pocket and removed his driver's license. "Here's all the detail you'll need. Full name, birthday, address, . . . no, we need to change the address." He handed the license to Jack.

"What if we need Turner to testify in court?" Jack challenged.

Stan took a deep breath before replying. "Look, Geoff Turner was trained in Special Ops, Intelligence Services. It was a stressful life, not to mention a bit dangerous. It even got him killed . . . not the kind of life I want, now. I will be glad to testify as his partner on this Cunningham investigation, but if you need his testimony, go dig him up and ask him to testify. I'm sure you can find his grave in White or Asheville," Stan replied calmly.

"I've got a question for Geoff Turner, before he disappears completely," Mary interjected, staring at Stan. "Was coming to my diner a coincidence?"

Stan put his fork down and placed both hands on the table. Looking squarely at Mary, he replied. "When I, excuse me - Geoff Turner, realized I needed a 'safe haven' away from Asheville, I made a few inquiries. Your departure to the Knoxville area came up and you were a bit of a legend among agents. I figured you could provide backup if I needed it, which you did." Reaching over and squeezing Siobhan's hand, he added, "I hadn't figured on meeting anyone like Siobhan." Taking a deep breath and exhaling peacefully, he turned back to Jack. "By the way, how did Marc Hendricks do?"

"Great," Jack replied between bites. "I asked how he liked being a Deputy Marshall. He said he preferred the quiet life of a small city detective."

Stan chuckled.

While everyone paused to eat a bite of breakfast, Mary began a new line of conversation. "So, Mister Winthrop, now that you have solved your big case, what are you going to do with yourself?"

"He's going to marry me, we are going to buy a house, and then help people find lost valuables," Siobhan replied while Stan enjoyed more ham and egg.

"You really want to marry a man who has a habit of disappearing?" Jack teased.

"Oh, he won't disappear, I'll be by his side," Siobhan replied.

"Are you leaving me?" Mary objected.

"Nope . . . well, maybe when we have a job out of town."

"Do I get a say in any of this?" Stan asked, trying to get into the conversation.

"Nope, you gave that up when you asked her to marry you," Jack laughed.

"They do make a pretty good team, though," Mary smiled. "Congratulations, you two."

"Yes, congratulations," Jack agreed.

After all finished breakfast, Jack used his phone to take a picture of Stan's driver's license and returned it to him. Stan retrieved a single ledger from his Explorer and handed it to Jack. Seeing Stan had included a key to read coded sections of the ledger, he smiled and quietly asked, "So, how much did you take Cunningham for? . . . off the record . . ."

"Enough." He then offered Jack his hand, which was accepted with much gratitude and respect.

Epilog

Thursday morning, a week later, a U. S. Mail carrier walked into Pearl's Diner and asked for Stan Winthrop. Stan was helping out on the grill so Horace could recover from yet another injury, this time a sprained wrist from changing a flat tire.

"Yes, what can I do for you?" Stan asked when he reached the carrier, still waiting at the front door.

"Are you Stan Winthrop?" the carrier replied. "I'll need to see some identification."

Stan produced his driver's license.

"Thank you, sir. I have a registered package for you, please sign here." The carrier held out his electronic pad for Stan to sign. Once Stan signed, the carrier handed Stan a cardboard envelope and left.

Seeing the carrier talking with Stan, Siobhan joined him. "What is it?"

"Let's see," he replied, pulling the tear strip. Looking inside, he looked back at Siobhan. "We can go get that marriage license, if you still want." He then removed a U. S. passport and Social Security documentation. Looking at the earning record, he recognized much of Turner's history.

Stan and Siobhan were married that Sunday afternoon at Pearl's. A retired judge who visited Pearl's every Sunday morning did the honors. They found a house two days later and paid cash for it, before leaving on a three-week honeymoon in Scotland.

Returning to "real life," the happy couple spent mornings at Pearl's and afternoons looking for furniture for their new house, but had to stop when Stan got a visitor at Pearl's during lunch.

"Mister Winthrop, I understand you find things . . . possibly things that are not perceptibly lost?" The man standing at Stan's table was in his late fifties, reasonably good physical condition, close cut salt & pepper hair, and wore a minister's collar.

"Please, sit down. What did you lose?"

Sitting opposite Stan, the minister continued. "Well, nothing lost, exactly. However I believe something has been replaced with a duplicate." He carefully watched Stan's reaction.

Curiosity peaked, Stan raised one eyebrow and grinned slightly. "What was replaced? Can you show me?"

The minister then opened a box he was carrying and removed an exquisite chalice. The cup was a stoneware bowl wrapped in a braid of gold and silver which also formed the stem and base. Wherever the braids met, they formed a pattern similar to Celtic knots. Three rubies adorned the base of the cup at the top of the stem. He handed the work of art to Stan, who examined it, even studying the hallmark under the base.

"It does look authentic, but is only two . . . possibly three years old. What makes you think it's a forgery?" Stan asked, setting the chalice on the table.

"How can you tell it is only a few years old?"

"The hallmark." Stan then lifted the chalice, turned it over and using a table knife pointed to the hallmark on the bottom. "The edges of the mark are still quite sharp. It could be quite old if it were sitting on a shelf somewhere and never touched. Even the gentlest cleaning would take the edge off the hallmark after a decade, or so. But I'm betting you use this regularly, in communion services."

"Only 'High Communion,' now days, but you are correct. It has been used for generations . . . or at least the original was."

"How did you discover this is a replacement?" Stan asked, again examining the artistic detail.

"First a bit of history, then you will understand how I spotted the change. Our church was founded by a family from northern England. A county land baron was ransacking churches to support his castle. The priest and a handful of devoted followers grabbed the wealth of their church and escaped to the colonies. They initially tried to setup in New Amsterdam, but soon moved west, their children finally settling in what is now Ohio. This chalice, its platen, and matching candlesticks were the entire wealth of the congregation from the very beginning. Years, decades, passed before representatives of the land baron they had escaped came after them. The service was then hidden beneath the church, survived two fires, and was brought out only for high service. The land baron's family eventually gave up, or so we thought, and the service was put on display in the sanctuary. Even though we used it only a few times each year, I have cleaned it every week for the past seventeen years. Then while serving communion, this past Easter, I noticed the balance was off. I mentioned this to our elders, but they all told me I was out of my mind.

"Two weeks ago I was at a reception for a second cousin, who is an author. He just released his second novel, not that his first was that great. He overheard me talking with a jeweler about my suspicions about the chalice, and told me he knew of a man who could find anything. You had found a signed copy of his first book, I believe. The inscription might prove embarrassing to some."

"Not that embarrassing, just a bit intimate," Stan responded. Looking around the diner, he spotted Siobhan cleaning a table and waved her to come over.

"Yes?" she said, wiping her hands on a towel.

"How would you like to investigate, excuse me, find a chalice that supposedly isn't lost?" Stan smiled.

"What do you mean, 'isn't lost'?"

"See, it's right here." Stan picked up the chalice and showed it to Siobhan. "Or at least a replica is here. We need to find the real one."

"Does Flib get to go, too?"

"Sure, but probably not if we go to England."